Fertile Ground

Also by Ben Mezrich
Threshold
Reaper
Skin

Fertile Ground

BEN MEZRICH

HarperCollins*Publishers*

FIRST EDITION

Designed by Joseph Rutt

Library of Congress Cataloging-in-Publication Data
　　Mezrich, Ben, 1969–
　　　　Fertile ground : a novel / Ben Mezrich. — 1st ed.
　　　　　　p.　　cm.
　　　　ISBN 0-06-018752-2
　　　　I. Title
PS3563.E986F47　　　　　　　　　　　　1999
813'.54—dc21　　　　　　　　　　　　99-22560

99 00 01 02 03 ❖/RRD 10 9 8 7 6 5 4 3 2 1

1

Ted Conners opened his eyes seconds before the sweaty, green-vinyl seatback smacked into the bridge of his nose. He blinked, shifting his head back and forth, struggling to remember where the hell he was. Then the mingled scent of diesel fumes and body odor quickly chased away the confusion. He rubbed his nose as he surveyed the cramped interior of the temporarily stalled bus. The aisles were full, a throbbing mass of bodies squeezed between the two rows of seats. The air was stiflingly hot, and the windows on either side had turned the color of misty, opaque cream.

"Figures," Ted mumbled, as he shifted back against his

seat, surprised that he had dozed off under such barbarous conditions. "The air-conditioning goes out on the hottest day of the summer."

The woman to Ted's left grunted in agreement. She was overweight, black, and wore a dress that looked more like a burlap sack than an item of clothing. Her enormous right thigh was squashing the hell out of Ted's hip—ruining the crease of his only good suit. Then again, the thick sheets of sweat enveloping every inch of Ted's body had already turned his pants from a light gray to something resembling charcoal, and his white shirt had gone nearly transparent against his chest. Served him right, for being stingy about a ten-dollar taxi ride to Cambridge.

As the bus jerked forward again, Ted pressed his face against the fogged-up window to his right. Through the crack above the glass—two inches, as far as it would go, just enough to let the hot breath of the city lick at his cheeks— Ted could see the skyline hovering above the Charles River. The low, quaint townhouses of the Back Bay lay in the twin shadows of the Prudential and the Hancock, and Ted could just make out the financial district in the distance, a handful of jutting steel columns huddled together against the hazy sky. A beautiful city, even in the dead of August, even from the cramped interior of an oversized steel coffin.

Ted sighed as the bus chugged to another dramatic stop. At the moment, the Number One was lodged like a clot in the center of the Mass Avenue bridge, trapped between two lanes of rush-hour traffic. It seemed as though half the world was trying to get out of Boston—and the other half was trying just as hard to get in. A din of car horns, pop radio, and colorful curse words rose like steam from the hot black asphalt.

"Gonna take two hours to get into Cambridge," the overweight woman to Ted's left mumbled, inadvertently pressing her enormous haunch harder against Ted's hip. Ted nodded, sliding as close to the window as possible. For a brief moment he felt strangely lightheaded, almost dizzy, and he reached for the top two buttons of his shirt. As he pulled the collar open, he wondered how long he'd been asleep. The bus had moved only a few blocks since he had boarded at the corner of Newbury and Mass Ave, but time and distance were unrelated concepts in the world of mass transit. The Number One could have stopped forty times since Newbury Street.

Ted experienced a moment of panic as he thought of the crowd of strangers moving through the aisle as he slept, and he quickly felt for the package beneath his knees. Then his fingers touched the edge of the Tiffany's bag and he smiled, relieved. Two months' salary had gone into the necklace inside the bag. Sandy, his girlfriend of three years, was going to flip when she saw the beautiful piece of jewelry, and Ted couldn't wait to see the heart-shaped slab of jade resting in the crevice between her wonderful breasts—

Ted coughed, his head jerking forward. The image evaporated as the sounds and smells of the Number One bus assaulted his senses, bringing him back to reality: Sandy was still miles away. He coughed again, then realized with a start that he didn't feel so good. His heart was racing, and there was a prickly, hot sensation running across his chest. He swallowed, trying to slow his breathing. *The heat*, he reminded himself. He had walked up and down Newbury

Street for three hours searching for the necklace—and it had to be close to a hundred degrees in the crowded bus. Almost hot enough to melt jade.

Ted managed a deep breath, calming himself. He felt a little better and slowly opened his eyes. For some reason, the interior of the bus seemed a bit bright, and he blinked rapidly. There was a sudden stinging in his right eye, and his vision swirled. A second later, he felt something warm running down his right cheek. The trickle didn't feel like a tear; it was thicker, tracking across his flesh in a slow, determined arc.

Puzzled, Ted reached up and touched the trickle with his fingers. *Sticky.* Ted held his fingers in front of his face, squinting through the blur.

Blood. Ted stared at his fingers, shock filling his insides. Had he cut his eye? He didn't even know that eyes could bleed. Well, some sort of cut would explain the sudden deterioration in his vision—and maybe even the lightheadedness. Perhaps he had cut himself when he hit the seat in front of him with his nose.

He moved his hands toward his pockets, searching for a Kleenex—when suddenly, a wave of nausea billowed up through his stomach. He retched, clamping his lips shut. His mouth filled from the inside, and the taste was unmistakable. *More blood!*

Christ. Blood from his stomach? An ulcer, maybe a ruptured organ? Panicking, Ted whirled toward the woman seated next to him. She gasped, pulling back. The look on her jowly face scared Ted even more than the mouthful of blood. Eyes wide, she pointed at his skin, whispering something under her breath.

Still holding his lips closed, Ted squinted at the back of his hand. His skin had turned a strange, off-yellow color. Suddenly, he felt trickles running both out of his nostrils and down the lobes of his ears. There was a warm seepage in his pants, more viscous liquid running across his upper thighs. It felt as if his insides were leaking out of his body. And there was nothing he could do about it.

"Mister," the woman finally managed. "You need to get to a doctor. Right away."

Ted stared at her—his mind unable to focus—when a new surge of nausea ripped up his stomach. The woman slid a few inches away, staring at Ted's bulging cheeks. Terrified, Ted tried to rise out of his seat. But his knees were weak, and he swayed back in his seat, his eyes drifting shut. *Christ, what the hell is going on? What is happening to my body?*

"Help me," he finally whispered, bubbles of blood spraying out over his lips. The overweight woman saw the blood and she started to scream. Suddenly, Ted's body jerked convulsively, and he gripped the vinyl bus seat. The right side of his body sagged, and he crumpled forward, crushing the Tiffany's bag beneath his knees. His jaw went slack, and there was a gush of liquid. The woman's screams multiplied in Ted's ears, and he struggled to open his eyes once more.

For a brief, horrible second his vision returned. The sight before him was worse than anything he had ever witnessed in his life.

The Tiffany's bag beneath his knees was floating atop a puddle at least an inch deep, a shimmering puddle of dark red blood. . . .

2

Jake Foster arched his back as the moment approached, his hands tight around Brett's waist, sweat dripping in heavy tear-shaped drops from his wavy, dark brown hair. Brett was splayed out on the hard mattress beneath him, her long legs hooked around his thighs, her ass raised on a throne of thick, stiff pillows. Brett's eyes were closed, her lips slightly parted. There was something basic and feral about the expression on her Slavic face, and Jake imagined that she was some sort of jungle creature, some sexy, hairless, catlike animal he had yanked out of the bushes and thrown to the ground. He slid his hands up her body, feeling the warm skin of her stomach, the angle of her rib cage, the soft, rounded curves of her pert breasts. She responded to his touch, her arms rising above her head, her shoulders curling back. Her stomach trembled and her voice slipped out from between her lips. "I'm coming. God, Jake, I'm coming."

"Now?" Jake whispered anxiously. He moved his hands back to her waist, sliding her pelvic region higher on the pillows.

"A few more seconds," Brett hissed back. "I'm right on the edge."

Jake took a deep breath, moving his hips a little harder, working his knees to get a better angle. His movements were more than sexual posturing, just as Brett's carnal dialogue was more than a casual cue of her impending release: her words were a warning.

"Okay," Jake said. "I'm almost there."

It was imperative that Jake come with her, that he timed his orgasm to match the muscular contortions of her own. Jake knew, better than anyone, that success was all in the timing.

At the thought, he reflexively tossed a glance at the wall by their bed. Three sheets of computer paper were tacked to the peach-colored wallpaper, just beneath a watercolor of the Nantucket shoreline. The jagged black line that stretched across the sheets of paper was a stark contrast to the soft blue waves of the watercolor, and Jake felt a tightness in his stomach as he quickly interpreted the sharp angles of the chart, the dips and ascensions Brett had carefully highlighted in bright yellow ink. For nearly sixteen

months, she had painstakingly recorded her body temperature, entering the numbers into a program specifically
designed for her physical parameters.

According to the chart, twelve hours ago Brett's basal
body temp had dropped a few degrees from norm, signaling
that she had ovulated, that the short window of fertility
had opened and it was time for Jake to do his part. In
another twelve hours her temperature would rise again, and
the window would close. Already, the precious egg had
started to age, deteriorating by minute degrees as it waited,
impatiently, in one of her fallopian tubes.

Over the past year and a half, Jake had learned to hate
that little red blister floating inside her body. And he hated
himself for hating it, because it was a part of the woman he
loved more than anything in the world. His partner for the
past seven years, his wife for five of those, and one day,
God—and science—willing, the mother of his children.

"Oh God," Brett murmured. "Okay, oh God, now. Now.
NOW."

Jake closed his eyes and let Brett's gyrations bring him
past the point of control. He felt his body stiffen, felt his
muscles clench as the moment hit. He could imagine the tiny
tadpoles of sperm rushing out of his epididymis, the twenty-
one feet of coiled tubing inside his scrotum. He could almost
see the little creatures flitting through his vasa deferentia,
picking up a comet's tail of lubricating fluids and sugar-fuels.
He exhaled, picturing the tidal wave of semen coursing
through his urethra, gaining speed, firing with the force of a
shotgun blast into the hostile, acidic environment of Brett's
vagina.

Two hundred million competitors in a life or death marathon with that damn, mocking blister at the finish line. To win the race, one of those two hundred million hopefuls had to penetrate the cervical mucus, find the small entrance to the cervix, race across the uterus—a cavern the relative size of the Atlantic Ocean—choose the correct fallopian tube, and be the first to penetrate the hard outer layer of the waiting egg. The odds against success were immense; even the sucking, vacuumlike contortions of Brett's orgasm and the tilt of her pelvic region did little to help ease the journey. Of the two hundred million sperm at the starting line, perhaps twenty would make it to the vicinity of the egg itself. And of those twenty, only one would hit the egg dead on.

Jake gasped in full release, imagining the moment. A burst of chemicals would spout from the chosen sperm's head as it tunneled like a snake through the egg's outer shell. As soon as it hit the inner membrane, a massive electrical charge would erupt through the egg's surface, suddenly hardening the outer shell to prevent any other sperm from entering. Then the single, tiny marathoner would rupture, spilling its genetic contents, fusing Jake and Brett, creating life.

Jake collapsed onto his wife, his face close to her cheek, the scent of her sweat and her hair in his nostrils. He could feel her chest heaving beneath him as the endorphins rushed through his bloodstream, overwhelming his system with what felt like a dozen Valiums. He listened to the last few gasps of Brett's quiet orgasm, then carefully slid out from between her legs. Brett stayed in the same position, pelvis raised, legs slightly apart, as Jake pulled a bulky white comforter over her body, letting it drift down over the tops of her breasts. Then he rose to a sitting position.

From the bright fingers of daylight traipsing through the venetian blinds, Jake guessed it was close to nine. Both he and Brett were going to be late for work—but that was nothing new. In his case, it didn't really matter. His lab functioned pretty well on its own, and he no longer scheduled clinical appointments before noon. For Brett, the morning ritual was more problematic. As a second-year ER attending at Boston Central, she had day-to-day responsibilities that far exceeded Jake's own. And even though she had two residents and three interns under her command, at thirty-three years old, she was the linchpin that kept Central's trauma department running. Every morning that she was late, she damaged her reputation with the hospital hierarchy—and especially with the surly chief of her department, Maxwell Cross. And every time Cross chewed her out, she came home more despondent, more withdrawn—and more desperate.

But the morning ritual wasn't a matter of choice. Male hormones were most active in the dawn hours. And morning sunlight stimulated the production of soltriol, a steroidal hormone that aided fertility. Jake had read all the studies, knew all the statistics. And even though the morning sex was his idea—it wasn't his fault. Although lately, pretty much everything wrong with their marriage and their lives *felt* like his fault.

He took a deep breath, letting his bare feet touch the cool floorboards beneath the bed. The monotonous hum of the central air-conditioning mingled with the soft orchestral chords rising out of Brett's clock radio, which sat on her low, wooden bed table. Next to the bed table stood their shared dresser, next to that Brett's bookshelf, an elegant, polished-oak antique they had bought on the Cape three years ago.

Jake moved his gaze to the other side of the room as he stretched his arms out in front of him. His bookshelf—a decade younger than Brett's antique but carved from similar oak—was more ordered than his wife's. The top two shelves contained copies of his two published textbooks, the first an expansion of his Harvard Ph.D. thesis, the second an updated edition he had co-edited with his best friend, an obstetrician at Boston Central.

Jake rubbed sweat out of his eyes and then turned to look at Brett. Her cheeks were still red from her orgasm, but her dark eyes were now open, and Jake could tell by their shape that she was thinking—something she did way too much of. For the moment, Jake was content to look at her in silence, hoping against hope that she kept whatever was running through her head to herself.

Silent, she was as beautiful as a porcelain doll. Her high, angled cheekbones were inherited from her Russian father, her exotic, almond-shaped brown eyes from her Icelandic mother. Her hair was short and sable, a dozen shades darker than her eyes. She had recently grown out her bangs, and the silken strands spilled over her eyes, giving her whole face a smoldering, Asiatic edge.

From the neck down, the image of the porcelain doll no longer fit. Beneath the white comforter, Brett was more angles than curves. Like Jake, she was a natural athlete, a track-and-field star at Harvard who had concentrated on the hundred-meter hurdles because her legs seemed almost twice as long as the rest of her body. Even these years later, her stomach had remained flat, if no longer defined, and her limbs were still well-muscled and flexible. Five years of intense medical training—her internship, residency, and first year as an ER attending—had not yet affected her body.

Still, Jake knew the changes were coming. He had his own body as a guide; the general softening of his athlete's physique, the cracked eggshells at the corners of his blue eyes, the streaks of gray hidden in the curls of his dark hair. He was only two years older than Brett, and already he could feel the difference in his joints and muscles. He had played soccer in college, but now his weekly pickup game on the lawn of the business school in Cambridge left him sore and exhausted.

He was no longer a kid: a few years ago, the realization would have cut into his psyche like a scalpel. But he had finally grown into the role. Hopefully it wasn't too late.

"You don't have to wait with me," Brett said, her hand touching Jake's bare arm. "There's no sense in both of us being so late."

Jake put his hand over hers. "I'm not in any rush. Daniel's got the lab under control."

Jake winced at the thought of his arrogant, ambitious graduate student left alone in the multimillion-dollar lab for the third morning in a row. Daniel Golden was a brilliant student—but as slippery as they came. God only knew what mischief he was getting into while Jake worked on his personal life. But Jake didn't dare leave Brett alone, not the way things were going. Research showed that she should remain in the same supine position for at least forty minutes after sex. Even though Jake's part was done, the marathon was still in full swing, the tiny competitors still swimming for their lives.

Brett sighed, pulling her hand out from under Jake's and crooking her long arms behind her head. "Wish I could say the same for Calvin. He tries to cover for me in the ER, but Dr. Cross hates him even more than he hates me."

Jake shrugged, slowly rising from the bed. The mention of Brett's resident, Calvin Johnson, made him uncomfortable, and he felt the sudden urge to change the subject. He knew it was foolish, a carryover from the jealous days of their courtship. Some handsome young doctor with a crush on his wife was nothing new, and even though Calvin spent six days a week with Brett in the pressure cooker of the ER, it didn't mean Brett wanted anything to do with him. Still, she did mention his name a hell of a lot, and he *was* a good-looking kid. But Jake would never dare mention his unease to Brett; they had been through this sort of thing before, and Jake had learned to keep his jealous reflexes to himself. Better a little discomfort than an argument about trust. Trust was an argument Jake could never win.

He crossed toward the dresser and searched the top drawer for a pair of clean boxers. "Coffee? I think we've still got a couple of croissants left over."

"Jake, really, you don't have to wait around while I lie here like an invalid. I can grab something at the hospital cafeteria."

"I told you, I'm not in a rush. And we're partners in this, remember?" He pulled on the boxers, then found a white button-down shirt in a dry cleaner's box in the second drawer. As he did the buttons, he noticed that Brett had gone silent. He recognized the way she was breathing, and he felt his lips tightening into a line. He knew what was coming next. After five years of marriage, he and Brett could read each other like radiologists reading chest X rays. Little, seemingly insignificant smudges were actually the first signs of cancer—inevitable and unavoidable.

"If we're partners," Brett finally asked, "why do I feel like some sort of science project?"

Jake shut his eyes. *Old territory.* He could tell by the sharp edge to Brett's voice that the storm wasn't going to blow past without a little lightning. "Brett—"

"I'm serious, Jake. Sometimes you look at me, and I can tell your mind isn't here. You're not seeing me, you're seeing my insides, my ovaries, my fucking fallopian tubes. You don't kiss me because you love me—you kiss me because you're trying to set off some hormonal reaction, trying to change the consistency of some fluid you think makes all the difference."

Jake finished with his shirt, trying to stay calm as he stepped back from the dresser. He crossed to the shallow closet on the other side of the room, and searched for a pair of dark slacks. "I can't help the way my mind works. And I'm just trying to increase our chances—"

"This isn't your lab, Jake. This is our bedroom. It's supposed to be fun, not work."

Jake tried not to roll his eyes. "You're the one who stapled the fucking ovulation chart to the wall."

"And you're the one who checks my cervical mucus every morning before we have sex. I swear, sometimes I feel like one of your lab rats."

Jake felt his face getting hot. It was the same old argument, in a slightly different form. Brett was telling him for the hundredth time that the romance was gone, swallowed up by their growing desperation. To Jake, it was more than an observation—it was an accusation. An indictment of the role reversal that had plagued them over the past year. He had turned their lovemaking into something procedural and passionless. Everything had to be perfect, everything had to be by the book. Because the truth was, he couldn't handle the failure one more day. It was eating him up inside.

"There's a science to this," he said, trying to sound calm. "We're not in the ER, and you're not in control. This is my area of expertise."

Even as he said it, he knew it was exactly the wrong thing to say—both from a relationship standpoint and from a medical perspective. The more one turned the search for fertility into something mechanical, the less chance one had of getting pregnant. There was an enormous emotional component to fertility, not entirely defined by the secretion of sexual hormones. Jake knew this with the certainty of an expert—because he *was* an expert, one of the top fertility scientists on the East Coast. His lab attached to the Sandler Wing of Boston Central was one of the best-funded reproductive clinics in the state. *And still, it doesn't seem to make any difference.*

"You don't get it at all," Brett said, turning away. "It's not a competition, Jake. It's not about control—or pride."

Jake tucked in his shirt, waiting for her to say more. But she had gone silent. She had withdrawn into herself, shut down. *As usual.*

Jake tried his best not to be angry as he trudged out of the bedroom, on his way to the kitchen on the first floor. He knew he had no right to be angry. It had been his idea to wait to get married, his idea to wait to have kids. It had been his inability to commit that had set them back the crucial few years.

And now, he couldn't give Brett the one thing she had always wanted. The one thing she had waited for all her life. And all the science and data in the world wasn't making any difference. All Jake's expertise was getting him nowhere.

He simply couldn't get his wife pregnant.

3

An hour later, Jake strolled through the lobby of the Sandler Wing of Boston Central Hospital. Outside, it was at least ninety degrees, so hot the dashboard of his 1973 Buick Skylark had started to give off that smoky, melted-plastic smell of a car way too old for another Boston summer. But inside the plush, carpeted interior of Central's newest construct, the air was crisp enough to taste.

Jake pulled his white lab coat over his shoulders as he crossed the vast, semicircular front atrium. Two rows of cushioned waiting-room chairs lined the wide front picture windows, and about half of the chairs were occupied by patients busily filling out computerized note-charts. Behind the waiting area stood a ten-foot-high statue of a pregnant woman holding an infant. The statue was surrounded by a Japanese-style fountain, complete with bonsai trees, tiny polished pebbles, and huge goldfish with bubble eyes and multicolored fins. The statue and fountain had been donated by Arthur Sandler himself, the attorney general of Massachusetts and a prospective candidate for next year's governor's race.

Twenty feet beyond the statue stood a pair of sliding electronic security doors. Built into the doors was a state-of-the-art metal detector, a last-minute addition in deference to the abortion clinic located on the third floor. Two security guards stood nearby, with X-ray batons and stacks of visitor IDs.

As Jake approached, one of the security guards—burly, black, with deep-set eyes and a neck like a tree trunk—held out a tray, a friendly smile on his lips.

"Hey, Doc," he said. "Know what the lil' tyke did today?"

Jake dropped his wallet and keys onto the tray, winking at the oversized guard. "Shat himself and smiled at his daddy?"

"You got it. Most beautiful thing I ever saw."

Jake laughed. Bernard Stoller and his wife had been patients of his a little over a year ago. Bernard had come to him nearly in tears after fourteen months of failure in the bedroom. Bernard had assumed that there was something wrong with his wife—and it had been Jake's petrifying task to explain to the ex-linebacker that it wasn't Mrs. Stoller's problem that was keeping her out of maternity clothes. To ease the blow, Jake had put it in the most scientific terms possible: Bernard suffered from *idiopathic oligospermia*— an explanation that seemed much safer than telling the man he had an exceedingly low sperm count. It was a condition that had become fairly common over the previous decade; in fact, in the past year Jake's research had led him to the conclusion that there was a growing, unexplained crisis in male fertility in the Boston metropolitan area— and Bernard Stoller's low sperm count was just another addition to his recent collection of statistics.

After a more detailed evaluation, Jake had prescribed a volley of clomiphene citrate, and just two months later, the security guard had shown up at Jake's office door with a box of Cuban cigars. He and his wife had conceived within weeks of Jake's diagnosis. From that day forward, Jake had been met in the Sandler lobby by Bernard's wide, grateful smile. It gave Jake a warm feeling to know that his efforts had caused such happiness in someone else's life. At the same time, he could not ignore the pangs of jealousy he felt when he thought about how simple, how *easy* the answer could be.

"I just pray the kid gets his mother's looks," Bernard continued, as he pushed a hidden button in the opaque Plexiglas, opening the sliding doors. "If not, I'm gonna ask you for my money back."

Jake stepped through the doors, retrieving his wallet and keys. "Sorry, Bernard. You didn't read the fine print. No refunds or returns."

The security doors slid shut, leaving Jake alone in the

blue-carpeted corridor that led into the belly of the Sandler Wing. He headed toward the bank of elevators at the far end of the hallway, thinking about Bernard and his little football-headed kid. He noticed a sudden tightness in his throat. Brett's voice reverberated through his mind: *It's not a competition, Jake.* Of course, she was right. She was usually right. But her words didn't make his ironic situation any easier to accept.

Still, Bernard's case should have filled him with hope. The truth was, ninety percent of the couples who came to see him ended up conceiving within twelve months. The scientific advances were spectacular, outpacing most other fields of medicine. Sooner or later, he and Brett would beat the odds. *Unless there's something seriously wrong, something previously undetected . . .*

Jake bit down on his lower lip, angry with himself for letting the sudden thought into his head. The discovery he had made one week ago couldn't possibly have anything to do with his and Brett's problem. They had been trying to get pregnant for nearly two years. And his recent discovery was unique—it had to be, because it was too crazy to imagine anything else. The discovery represented an aberration, maybe a good journal article, even a lecture at the upcoming National Fertility Conference in Chicago—nothing more. It couldn't possibly be related to his own infertility.

Even as he discarded the idea, he realized that there was only one way to know for sure. Only one way to rule out the possibility, once and for all.

He stepped into the elevator and hit the button for the second floor.

• • •

Heavy guitar licks filled the room as Jake crossed the threshold of his lab. He could see himself reflected in a dozen polished surfaces, and he felt like he was trapped in some sort of space-age prism. The loud music only added to the surreal experience, and Jake sighed, trying not to feel old.

Even after six months, he hadn't gotten used to the new lab. Science was supposed to take place in dark, dingy basements cluttered with wires and exposed pipes—at least that's what Jake had been raised to believe. His father had been an electrical engineer, his mother a chemist. He had grown up on university campuses all over the United States, and he had seen dozens of laboratories, had played hide-and-seek behind test-tube racks, steel equipment shelves, and Univac computer cabinets. Even during his time at Harvard Med School, the labs had always felt like labs. In four years, Jake did not remember seeing one window—let alone anything like the Plexiglas monstrosity that bordered the entire right side of his vast new digs.

According to the building specs, the picture window was five inches thick, impervious to wind and weather. Still, it didn't *feel* right. The soft orange glow of natural light reflected oddly off the polished marble surfaces of a dozen counters and cabinets, and as the sun rose higher, the lab often took on a nearly tropical glow.

The guitar music grew louder as Jake moved deeper into the lab, and he glanced toward the ceiling. A half-dozen wireless speakers were embedded behind the circular halogen tiles that ran the length of the ceiling. By the cacophonous wail, Jake could easily guess which of his graduate students had gotten to the stereo in his office first.

He reached the partially open door to the computer room at the back of the lab, and his suspicion was confirmed. Daniel Golden was seated at the IBM mainframe in the far corner of the room, his small body caught in the conical blue glow pouring out of the three-foot-high flat screen. Daniel was hunched forward on an ergonomic three-wheeled stool. His short, wiry frame was perfect for the Japanese design.

Daniel was the sort of kid you expected to graduate summa cum laude from MIT. His thick, plastic-rimmed glasses matched his jet black hair, and his cheeks and jaw were perpetually scruffy. He was wearing his trademark MIT Chess Team sweatshirt and a pair of tattered green shorts. Jake had spoken to him numerous times about the outfit—but had finally given up. Daniel was working toward a Ph.D., not an MD; he didn't have to see patients—in fact, he never really needed to leave the confines of the lab. It didn't matter what he wore, or what he looked like—just how facilely his mind worked.

On that count, Daniel Golden was as distinguished as his resume. From the first day he had joined Jake's team, he had happily lodged himself in the high-tech lab. Fifteen- to twenty-hour days, seven days a week. Other than a network of e-mail confidants, he had no social diversions; as far as Jake could tell, his life revolved around his Ph.D. project, an innovative search for the chemotaxin at the source of fertility—the elusive protein that the egg supposedly secretes to attract sperm. If Daniel ever succeeded in actually finding the protein, it would no doubt win him a Nobel Prize and get him a lab of his own.

Jake cleared his throat as he stepped into the small, cubic computer room. Daniel looked up, his compressed, pug-nosed face momentarily confused. Then he saw Jake's chiseled visage reflected in his computer screen, and his hand whipped toward the keyboard. The screen went instantly blank.

Jake had to keep himself from laughing. Daniel was always like this around him—secretive to the point of absurdity. As if the kid were in some sort of constant competition with his own Ph.D. adviser. Jake tried to make his voice as amiable as possible.

"You don't mind if I turn the music down a touch?" he asked. "If it stays this loud, it's going to curdle our sperm samples."

Daniel faked a laugh, then gestured toward Jake's office on the other side of the lab. His voice was high-pitched, irritating, like a rusty gear. "You got a message from Dr. Stern. He says the game's been moved to seven-thirty."

Jake nodded; his weekly pickup soccer game had been starting later and later as the weather turned hot. But he was surprised that Alex Stern had been the one to call him. Alex was his closest friend, his former med-school lab partner and co-conspirator, but he wasn't the type to pass along scheduling messages. "Did Alex say anything else?"

"He wanted to speak to you as soon as you got in."

Daniel's voice had ratcheted up another octave, and Jake understood. Daniel hated Alex Stern. Alex was a congenital smart-ass, and the few times he had visited Jake's lab, he had gone out of his way to give the awkward kid a hard time.

"Okay, thanks. Anything else?"

"Nope." Daniel turned back to his computer, his thin shoulders shrinking under his sweatshirt. Jake watched him for a moment more, but the kid was obviously waiting for him to leave before he powered up the computer. It was ridiculous—this was *Jake's* lab, after all. But if Jake really had a problem with Daniel, he could always speak to the dean. As it was, Daniel did his work, ran whatever samples Jake asked him to test, and stayed out of the way. So what if he had his secrets?

Jake exited the computer room and headed toward his office. His office door was open, and the scent of bad coffee drifted in the gusts of frozen air coming from the twin vents just inside. Once through the doorway, Jake ignored the coffeepot on the windowsill and headed straight for the stereo on the bottom shelf of his bookcase. He turned the volume to a less painful level and then crossed toward a locked bookcase on the other side of the kidney-shaped room.

The lock was a standard combination model, and Jake quickly twirled to the correct numbers. The doors clicked open, and he reached into the bookshelf and retrieved a heavy steel-and-plastic device, two feet high, trailing a long power cord. The device weighed at least thirty pounds, and was about the size and shape of a binocular microscope. Jake set the device down carefully on his desk, then plugged the power cord into the nearby outlet.

A low whirring filled his office as the device powered up. A small internal light blinked on, and Jake could smell the twin heating coils warming up the thick plastic base. A flicker of excitement moved through him as he listened to the whirring. The long hours he had spent working on the device had been cathartic—a way of taking him away from the troubles in his personal life.

He ran his hands down the sides of the device, pride rising within him. Much of the device did, in fact, consist of a microscope, with two high-powered lenses, a built-in camera, a dozen focusing gears, and three separate bulbs for optimum light. But the base of the device was entirely Jake's own invention. The specimen receptacle was unlike any other, protected inside a spherical container made out of the purest blown glass. Running through the glass were six copper contact wires, attached at two ends to a maze of transistors and resistant coils. It had taken Jake nearly four months to construct the machine, another two to get it to work properly. He had only used it for the first time a week ago—on three samples from male patients with perpetual, unexplained infertility.

He hadn't expected the device to unearth anything groundbreaking. The prototype was just meant to add another dimension to the tried and true tests of his trade. Simply put, the device was designed to recreate the natural electrical currents found inside a woman's reproductive tract. The specimen receptacle in the prototype's base was filled with solution that mimicked a woman's vaginal secretions, and the copper wiring was tuned as closely as possible to the ionic charge present in the female womb.

Jake had chosen his trial samples carefully. All three men had high sperm counts and Grade IV motility—sperm that were active, straight-swimming, intrinsically capable of insemination. All three were from men who should have been able to conceive, but for unknown reasons, could not. In the past year, Jake had seen more and more such patients; in the last two months alone, the rate of unexplained male infertiles coming into his clinic had jumped a full ten percent. It was a stunning rise—one that Jake could not yet explain.

When he had placed the first two samples into his device, they had behaved exactly as he had anticipated. High motility, high mobility, no deviation from their already recorded characteristics. The special environment had made no difference; they acted exactly as they had under a normal microscope.

But the third sample had exhibited activity that had shocked Jake to his core. In fact, in all his years as a doctor, he had never seen anything quite like it. A brand-new disorder—a vivid pattern of sperm behavior that had never been documented before.

Now, a week later, he couldn't get the memory of the discovery out of his head. He knew he needed to run more samples through his prototype. There was a chance he had stumbled on a brand-new paradigm—one that might explain the falling male fertility rate in the Boston metropolitan area. But before he began running random samples, there was something more personal he had to do. *I have to set my mind at ease.*

He thought about Brett, lying silent on their bed, her face turned away. Then he clenched his jaw, rising from his seat. He quickly crossed his office and shut the door. The lock clicked automatically, and he wondered what Daniel would think if he happened to stroll by: *Could the boss actually have his own secrets?* Jake smirked as he moved back to his desk.

He reached into the second drawer and retrieved a wide-mouthed, plastic specimen cup. The cup was sealed in clear cellophane, and he hastily ripped the covering away, tossing it under his feet.

Normally, he should have remained abstinent for two days before collecting a sperm sample, so that his body would have time to restock its supply. But Jake wasn't concerned with his count; he had tested himself dozens of times, and knew that he was producing close to one hundred million sperm per ejaculation—high enough to keep him at a fertile level without any period of abstinence. Besides, at the moment he wasn't interested in how many sperm he was producing—rather, he wanted to know why they weren't doing their job.

He quickly undid his belt buckle and lowered his pants to his knees. He felt mildly uncomfortable, his pants down in the middle of his office—but he didn't want to risk running into Daniel on the way to the collection room on the other side of the lab. He closed his eyes as he went to work, keeping the plastic container firmly gripped in his left hand.

At first, he pictured Brett on the desk in front of him, her naked body writhing in coordinated rhythm with his moving right hand. But slowly, the picture changed, and he cycled through his standard visuals. Brett on her knees on their bedroom floor, on her stomach on the leather couch in their study, in the shower, her hands against the foggy glass door, her lips wrapped around his—

The moment came quickly, and Jake gasped, careful not to miss any of the crucial first spurt, the portion of the sample with the highest concentration of healthy sperm. He knew he had to act quickly: within sixty seconds, his semen would coagulate into a gel the consistency of tapioca, a process known in the lexicon as "clumping." Ten minutes later, it would liquefy again, but Jake did not want to wait for the subtle chemical changes. He wanted to know what his sperm were doing the second they left his body— what they were doing as they traveled up Brett's system.

He took a deep breath, slowing his heart as best he could, carefully pouring his sample into the spherical receptacle at the base of his viewing device. Then he put his eyes against the twin lenses.

It took him a second to get used to the bright light streaming out of the high-intensity bulbs. Then his eyes focused, and the microscopic sample began to take shape. He could see the tiny, tadpole-like sperm swimming at unbelievable speeds through the receptacle, their tails wriggling back and forth as the glucose powered them along. As he had witnessed before, his sperm were moving straight and strong—but now there was something noticeably different about them. Sweat rose on Jake's back as he focused his vision on a single sperm, following its oval head with his eyes. As he watched, the sperm took a sharp right—and smashed directly into the head of one of its colleagues. Both sperm ruptured on contact, their long tails twirling off, wiggling uselessly.

Jake's stomach clenched as he shifted his eyes to another tiny subject. Again, he watched the same macabre display. The sperm was going along at breakneck pace, driving straight across the receptacle—when suddenly it twisted to the left, slamming headlong into another sperm.

Over and over, he watched his tiny sperm crashing into one another. Within a few seconds, not a single living sperm was left in the receptacle. Jake found himself staring down at a bloodless battlefield, filled with the corpses of his hapless, suicidal marathoners.

Traumatized, he rocked back in his chair. He was suddenly having trouble catching his breath. It was exactly what he had feared—the same display he had witnessed with the test sample. It seemed impossible, incredibly coincidental—but there it was, right in front of his eyes. A horrible answer to his infertility, to two years of frustrating struggle. It wasn't the number of sperm he was producing, or the strength of their motility. It was their vicious, suicidal behavior.

A week ago, Jake had given the horror a name.

Apoptotic Sperm Dysfunction. A disorder perhaps never seen before—because the device on Jake's desk was his own invention, utilizing familiar science in an unfamiliar way.

"Christ," he said, coughing, his head suddenly in his hands. On a personal level, ASD was a tragedy, a strange mutation in his sperm that had obviously affected his fertility. But on a professional level, it was enormous, unbelievable. Now he had two cases of the strange disorder in only four samples. The odds against such a finding were staggering—unless the syndrome was more common than he had realized.

Two samples did not define an epidemic. But Jake's recent research convincingly showed a rising rate of male infertility in the Boston metropolitan area. The average sperm rate was falling, sperm motility was slowing—and unexplained infertility was becoming more and more the norm. Was it possible that Jake had stumbled onto the answer?

Was ASD somehow linked to the city's fertility crisis?

To answer that question, Jake needed access to a much larger set of sperm samples.

He knew just where to go.

4

Brett closed her eyes, letting the steam from the Styrofoam cup on the table in front of her gently caress her cheeks. The antique rocking chair felt good against her tired hips, and she kicked off her bloodstained sneakers, wriggling her stockinged toes. Soft violin music echoed through her ears, and she felt herself drifting, carried by the undulating notes. She could just barely hear the screech of steel stretcher wheels in the distance—but she ignored the sound, pretending it was coming from miles away. As long as she was in the rocking chair, nothing could touch her. It didn't matter that the double doors that led back into the chaos of the ER were only ten feet away, or that her beeper squatted ominously on the table, inches from her cup of coffee. This was her oasis. For the next seven minutes of midmorning break, the rest of the world simply did not exist.

Sometimes it amazed her, how fast she could shift gears. She knew it was a skill common to emergency physicians— an adaptation to an insane way of life. One minute, you were holding a shattered, bleeding body together with your gloved hands. The next minute you were stretched out in the intern lounge, listening to Vivaldi as you contemplated what you were going to eat for lunch. It was a bizarre style of living—and Brett wouldn't have traded it for anything in the world.

Well, that isn't exactly true. Brett's hands moved to her stomach, and her fingers roamed across the soft material of her dark blue scrubs. She pretended that she felt something—a new layer of fat, a bulging thickness that wasn't there before. Then her shoulders sagged, and she shifted her hands back to the table. Who was she kidding?

It had been two years since she'd gone off the pill. She and Jake had done everything by the book, had followed every suggestion from every expert Jake knew. They had suffered through a barrage of physiological tests, had given samples of every damn fluid in their bodies. And still, nothing. Jake had assured her that it was normal, that two years for a couple their age wasn't unusual—but Brett knew better. She had read the same manuals as Jake. There was something wrong, and Brett knew there was a good chance she would never get pregnant.

Her fingers shook as she lifted the cup of coffee to her lips. The liquid was searingly hot, but she didn't jerk away, she let the pain add to the agonizing ache inside her body. The ache was a constant, something she had endured for a very long time. She knew it was tearing at her marriage, breaking down everything she and Jake had worked so hard to build. But the ache was something she couldn't control. It wasn't merely her biological clock; it was something much deeper, something so powerful she couldn't face it head on—

Warm hands landed on her shoulders, rocking her chair back from the table. Suddenly she was staring up into a pair of dark eyes. She gasped, startled—and then she started to laugh. Calvin Johnson beamed down at her, his smile wide as a Cheshire cat's. He winked playfully, his smooth black features made even darker by the soft light of the cozy intern lounge.

"You looked so fucking relaxed," he said, his face still inches from hers. "I had to make sure you were still alive. Should I call in a cardiac team?"

Brett kicked her feet against the table, shoving the rocking chair back into Calvin's chest. He grunted dramatically and let her shoulders go. He pretended to stumble back across the small lounge, toppling into the soft gray couch in the far corner. Then he hooked his long, muscular legs over one of the couch's armrests, his arms crossed behind his cleanly shaven head.

"A contemplative moment," he said, "and it's not even noon. Maybe you really are getting old."

Brett considered tossing her coffee at the smiling resident. "One day you'll understand. With all the helpless residents nipping at our heels, it's a wonder we attendings don't go completely crazy."

Calvin laughed, his head falling back against the couch. "You won't go crazy—you'll just end up like Chief Cross. A stick up your ass and a sneer on your pretty white face."

Brett coughed, glancing at the double doors that led to the ER. Sometimes, Calvin pushed their banter just a little too far. But it didn't really bother her—over the past year, she and her senior resident had developed a unique, extremely close friendship. It was a relationship Brett treasured, especially now that her marriage had become so troubled. Calvin was someone she could talk to, confide in, and trust.

Although they came from completely different worlds—Calvin from a rough childhood in downtown Detroit, Brett from a Boston family that dated back more than a century—they had developed a remarkable closeness. Perhaps that was because they both knew a bit about childhood scars.

Brett's thoughts froze as the sound of two beepers going off simultaneously echoed through the intern lounge. Before either she or Calvin had a chance to check who was paging them, a high-pitched voice sprang out of the intercom attached above the double doors.

"Doctors Foster and Johnson to Emergency. Ten–thirty-three en route, Unit Three-one-six arriving with a code two-nine-four. ETA three minutes."

Brett slid her shoes on and sprang to her feet. Calvin was already on his way through the double doors. The ER had been quiet all morning—but now that was about to change. Brett felt the adrenaline pulsing through her veins. She was a trauma specialist, one of the best in the country. The intercom call had instantly caused her to switch gears yet again.

10-33 en route. That was the dispatch code for a serious emergency. A paramedic team was rushing toward the hospital, a grievously ill patient in the back of their wagon. Worse yet, the ambulance had radioed in a code 2-9-4. That meant the patient was bleeding profusely from multiple areas and was near death.

On its own, the situation was enough to get Brett's heart pounding. But this particular call sent shivers down her spine. And she could tell by the way Calvin held the double doors open for her—his eyes averted, a tremble in his shoulders—that he was thinking the same thing.

It was their third code 2-9-4 in five days.

"Jesus," Brett gasped, as three blood-soaked paramedics and two trauma nurses burst through the ER front doors at a full run, stretcher leading the way. One of the paramedics was breathing the patient with an ambu bag, while another held two plasma bags over his head, trailing long IV tubes down to the patient's right arm. The third paramedic was pushing the stretcher, shouting orders at the two trauma nurses rushing to keep up.

Brett's trauma team moved instinctively in a semicircle around the ER table to her left. "I need a chem cart," she shouted, "EKG, respiratory cart, and a transfuser—stat. O-negative whole blood, as much as we've got on hand."

She rushed forward, Calvin a step behind her. As she reached the head of the moving stretcher, she immediately shifted her eyes to the patient, taking everything in at once. The man's mouth was partially hidden by the ambu bag and the long, plastic endo tube—but Brett could see the blood bubbling out around the corners of his lips, covering his chin, soaking the stretcher beneath him. More blood streamed from the man's eyes, nostrils, and ears, and his hair was completely drenched, sticking to his skull in dark red clumps.

The paramedics had already ripped his shirt open, and there were EKG leads running in spaghetti twists from his bare chest. Trickles of blood dripped down from his nipples, more blood oozed from his navel. Where his torso wasn't covered with blood, the man's skin had turned a strange off-yellow color. Brett stowed that clue away for later.

"Picked him up in the Public Garden," the lead paramedic began. "Witnesses say he was sitting on a bench, reading a book, when suddenly he started bleeding out of his nose, eyes, and ears. Then he collapsed, went into convulsions, started vomiting blood. We were driving by, got to him just as he went into full shock."

Brett nodded, noticing out of the corner of her eyes that all three paramedics were wearing double-gloves and that the sleeves of their uniforms were banded shut. All three men were doused in blood, their uniforms looking like something from a Jackson Pollack nightmare.

"Current condition?" Brett asked, as the stretcher skidded to a stop next to her trauma team and the waiting ER table.

"Unresponsive. Got an endo tube in blind, started breathing him with the ambu bag. Then we got him on full plasma—but no matter how much we put in, he just bled it out. Nearly ran through our whole stock before we got here."

The paramedic was breathing heavily, clearly shaken. That scared Brett more than anything else. These guys were hardcore—nothing was supposed to faze them. This one—his name was Kyle Van Epps—had pushed a half dozen subway-accident amputees through those double doors, barely breaking a sweat. But now he was panicked—and Brett understood why.

The patient was a healthy, athletic-looking young man—and he was bleeding out at an alarming rate. The sheer viciousness of his condition was staggering to watch—and more than a little frightening. Extensive bleeding from a gunshot wound or a violent amputation was one thing; intense bleeding without an obvious cause was a trauma specialist's nightmare.

At least Brett knew it wasn't anything viral or contagious. She and Calvin had seen this exact condition two other times in the past week. All young men, all in good physical shape—and all gushing blood. Infectious disease specialists from the CDC in Atlanta had already checked the samples, and though the cause of the condition was unknown, there seemed to be no danger of contagion. But for Brett, that didn't make it any easier to deal with. The man on the stretcher in front of her was dying.

Her trauma team surrounded the stretcher, each person grabbing a section of the blood-soaked sheet beneath the patient. Brett caught Calvin's eye, then joined in.

"One, two, three—lift!"

Her team quickly pulled the patient off the stretcher, transferring him to the ER table. With the motion, a new gush of bright red blood fountained out around the endo tube, soaking the paramedic still working the ambu bag. Adam Stanhope, the respiratory tech, quickly took the paramedic's place, making sure there was no pause in the breathing rhythm. The paramedic staggered back, shaking his head. Like Kyle's, his entire uniform was covered in blood.

Brett pushed past him, her attention focused on the patient in front of her. "Calvin, get the EKG lines hooked up. Barbara, start the O-negative whole-blood transfusion. Four units of fresh plasma, six units of platelets. Katherine, start a second IV, and get a chem 7, a red blood smear, and a platelet count, stat!"

As her team rushed to carry out her orders, she grabbed a syringe from the chem cart at the head of the stretcher. She wasn't going to wait for the smear or the platelet count—because she had a pretty good idea what they would indicate: *Microangopathic red blood cells, a falling platelet count, abnormal fibrinogen numbers, a high level of fibrin degradation products, low plasminogen levels.* Although the cause of the patient's terrifying condition was a mystery, the character of his condition was not.

"DIC," Calvin stated, as Brett jammed the hypodermic full of heparin into the second IV line. Brett nodded, her face pale.

Disseminated Intravascular Coagulation. She and Calvin did not need the lab numbers, because they had seen them before. DIC—uncontrolled, intravascular coagulation, which leads to unstoppable hemorrhaging. In simple terms, massive coagulation inside the patient's bloodstream was rapidly depleting his platelets, making it impossible for his blood to clot. Every pore became a one-way valve, every orifice a broken dam. Unless, by some miracle, the injection of heparin or the infused platelets reversed the process, he would bleed until there was no blood left in his body.

"Just like the others," Calvin was saying, shaking his head as he finished attaching the EKG leads to the cardiac machine on the cart next to his hip. "And there's not a damn thing we can do about it."

Brett tried to ignore the desperation in Calvin's voice. Though she knew there was almost no chance of saving the man's life, she didn't need to be reminded that there was no real cure for DIC—that the only way to successfully treat the syndrome was to eradicate the underlying cause.

Her stomach clenched at the thought. It was a horrible, helpless feeling, hovering over a dying man she couldn't, for all her training, help. *His condition is incompatible with life—*

"Jesus," Calvin hissed, and Brett quickly turned in his direction. He was staring at the cardiac monitor, and his face had gone a shade darker. Brett saw the jagged green line, and realized there wasn't much time.

"More platelets!" she shouted, but she knew it was hopeless. The man's body was deteriorating right in front of her eyes. Any second, his organs would start to shut down, as he literally drowned in his own blood. Desperate, Brett was about to go for another blast of heparin, when she heard a hideous, metallic squeal. Suddenly, the patient thrashed upward, his body convulsing, every muscle going instantly taut. Brett dove forward, her hands pushing the man back down as streams of dark blood sprayed from his mouth and nose, drenching her scrubs. A second later, the man's entire left side went limp.

"He's stroked out!" Brett yelled. "Get me two cc's of—"

"He's crashing!" Calvin suddenly interrupted from the cardiac machine. "He's going into v-fib!"

Brett immediately forgot about the stroke, as she grabbed the defibrillator paddles off the cardiac cart. The stroke had become secondary, because now the man's heart was responding to random electrical impulses and was no longer capable of pumping blood to his body. He was dying, fast.

"Two hundred joules!" Brett shouted, rubbing the paddles together to spread the conductive jelly. "Clear!"

Everyone stepped back from the table, and Brett slammed the paddles against the man's blood-slick chest. She depressed the triggers, and the man's body jerked against the table. She looked at the EKG machine—and her heart fell.

"He's down!" Calvin shouted. "Flatline."

Fuck. Brett cleared her throat, struggling to remain calm. "Give me three hundred and forty joules! Clear!"

Again, everyone stepped back. This time, the patient arched a full inch off the table as the electric charge ran through his body. Without pausing to look at the cardiac machine, Brett tossed the defibrillator paddles and leapt forward, starting intense CPR. The patient's chest felt warm and slick beneath her gloved hands, and she tried not to look at his bloody face as she counted out the rhythm. *One one thousand, two one thousand, three one thousand, come on damn you, come on you fucking bastard don't you fucking die—*

"Brett," Calvin said, quietly. His gloved hand touched her shoulder.

Brett paused, looking at him, her hands still moving against the man's chest. Then she shook her head. "Not yet. Give me a scalpel and an aortic clamp."

Calvin raised his eyebrows. "Brett—"

"Now, Calvin. I'm going to crack his chest, clamp off his aorta."

Calvin handed her the scalpel and the clamp, and she quickly made the deep incision, cutting the man open on the midaxilliary line, between the fourth and fifth rib. A wash of blood poured out over her gloved right hand as she reached deep into his chest cavity, feeling upward toward the cardiac sac—and then her eyes went wide.

She couldn't even find the fucking heart. The man's entire chest cavity was filled with blood. It was spilling out of every organ, as if his interior blood vessels had simply disintegrated.

Brett withdrew her hand, looking at Calvin.

"Well," she finally said. "That's that."

Calvin glanced at the clock above the double doors. "Call it two-fifteen."

Brett nodded, stepping away from the stretcher, yanking off her gloves and tossing them toward the floor. Her entire body felt numb. She straightened her back, forcing the tension out of her voice as she faced her trauma team. "It was a good try, everyone. Let's get him cleaned up and moved to an autopsy room right away. Barbara, page Dr. Kelly down in Path, get him in as fast as possible."

"Four in a week," Calvin said, as he followed Brett toward the changing room. "The CDC's got to get somebody down here."

Brett shrugged, trying to appear calmer than she felt. "It's not viral or bacteriological—so they're not going to rush. And four DICs in a city as big as Boston isn't exactly an epidemic. Still, these are young, healthy-looking men. This shouldn't be happening."

They passed through the doors leading to the changing room. The room was large and brightly lit, with white, cinder-block walls and a tiled, porcelain floor. Two oversized stainless-steel sinks took up most of the far wall. To the right, another door led to the co-ed locker room.

Brett headed directly for one of the oversized sinks. She felt lightheaded as the adrenaline rush finally began to subside. Calvin sidled up next to her, turning his faucet on high. Steam erupted as the water hit the cold steel bottom of the sink basin. Brett watched the steam billow upward, vanishing as it hit the gusts of antiseptic, air-conditioned air coming out of the room's ceiling vents.

"DIC's a symptom," she said, thinking out loud as she scrubbed the blood off her hands. "It's not a disease. Something's got to set it off. Tumors, severe intracranial damage, severe infection, extensive surgery, deep skin burns, leukemia—"

"An interrupted pregnancy," Calvin added, and Brett shot him a glance. All four of the recent cases had been young men. Still, his comment tweaked at her thoughts, and she paused, holding her hands still beneath the warm jet of water.

"Or a dirty tampon."

Calvin stared at her. She continued her line of thought. "Toxic shock syndrome back in the seventies. Strep and staph bacteria on the surface of feminine products caused a fairly large number of unlucky women to crash out, all textbook DIC cases."

"You think that's what we're looking at?" Calvin asked, grabbing a towel off the rack next to the sink. "Toxic shock syndrome?"

"It's possible," Brett responded, taking the towel from him. "TSS is essentially an overwhelming immune response to some sort of antigen. Something that's normally harmless sets off a massive reaction—like an allergic response, only much worse. The body tries to overcome the antigen with massive coagulation—and when the coagulants and platelets are depleted, massive bleeding begins. Once the process starts, it's extremely difficult to stop."

Incompatible with life. Brett wrapped the towel around her hands, hiding her sudden fists. She pictured the body on its way down to the autopsy room, still leaking blood from every open pore.

"Calvin," she said, "we have two choices. We can wait for the CDC to finally send somebody down here. Or we can look into this ourselves."

Brett knew the quest came at an opportune time for her.

For too long, everything in her life had revolved around her inability to get pregnant. The mysterious DIC deaths might very well be the thing to keep her mind out of her bedroom.

"First," she said, as she tossed the damp towel into a disposal bin beneath the sinks, "we need to try and figure out what links our four DIC deaths. Four young, healthy men shouldn't have died like this. We need to find out why they did."

Calvin nodded, pulling at his bloody scrubs as he headed toward the locker room. "Somehow, I don't think the answer is going to have anything to do with tampons."

5

Dr. Eric Heidlinger saw the taxi but didn't stop running, his heavy briefcase pressed tightly against his chest, his white lab coat flapping out behind him like some sort of cut-rate superhero's cape. The taxi's horn blared, the tires sending up dust and smoke as the driver frantically slammed the brakes. Heidlinger kept his head down, his teeth clenched, shoes churning against the gravelly blacktop. The taxi was still coming toward him, the driver's eyes wide, a scream caught in the poor man's throat. Then, at the last second, the cab swerved to the right, slamming headlong into the concrete barrier with a sickening crunch of metal.

Heidlinger kept moving, refusing to look back. He prayed that the driver was all right—but he couldn't stop to check on the man. Tears streamed down his wrinkled cheeks as he reached the other side of the street and vaulted the low railing. His feet touched grass and he fell, toppling down a steep, muddy embankment. His arthritic joints cried out— but he held onto the briefcase, accepting the pain, letting it chase the exhaustion and sorrow out of his body. He had to keep moving. He had no choice.

A second later he was on his feet, leaping over a low bush, heading toward the tourist-infested streets of the Boston waterfront. Sweat ran down his back, and his chest heaved from the exertion. Heidlinger was two days past his sixty-third birthday. He hadn't run like this for more than twenty-five years and he doubted his body would ever recover from the strain. But he didn't care. He was almost certainly a dead man already.

He pressed his briefcase harder against his chest, heading directly toward the harbor, approximately a hundred yards in the distance. A half dozen boats rocked up and down in the dark water, resting in the shadows of the waterfront hotels and restaurants. It was rush hour, he realized: he could see the cars full of people heading home from work. *Innocent, unknowing people—heading home to their wives and children, heading home without the slightest knowledge of what I've done.*

Heidlinger lowered his shoulders and kept on running, telling himself that it wasn't over yet, that he still had a chance to fix things, to make things right.

To make things right. Heidlinger reached the edge of the

crowded street, slowing as he searched for a hole in the traffic, somewhere he could get across to the packed sidewalk on the other side. For so long, Heidlinger had tried to live with the guilt of what he had created. And then, just twenty minutes ago, sitting in his office with the door closed, reading the birthday card his grandson had sent him from Indiana—he had suddenly snapped. A moment later he had rushed out the door, moving faster than his old legs had ever carried him.

He had assumed they'd stop him in the elevator—take him out before he ever reached the ground floor of the vast glass-and-steel building in the heart of the Back Bay. He knew they had been watching him for some time—watching him in his office, at his home on Beacon Hill, from a tiny fiber-optic camera attached to the glove compartment of his car. They were onto him—but for some reason, they had let him out of the building, out into the sweltering streets of the city. And that meant he still had a chance.

He leapt forward again, hitting the crowded street at a dead run. A two-door sports car swerved past, horn blaring, and a Volvo screeched to a stop just feet from his right hip. Then he was across to the other side, trying to lose himself in the crowd of well-dressed men and women.

If he was going to make things right, he had to do it himself—and quickly. And that meant he needed to find someplace isolated and safe, someplace crowded enough to give him shelter but quiet enough to let him work.

He continued down the street, half-carried by the bustling crowd. Most of the people around him were wearing business suits, even in the extreme heat. The waterfront was Boston's new up-and-coming yuppie neighbor-hood, and these were the working chic, the men and women who staffed the enormous pincushion of buildings that made up Boston's financial district. Some of them probably worked in the very same fifty-story tower from which Heidlinger had just escaped.

The thought filled Heidlinger with dread, and he whirled forward, shoving people out of his way. Then his eyes settled on a massive modern building twenty yards to his right, jutting out over the harbor. His face brightened as he recognized the building, and he rushed forward.

He glanced at his watch as he reached the back of a small line of tourists in front of the building's glass doors. It was ten minutes to eight—he had made it just in time to catch the extended summer hours. He knew this for a fact—because a month ago, he had waited with his grandson in this very same line.

He rocked forward, picturing little, blond-haired Brad holding his hand as they waited for the line to get moving. His eyes burned as the guilt and shame rose inside him.

"Sir? Are you all right?"

Heidlinger shook his head, struggling to clear the tears out of his eyes. Now he was at the front of the line, staring through a sheet of glass at a woman with frizzy orange hair. He nodded quickly, then reached into his pocket and pulled out a ten-dollar bill. He shoved the bill through the slot at the bottom of the window.

"Sir," the woman said, gesturing toward the clock behind her shoulder. "Are you sure you don't want to come back another day? The aquarium closes in ten minutes."

"That's all I need," Heidlinger croaked. The woman stared at him and then shrugged, handing him a ticket.

A minute later, he was through the glass front entrance of the New England Aquarium. He took a brief moment to catch his breath, his eyes adjusting to the dark interior of the building. He was standing a few feet from the wooden railing that looked out over the enormous penguin tank. He could hear squawking and splashing coming from the other side of the railing, and he assumed it was feeding time. A crowd of tourists stood with their backs to him, pointing and laughing, some holding children up over the ledge for a better view.

To Heidlinger's left was a new, brightly lit exhibit, something about the ecology of marshes. To his right, the aquarium store, its glass windows cluttered with stuffed animals of every conceivable size and shape. And just ahead, following the curve of the penguin tank's railing, was the carpeted walkway that led into the belly of the aquarium, lined on either side by huge glass tanks. The walkway extended upward in a slow spiral, rising high above the penguin tank to the top of the building. Heidlinger and his grandson had spent hours wandering up and down the walkway, losing themselves in the dark, contemplative atmosphere.

Now, Heidlinger again intended to lose himself inside the aquarium—but not in order to contemplate. He rushed toward the blue carpeted walkway, past a pair of teenagers holding hands, winding through a group of school-age children following a woman with a whistle in her mouth. He continually glanced back over his shoulder, trying to see if he was being followed. Of course, he wouldn't see them until it was too late. They were professionals—led by a maniac, but a *brilliant* maniac, a man who had been a high-ranking member of one of the most elite corps in the U.S. military. Heidlinger had made the foolish mistake of under-estimating the man's psychosis once before.

Heidlinger turned abruptly to the right, entering a dark alcove set between two dimly lit fish tanks. The larger of the two tanks contained a single, enormous grouper, drift-ing just inches from the glass, its mouth wide open. The smaller tank was full of fluorescent jellyfish, floating like tiny parachutes in the computer-controlled artificial cur-rents. A young man in blue overalls stood near the jellyfish tank, headphones over his ears. A child—maybe eight years old—was by the grouper tank, his face close to the glass. A few feet behind the kid was a recessed doorway. There was a heavy, metal padlock on the door—but the recessed door-frame provided a few feet of privacy—enough for Heidlinger and his precious briefcase.

He quickly slid between the child and the man in over-alls, pressing himself against the locked door. Neither of the gawking fish-watchers seemed to notice him, and he quietly moved into a crouch, wincing at the pain in his arthritic knees. Then he placed the briefcase down in front of him and undid the latch.

The briefcase came open with a pop. Heidlinger's fingers shook as he reached inside, carefully withdrawing four items: a small laptop computer, an external modem, a palm-sized cellular phone, and a single, shiny CD-ROM.

Sweat dripped from his wild hair as he opened the laptop.

It instantly powered up, the screen shifting through a rainbow of colors. Heidlinger turned his attention to the modem, unstringing a pair of wires from its base and inserting them into a plug in a corner of the laptop. Finally, he attached his cell phone to a jack in the modem, and hit the send button.

As the cell phone dialed a preprogrammed number, Heidlinger rocked back on his heels, his tired shoulders touching the hard wooden door. He could just barely see the young kid's bright sneakers about eight feet away—and the sight made him think of his grandson again. He took a deep breath, wondering how he could have been so stupid. How he could have made so many mistakes.

In the beginning, his recklessness had been powered by greed. He had given up his easy, peaceful life in academia for the money of the corporate world. Alaxon's offer had seemed too good to be true; he was simply going to continue the work he had been doing at Harvard—for truckloads of money.

But what had started as a dream job had quickly revealed its darker side. With the upgrade in funding, Heidlinger had made enormous leaps in his work on Compound G—without realizing that Alaxon was monitoring his every move, salivating over his results. What they were planning—what they had been planning all along—was unethical, irresponsible, and horribly dangerous. Six months ago, Heidlinger had finally understood how they were using him—and then he made the mistake that would, in all probability, cost him his life.

Instead of going to the newspapers or to the police, he

had chosen what he had considered at the time a less dangerous route of action. First, he had sent an anonymous, single-page fax to one of the most powerful men in Boston, detailing the discovery he had made. Then he had headed straight to the VP in charge of Alaxon's research department—Malthus Scole. Just as in the fax, he had explained the problem with Compound G, expecting Malthus to immediately cancel the project—or at the very least, turn the situation over to his father, Simon Scole, Alaxon's CEO. In short, he had expected Malthus to act rationally.

Heidlinger bit down on his lower lip, cursing himself for being so stupid. He closed his eyes and took another slow breath. Of course Malthus hadn't shut down the project. Instead, he had set up twenty-four-hour surveillance on his skittish employee. Heidlinger had begun to notice dark sedans following him on his way home from work, echoes when he picked up his phone to call his children, tiny fiber-optic cameras left menacingly unhidden in his car, in his closets, even in his bathroom. Malthus had wanted him to know that he was not playing games.

Heidlinger opened his eyes. He didn't care how dangerous Malthus was—he was smarter, and he was determined. Compound G was his invention—and he was going to expose it for the horror that it was.

A quiet beep sounded from the laptop. The screen shivered, then changed: a colorful insignia appeared across the center, followed by bright blue lettering. Heidlinger instantly recognized the seal of the National Institutes of Health. He was now connected via the Internet to the NIH's enormous database.

He quickly attacked the laptop keyboard, using password after password to delve deeper into the NIH's mainframe. He knew all the passwords from memory; he had spent two years as an assistant researcher at the NIH headquarters while on sabbatical from Harvard, and he had kept many connections in the federal center's main offices. It took less than a minute for him to navigate through the NIH mainframe to his goal—the ultimate encyclopedia of biogenetic information, the GenBank of the National Center for Biotechnology Information.

He leaned back from the computer, breathing heavily. Then he reached for the CD-ROM, the fourth object he had stolen from his office. It was the key to his plan: a few million gigabytes of information loaded into a tiny Trojan horse program. He had written the program months ago— but had never believed he'd actually have the guts to use it.

Adrenaline pulsed through his body as he slid the CD-ROM into the laptop. Two more keystrokes—and it was done. The Trojan horse had attached itself to the NCBI GenBank—the perfect hiding place. When the right person looked for it—and only the right person would be able to access the information—the truth about Compound G would come pouring forth. *And Alaxon will be finished.*

Relief flowed through Heidlinger's shoulders as he shoved the four items back into his briefcase. For the first time in six months, he felt like he could breathe. The guilt was gone, in its place a sense of calm, even pride. He didn't have to risk his life or the lives of his family by challenging Alaxon himself—and Malthus Scole would never know what he had done.

Heidlinger rose to his feet, then stepped out of the alcove. The young child was no longer standing in front of the grouper tank—but the man in overalls was still staring at the jellyfish, his head bobbing as tinny music leaked out of his headphones. Heidlinger slid past him, wondering how anyone could stare at jellyfish for such a long time. Then a thought hit him, and he paused, glancing back at the man. He noticed that the man's lips were moving—but not in tune to the music.

Panicked, Heidlinger spun toward the exit—and nearly collided with a tall man in a poorly tailored gray suit. He staggered back, his eyes wide, his breath labored.

Malthus Scole nodded at him, his round face glowing in the soft light from the grouper tank. His platinum hair was cut tight against his spherical head, and his long arms hung stiffly at his sides. He had a gawky, elongated look—except for his eyes. His eyes were the color and intensity of a lit butane torch. There was something horribly unnatural about those eyes—something cold and suffocating and impersonal. They didn't seem connected to anything underneath, as if Malthus's optic nerves had tangled together, leaving the tiny orbs trapped, strangling in their sockets. They were the eyes of a killer.

Heidlinger stared at those untracking blue eyes as he backed away, lifting his briefcase like a shield in front of his chest. Before he could cry out a strong arm slid around his throat, yanking him off his feet. He gasped, choking, and the arm loosened slightly. He shifted his head and saw his second assailant reflected in the glass of the grouper tank. It was the young man with the overalls and the headphones.

But from this angle, his face didn't look so young—because it was covered in scars. At least five that Heidlinger could count, running in a brutal, star-shaped pattern from the left corner of his upper lip to the bridge of his nose.

Heidlinger turned his attention back to Malthus, trying to remain calm. "Malthus, please. This isn't necessary—"

"You left the office in quite a hurry this afternoon, Dr. Heidlinger. And you seem to have disregarded company policy. You removed four items from the building's premises. A laptop. A modem. A cellular phone. And a CD-ROM."

Heidlinger's heart pounded. He could feel warm breath against the back of his neck, and he imagined the scarred face was smiling. He swallowed, feeling the man's tight bicep against his Adam's apple.

"I was going to bring them back," Heidlinger tried, although he knew it was useless. His only hope was to stall long enough for someone to walk past. "I'm sorry—it won't happen again."

"Well," Malthus said, opening his suit jacket. "I'm sure you're sincere in your remorse. But you understand—we can't have people flouting the rules. Rules keep us civilized."

Malthus reached into his jacket and pulled a syringe out of the inner pocket. Heidlinger's stomach dropped as Malthus removed the plastic guard that covered the long, glistening needle. The syringe was filled with some sort of clear liquid. Heidlinger instinctively shuffled backward— and again the arm tightened around his throat. Malthus's dead blue eyes locked like fangs into Heidlinger's face.

"When we break the rules," he said, his words slow as molasses. "We must be punished. Wouldn't you call that a fair policy, Doctor? A good, *corporate* policy?"

Heidlinger's head was spinning. He tried to struggle against the stiff arm at his throat, but he was too weak, too old. His shoulders sagged, and his hands went limp. The briefcase dropped to the floor, landing with a loud clatter. Malthus glanced at it and then sighed.

"Now you've gone and damaged company property," he said. "Another infraction, Doctor. As VP of your department, I'm inclined to call this cause for termination."

6

"Chicago, baby. The Rainman Suite at the Excelsior Hotel. The Bulls, the Bears, the Blackhawks, fried onion rings, and two-pound steaks. Can't think of a better place to make ourselves famous."

Alex Stern smiled as he slapped his thick hands down on the desk in front of him. The concussion sent Jake's glass of Scotch two inches into the air above the polished mahogany. The crystal glass landed, teetered, but somehow righted itself without spilling any of the potent brown liquid. Jake leaned back in the weathered two-seater that squatted in the center of his friend's cluttered office.

"When you're done celebrating, you think I can get my credit card back?"

Alex rolled his eyes, then lifted Jake's AmEx out from under his phone and tossed it over the desk. Jake reached for it but missed, his fingers hitting the edge of the gold plastic, sending the card spiraling toward the bright red Oriental rug that covered most of the office floor. As he bent to pick up his card, his eyes flickered across the disordered room. His friend's sense of style had not changed much over the years. Huge, framed roster photographs of all three of Boston's professional sports teams took up most of the plaster walls, and the windowsill behind Alex's chair was covered with a collection of sports paraphernalia— including a baseball signed by Mark McGwire, a Louisville Slugger signed by Hank Aaron, a football from the 1987 Super Bowl, and Alex's prize possession—a signed hockey stick that had once belonged to Wayne Gretsky.

The place did not look like a doctor's office—certainly not the office of a respected obstetrician, a man people trusted during the most precious and personal moments of their lives. Instead, it looked like the office of a high-school football coach.

Jake smiled to himself as he shifted his gaze toward Alex Stern: big, bulging, his thick shoulders testing the material of his white doctor's coat. Alex *looked* like a high-school football coach; even his bulbous, perpetually red-cheeked visage fit better on the sidelines than in a doctor's office. In the white coat he seemed constrained, chained, a bull pretending to be a lamb—except when he smiled. When he smiled, you realized he really was a lamb. Deep inside that packed muscle lurked a heart. His patients knew it, the hospital hierarchy knew it—and his friends relied on it. Alex Stern was a man you could trust. It just wasn't such a good idea to share a drink with him—unless you wanted to end up skinny-dipping in the Charles, or getting tossed out of a restaurant for urinating in the salad bar.

Jake laughed and reached for his Scotch. Truth was, Alex hadn't urinated in a salad bar in at least five years. He was a respected doctor, the father of two chubby potential football stars, and a happily married man. He just had a tendency to get a little *enthusiastic*. And sometimes, that enthusiasm was infectious.

At the moment, even after two days of almost no sleep, Jake could feel the sparks of excitement running through his limbs. Alex was right—they were going to become famous in Chicago. They were going to turn the National Fertility Conference upside down with their co-authored revelation. The stack of manila folders on Jake's lap contained all the proof they needed to galvanize the most conservative experts at the conference.

Apoptotic Sperm Dysfunction was real—and it was epidemic.

"You want another Scotch, cowboy?" Alex asked as he lifted his bulk out of his chair, heading for the file cabinet where he kept his liquor. "Or are you getting soft on me?"

"It's not even noon, Alex."

"Suit yourself. I've canceled all my appointments until we get back from Chicago. And my wife is in California at another sales conference. I can drink without guilt. Not that it's any better than drinking *with* guilt. At least then, you've got company."

Jake ran his fingers over the manila folders as he watched Alex pour himself another drink. He had to admit—despite the early hour—the Scotch felt good.

The past two days had been a wild blur. From the moment he had first watched his sperm crashing into one another inside his homemade viewing device, he had thrown himself headlong at the syndrome. First, he had tested the device itself, making sure it was working properly, that the electric charge had been correctly calculated. When he had finally convinced himself that his device was sound, he had begun to search for a larger base of samples. His first move in that direction had been to return Alex Stern's phone call.

As a private clinician and lab director in the Sandler Wing, Jake had enormous financial resources at his fingertips. He had a cutting-edge lab and as many high-tech gadgets as he'd ever need. But what he didn't have was access to the general population—he worked only with those rich enough or connected enough to afford his services. He could run twenty or thirty samples from his weekly stock of infertile patients, but if he wanted to run real numbers, he needed Alex's help.

Alex was the Vice Chair of Obstetrics at Boston Central. He had complete access to Central's enormous facilities—including its public clinics. Hundreds of patients passed through Central's clinics every day, and thousands of samples were stored in the hospital's vast labs. With Alex's help, Jake could use his device to test hundreds of infertile specimens.

Alex had listened intently to Jake's description of the suicidal sperm. Then he had whistled, immediately grasping the significance of the discovery. As an obstetrician, he was aware of the recent fertility crisis in the Boston area; he also knew that discoveries like Jake's could quickly translate into career gold—not to mention book deals and wonderful paychecks from pharmaceutical companies hoping to trademark reproductive magic. During the initial phone call, Jake had glossed over the personal side of his discovery—at the moment, his own sample was in a vial marked John Doe, stored in the specimen refrigerator in his lab along with his small group of infertiles. He had quickly enlisted his friend as his research partner, and had invited him over to the Sandler Wing to see the viewing device in action. Then the two of them had canceled their appointments for the next few hours and headed straight to Central's storage labs. At the time, neither of them had realized they were about to make history.

"Christ," Alex coughed, as he dropped back into his chair, a fresh glass of Scotch in his bearish hands. "When you returned my call, I figured the best I was going to do was a free trip to Chicago. Tag along to the conference, use your name and credit card to get away for a few days. I didn't know you'd be offering me immortality. Jake, do you realize what a splash this is going to make?"

Jake nodded. The numbers were staggering. Nearly thirty percent of the samples he and Alex had tested had shown signs of ASD. When the numbers were extended by means of the extrapolating software, that meant they were looking at an epidemic that could be affecting tens of thousands of people in the greater Boston area. Furthermore, the syndrome seemed to cut across racial and class lines, striking men from nearly every walk of life. The incidence of the syndrome roughly paralleled the Boston infertility crisis itself—and Jake now had no doubt that ASD was the crisis's major cause.

Jake straightened the manila folders and rose from the two-seater couch. His legs felt stiff, his body exhausted. He hadn't returned home either of the past two nights before three A.M.—and he had left each morning before six. Brett had been keeping similar hours, chasing some sort of mystery in Central's trauma department, something about a handful of unexplained bleeders who had died in the ER in the past week. They had barely spoken in forty hours.

Jake wasn't ready to tell her about his discovery—because he wasn't ready to face the possible implications it would have on their marriage. He still had no idea what was causing his ASD—whether it was congenital, viral, or bacterially based, or whether it was caused by another type of external antigen. And he was still a long way from beginning his search for a cure.

If his ASD was something he couldn't cure . . . He blinked hard, making the thought disappear. That was something he didn't want to contemplate. He wanted to understand more about it before he sat down with Brett to talk about what it would mean for their future.

"Six-thirty at Logan," he said, as he headed for the door to Alex's office. "I'll bring the data and the equipment from my lab."

"And I'll bring the Scotch," Alex responded, raising his glass.

Jake smiled as he exited the office. He had a good six hours before he had to leave for the airport, and he was going to use the time effectively: he was going to go home and sleep. Brett was on call until two A.M., which meant there was no chance of another argument until he returned from Chicago.

By then, he expected to be armed with the expertise—and accolades—of his entire profession.

He'd be ready to face his wife.

7

Daniel Golden stared at the computer screen with wide eyes as a guitar solo caterwauled through his ears. His trembling left hand snaked forward and he quickly adjusted the contrast on the computer screen, expecting the thing to disappear—but it only became brighter, more defined. *The Holy fucking Grail.* Daniel's jaw unhinged and suddenly he was laughing, the high-pitched sound rising toward the ceiling of the computer room, mingling with the guitar solo and reverberating off the cinder-block walls. Soon Daniel was laughing so hard that tears crawled down his stubbly cheeks, dampening the collar of his MIT Chess Team sweatshirt. His vision blurred and he leaned back from the screen, his knees clinging to the ergonomic stool beneath him as his body swayed back and forth.

"Oh my God," he finally whispered to the empty room. "I've found it. I've actually found it."

At the sound of his own voice, Daniel was struck by a sudden paranoia, and he glanced back at the half-open computer-room door. Of course, there was no one there. Dr. Foster had taken the rest of the day off, in preparation for his trip to Chicago. And the other two graduate students who supposedly worked in the lab were probably out drinking or chasing girls. Certainly, they had no reason to lurk around Daniel's computer room.

Daniel turned back to the screen. His eyes stung from his tears, and he wiped a soft sleeve across his runny nose. He was smiling so wide that his lips cracked at the edges. He still could not believe what he was looking at. After all his work, after all the time he had spent in the lab—he had finally found the elusive protein. And it had been Dr. Foster who had shown him the way. The big, moronic jock— Daniel shook his head, amazed at how strange fate could be. For six months, he had thought of his Ph.D. adviser as nothing more than a necessary nuisance. And then two days ago, he had begun to notice a change in the oaf's demeanor. Dr. Foster had begun to stay late at the lab, working on some sort of secret project in his office—with the door closed.

Curious, Daniel decided to find out what his boss was hiding. Daniel had assumed it couldn't be anything significant—after all, Foster was more muscle than brains.

But Daniel had assumed wrong.

The revelation had come at about three-thirty that morning. Jake had finally left him alone in the lab, and he had quickly sequestered himself in his boss's office, attacking the locked cabinet with a small sonar lock pick he had designed himself. Once inside, he quickly found the strange-looking microscope on the bottom shelf, sitting next to a stack of photographs and a pile of handwritten notes.

He had read the notes with a high level of skepticism. What Foster was claiming was hard to believe—but looking at the viewing prototype, Daniel had been forced to grudgingly admit that the engineering seemed sound. So he had decided to see if Foster's notes had any basis in reality.

He had quickly rushed to the specimen refrigerator and had retrieved one of the infertile samples, a specimen marked with a bright red John Doe label. Then he had placed the specimen in Foster's viewing device and pressed his eyes against the lenses.

He had stared, shocked, at the crazed, suicidal sperm.

The handwritten notes in Foster's locked cabinet had described a true phenomenon, a syndrome that had never been reported before. But Daniel knew it was more than a disorder—it was the key to something much, much greater.

Dr. Foster clearly had no idea what he had stumbled upon. Based on his notes, he believed he had discovered nothing more than a spermatic syndrome that was making men infertile. He didn't realize that the disease, on its own, was *insignificant*. He had raced off with that monstrous friend of his, Alex Stern, to tell the world about his discovery—without ever pausing to actually *think* about the big-picture implications of what he had found.

The sperm inside the viewing prototype weren't simply crashing into one another. They were *attracted* to one another.

They were seeking each other out, like guided missiles, like magnets with the same polarity—*like bees to pollen*. Daniel had realized this central fact the second he had put his eyes to the lenses. It was the same mechanism that fertility specialists had hypothesized brought normal sperm in contact with the female egg—except on a much more frenetic scale. Instead of chasing eggs, the sperm were chasing one another.

This was the breakthrough Daniel had been looking for all along. If the sperm were attracting one another, that meant they carried within their nuclei the chemotaxin that made fertility work—the unknown protein contained by the egg that attracted human sperm.

For Daniel, the next step seemed foolishly simple. For two years, he had been struggling to find the protein through a process called biochemical fractionation—using enzymes to slice female eggs into smaller and smaller pieces, searching for any trace of an unknown protein. The process had been frustratingly slow, and in the past year he had gotten absolutely nowhere. The problem was, the female egg was an exceedingly large cell—the largest human cell there was.

Spermatozoa, on the other hand, were exceedingly small cells. Biochemical fractionation of a sperm cell was a relatively simple procedure: by the time the first trickles of dawn poured through the huge Plexiglas picture window, Daniel had the sperm slices down to single microns. He had then taken the segments and placed them in Foster's viewing chamber with other sperm samples, searching for the smallest atomic particle that still attracted sperm. In theory, the fractionation process would leave him with the isolated protein itself, the chemotaxin. The Holy Grail.

And that's exactly what had happened. By six A.M., Daniel had isolated, purified, and cloned through PCR a tiny protein he had never seen before. Then he had quickly begun the process of crystallizing the protein with ammonium sulfate, reducing its solubility and preparing it for the final stage—X-ray crystallography, which would give him a three-dimensional picture of the protein itself—one that he could photograph, document, and check against the national data bank of recorded proteins to see if he'd really and truly found something new.

Twenty minutes earlier, he had loaded the purified, crystallized protein into the crystallography machine in the back of the lab. The rectangular steel instrument was one of the lab's most expensive pieces of equipment, with a price tag near a million dollars. Daniel had used it dozens of times before—but he was by no means an expert. He had taken great care to make sure the protein was correctly positioned in the machine so that the X-ray beam would strike the sample dead on, pinning it against the copper target with exactly 1.45 angstroms of energy. Then he had hurried to the computer room and powered up the IBM, waiting for the digitized X-ray photograph to appear.

Now, twenty minutes later, he gripped the ergonomic

stool beneath his knees as he rocked back toward the screen. The glowing picture seemed incredibly beautiful to him. He had set the computer to give off mainly blues and reds, and the picture looked like a frozen slice of a July fourth sky. In the center of the screen, Daniel could make out the protein itself—a strange compound of six amine functional groups twisted around a cyclic hydrocarbon. From certain angles, the photograph seemed vaguely familiar—but at the same time unique. Daniel's pulse hammered as he traced and retraced the structure with his eyes. Was he really looking at the Holy Grail? Was this *his* protein to name and publicize?

To be sure, he needed to run the picture through the NIH database, to make sure there was no match. He quickly rolled his stool over to the main IBM processor and flicked the switch that connected his computer to the lab's Internet server. He rolled back to his terminal and saved the crystallography photo as an image file. Then he tried to calm himself as he waited for the connection to complete. Inside, his mind was already whirling ahead, planning out the next few years of his life.

For so long he had been asking: *When is it going to be my turn?* Through high school and college, every time a woman looked at him funny or some jock made a joke about his appearance—he had asked the question: *When will I get what I deserve?*

Well, now things were finally going to change. For too long, he had been pushed around by people like Jake Foster. Neanderthal throwbacks with perfect hair and winning smiles, men who proved the rule about looks being inversely related to brains. Now, it was Daniel's turn to push back. He would use his discovery as a stepping stone; soon he would make history and earn a lab of his own. He would take his place among the panoply of famous scientists, his very name synonymous with greatness—

A high-toned beep interrupted him, and he cleared his mind, focusing on the bright blue insignia in the center of the screen. The colorful NIH seal sent new tremors of excitement through his body. Another few minutes and he would make history.

He entered his name and MIT grad school ID number, then cycled through the menus in search of the GenBank encyclopedia—the massive data bank kept by the National Center for Biotechnology Information, where every known protein was logged. A few seconds later, the NIH insignia was replaced by the GenBank logo. A prompt asked him for his name again, and this time he depressed the keys carefully, each stroke sending sparks up his spine. After his name was entered, he used the mouse to reopen the protein image file, and then he hit the command that would send the computer searching for any match.

He leaned back, waiting for the machine to tell him what he already knew—that there was no match, that Daniel Golden had just changed the world of fertility studies, that Daniel Golden had just thrown the biggest fucking pie in the face of every Jake Foster—

Suddenly, the screen in front of Daniel started to flicker. His eyebrows wrinkled as he tried to figure out what the hell was going on. He glanced back at the processor and modem, assuming that somehow the connection was deteriorating—when the screen cleared, turning a bright red color. A second later, a video image filled the center of the screen: a full-motion MPG file, highly defined, filmed with some sort of advanced digital camera. The video was being downloaded directly into Daniel's computer from the GenBank, a massive influx of gigabytes sweeping down through the Internet at near light-speed.

Daniel's eyes widened as he stared at the shifting video image. *This isn't supposed to be happening.* The GenBank was a database of stored information—not some sort of interactive mainframe. Someone had obviously stuck a virus of some kind into the data bank—a virus that Daniel had somehow triggered. He quickly reached for the keyboard, intending to break the connection—and then his hand froze inches from the keys. He stared at the screen as the video image continued, his face growing pale in the shifting red light.

"My God," he finally whispered. "I think I understand."

Twenty miles away, Malthus Scole tapped his fingers against the inlaid computer screen in the center of his black-glass desk. His blue eyes burned from staring at the shifting pixels, and he stretched his neck back and forth. A few more seconds, he told himself. *Just a few more seconds.*

Finally, the screen changed, and four lines of text appeared in front of Malthus's eyes. He quickly memorized the information and then hit a button on the side of his desk. The screen went blank, his desk again becoming opaque, and he hit a second button, this one located just above his knees on the bottom of the glass desktop. There was a soft click as the door to his office automatically unlocked.

Malthus pushed his chair back from his desk, stretching his legs. He could see himself reflected in a dozen glass surfaces, but he ignored the images; unlike his father, vanity was not one of his faults. He knew that his head was a little too round, that his face had a strange, almost angelic flatness, that his wiry frame was a few inches too gawky. He knew his ears were too big for his head, that his jaw distended outward at an unnerving angle. And he knew all about his eyes. *Maya mayta*, the Iraqis had whispered again and again, staring at his eyes. *Dead pools.*

Malthus felt a twinge of emotion—such a foreign sensation that he had no way of interpreting it, no way of knowing if it was fondness or regret. He let his hand drift into his front suit pocket, retrieving the six inch-long white sticks inside. He cupped the sticks in his hand, then tossed them across the smooth surface of his desk. They landed with a clatter, bouncing together in a chaotic, geometric shape. He tried to read the configuration but quickly gave up. It didn't really matter; he had never believed in the whore's witchcraft anyway. He had only pretended to believe, for the sake of their relationship. At the time, he had needed her comfort.

He had met the whore two weeks after his dishonorable discharge from the Airborne Rangers. She had approached him in a bar in Marakesh, perhaps recognizing the drunk, dazed desperation in his eyes. She had offered to make the pain go away. Staring at her young, dark, Arabic features, her long lashes, her cunning, overly made-up smile—he had decided not to kill her. Instead he had taken her home and made love to her, wiping the smile away with the back of his hand as he turned her body inside out. They had been kindred spirits; lost souls in a foreign country, both trying to escape unfair pasts.

In the end, of course, he *had* killed her. But that was years later, after he had accepted the job from his father and entered the corporate world. Such a woman would never have fit in the environment of fifty-story skyscrapers and tailored Armani suits.

Malthus picked up the sticks, shook them in his hand, and then tossed them again. This time they bounced a few inches off his desk, landing near the edge of the opaque glass. Their polished, white surfaces were a stark contrast to the shiny blackness, and Malthus smiled, enjoying the aesthetics.

His office had been decorated in tune to those same aesthetics: the black glass desk; his black leather chair; the tall, ivory white bookshelf standing against the equally white marble wall; the obsidian, art-deco clock in the far corner by the darkly tinted picture window that looked out over the jutting, tightly packed skyscrapers of Boston's financial district. Malthus had considered having the windows painted completely black—but he knew his father would not have approved. This was, after all, the office of Alaxon's VP of Research and Development. Not the war room of an Airborne Ranger, or the cockpit of an F–9 bomber on a mission over southern Iraq. There was no *rational* need to black out the windows.

Malthus sneered, again reaching for the white sticks. As

his palm closed over them, there was a quiet knock on his office door. He cleared his throat. "Enter."

The door opened and Michael Pierce slid into the office. Pierce was wearing a dark blue suit, a similar cut to the suit that hung awkwardly off Malthus's gangly body. The suit fit Pierce's muscularity well, and if it were not for the horrible scars that marked his young face, he would have cut a striking figure. "You sent for me, Major?"

Malthus nodded, waving Pierce deeper into his office. Pierce shut the door behind him, then stood at attention, his hands clasped behind his back. Malthus rose from the desk, the white sticks still tight in his palm.

"We've got another situation, Mr. Pierce. Please prepare the car."

Pierce nodded, then started to salute. Malthus glared at him—and Pierce's hand stopped a few inches from his forehead. His scarred cheeks turned red, and he quickly exited the office, the door clicking shut behind him.

Malthus shook his head, sighing. Even after two years, Pierce could not adjust to the different surroundings. Malthus had trained him too well. He was completely loyal, efficiently skilled—and brutal. Every Fortune 500 company needed a man like Michael Pierce. Especially during times like these.

Malthus closed his eyes, picturing the computer screen from a few minutes ago. He could still see the name at the top of the screen, glowing in bright green letters.

Daniel Golden. A scientist in a fertility laboratory in downtown Boston.

Malthus grew angry with himself. It had been a major

snafu, letting Dr. Heidlinger out of the building. But Malthus had wanted to follow the old man, to see if he had already made contact with someone on the outside. When it became apparent that he had not, Malthus had acted as quickly as possible. But obviously, he had not acted quickly enough.

Heidlinger had been able to upload some sort of Trojan horse computer virus into the NIH's mainframe. Malthus had put his best people on the job of eradicating the program—but Heidlinger had been too good a programmer, and they had been able to excise only a portion of the uploaded information. Still, they *had* managed to attach a homing program to the Trojan horse, a program designed to alert Malthus whenever the program was activated.

The homing program had gone off less than five minutes ago. Twenty seconds later, the program had given Malthus the name and address of the offender. There was no way to know if Daniel Golden had understood the abridged information from Heidlinger's CD-ROM, but Malthus couldn't take any chances. The man was, after all, a fertility expert.

Malthus had to handle the situation—immediately. Just as he had handled Heidlinger. If his father ever found out there was such an immense leak—Malthus clenched his teeth, then forced the anger out of his body. His father would never find out.

Malthus opened his palm and let the tiny white sticks clatter against the surface of his desk. He stared at the configuration, then picked them up and shoved them back into his pocket. *The fucking whore and her fucking witchcraft.* Malthus did not need her tricks—he had magic of his own.

Besides, these were not the sticks the whore had given him shortly after their first evening together—these weren't really sticks at all.

They were the severed finger bones of six Iraqi soldiers, boiled clean and polished with a steel sponge.

Malthus patted his pocket and then headed for the door.

8

"I thought New York was supposed to be the city of strangers, not Boston," Calvin said, poking fearfully at his plate of radon-green Jell-O with a spoon. "But from the looks of things, these four guys could have come from different planets."

They were sitting kitty corner to one another in the back of the dismal hospital cafeteria, sharing a tray from the dessert cart at the front of the long, rectangular room. The place reminded Brett of high school: light-green metal tables set a little too high, making it impossible to eat comfortably. The atmosphere was made worse by the constant scraping of metal against metal—cutlery against institution-style plates, plates against trays, trays against tables. It was almost impossible to concentrate while trapped in the cafeteria—which was the very reason Brett and Calvin had planted themselves in the back corner of the vast room.

They had been concentrating for nearly two days—and the DIC cases were still a mystery. The only good news was that there hadn't been another bleeder since the young man from the Public Garden. But the next case could appear at any moment, and Brett and Calvin feared they wouldn't be able to do anything but stand by and watch another bloody death. As long as the syndrome remained unexplained, the DICs were like an ax poised above Brett's ER.

She pushed the tray a few inches away, turning back to the small stack of Medical Examiner reports sitting next to her fork. The ME's office had conducted a thorough investigation into the four deaths, at Brett's request. She knew she was going to catch hell from Chief Cross when he found out about the expenditure, but she wasn't going to wait for the CDC to finally order a similar investigation. When there wasn't a viral or bacteriological threat, the CDC could be notoriously slow. A few DICs meant little to them; *they* didn't have to watch the poor victims bleed out.

Brett picked up the ME reports and leafed through them for the hundredth time. Calvin was right, the four patients couldn't have had less in common. All four were employed in different professions in geographically distinct parts of the city. Two were Caucasian, another part Indian, and the third African American. Two were single, in their late twenties. Two were married, and in their mid-thirties. None of the men exhibited any of the red flags the ME's office usually looked for: no foreign travel, no exotic pets, no abnormal history of family disease, no drug use. In fact, there was only one smoker in the bunch.

All four men were healthy, athletic, and well-fed. There was nothing Brett could see that linked them together— which made the four DICs seem impossible. The ME's reports stated that the four cases in one week were coincidental; a string of unexplained DICs in a city as big as Boston was statistically possible. People died all the time, and sometimes their deaths didn't have any noticeable cause. The ME's office even had a stamp for it, which they had plastered across the bottom of all four reports: REASONS UNEXPLAINED.

But Brett refused to accept the ME's findings. There had to be *something* that linked these four men. And if it wasn't on the outside, if it wasn't in the way they lived or their family histories—then it had to be on the *inside.*

Their bloodstream, their organs, their soft tissues, their immune systems . . .

Brett paused, placing the stack of ME reports back onto the table. She watched Calvin take a hesitant spoonful of the Jell-O, then put it back on the plate, shaking his head.

"Really, Brett. I don't know how you can put this garbage in your body."

Brett's gaze remained pinned to the Jell-O. "You know, Calvin, I think we've been going at this all wrong."

Calvin raised his eyebrows. "How do you mean?"

"We've been looking for some disease or trauma that could be causing the DIC. Some external factor that we can point at and say that's it, that's what's caused these deaths. Maybe we should be focusing on the DIC itself."

Calvin wrinkled his forehead. "DIC is a symptom, not a cause."

"True. But sometimes we need to focus on a symptom— to *find* the cause."

Calvin paused. "Okay, Brett. I'll play your game. Let's focus on DIC. Disseminated Intravascular Coagulation. An overwhelming reaction of the body—"

"Not of the body," Brett corrected. "Of the immune system. Or more accurately, of the immune response mechanisms. Normally, the immune system works by identifying foreign—or enemy—proteins, and then reacting to them."

Calvin yawned, using his hands to tell her to get to the point. He didn't like it when she simplified things—but she had learned that sometimes, simplifying the science made you notice things you had missed. She plugged ahead, ignoring Calvin's expression. "Foreign proteins are picked up by MHC class I and II molecules—which then activate T and B cells—"

"Which lead to the production of antibodies to destroy the invading proteins," Calvin finished for her, his hands on the table. "Thanks for the immunology lecture, Brett. Now can I get back to my Jell-O?"

Brett pointed toward the tray. "What if you were allergic to the green coloring, Calvin? What would happen inside your body?"

Calvin sighed, exasperated. "Why don't you get one of the med students in here, if you're so keen on teaching—"

"Calvin, just answer the damn question."

Calvin rolled his shoulders. "Fine. Using the DIC model you've just so eloquently described, *Dr. Foster*, if I were unlucky enough to have a predetermined matrix of MHC class II molecules that makes my body unaware that green Jell-O is not, in fact, a dangerous poison—my lymphocytes would send signals throughout my body that there was a deadly protein lurking around. A mass of antibodies would be produced—and theoretically, my immune system could freak out. Which could cause anaphylactic shock—"

"Or DIC," Brett said, nodding. The mechanism was simple. If you're allergic to peanuts, your receptors misidentify peanuts as an enemy protein—and your immune system overreacts.

"That's exactly what happened during the toxic shock syndrome outbreak related to tampons. A small percentage of women had the genetically predetermined matrix of MHC class II molecules for a particular bacteria on the tampons, and those class II molecules set off their immune responses."

Calvin nodded, his expression softening.

"We shouldn't be looking for a disease," Brett said. "We should be looking for a misidentified protein. We should be looking for green Jell-O."

"The ME's office did tox screens and blood workups—"

"And tissue cultures and so on, yes, I know. But from the severity of these cases, I'd say this protein is something we've never encountered before. The ME's office was testing for known contaminants. Not unidentified antigens."

Calvin touched his Jell-O with a finger. "I guess we could go back to the blood workups and the tissue cultures. But it's going to take a long time to look for something we've never seen before. We don't even know where to start."

Brett paused, her eyes moving from the Jell-O to the ugly

pink walls of the cafeteria. Then she looked at Calvin.

"Maybe we do. Calvin, I'm sure you noticed that all of the DICs were jaundiced, with yellowed skin."

Calvin nodded. "I thought we wrote that off to liver failure. The uncontrolled bleeding killed off these patients' livers pretty fast."

"Maybe we wrote the jaundice off too quickly. Maybe these patients' livers were dying even before they succumbed to the DIC."

Calvin clapped his hands together, understanding. "Because the foreign protein was pooling in their liver cells. If that's true, if a large concentration of the protein is in those livers—then there's a good chance we can track it down."

Brett was already rising from her seat.

Six hours later, Brett held her breath as she waited for the computer screen to clear. Calvin was leaning over her right shoulder, his shaved head glowing in the soft light from the fluorescent panels up above. He had taken his doctor's coat off, and his scrubs were untucked, hanging down around his waist. Brett's shoes were off, her toes touching beneath the computer table. Her body was just beginning to feel the effects of the long hours they had spent in the basement autopsy lab—and she knew Calvin was equally fatigued. But with any luck, their efforts were about to be justified.

"The suspense is killing me," Calvin said, shuffling his shoes against the smooth cement floor. "Is it supposed to take this long?"

Brett shrugged. "I haven't run an X-ray crystallography since medical school."

"Should I get Dr. Kelly?"

Brett glanced back over her shoulder. She could just see the main area of the basement autopsy lab beyond the plastic foam cubicle wall that surrounded the small computer area. The lab looked empty, the steel autopsy tables and blood gutters covered in plastic tarps. Brett assumed Dr. Kelly had disappeared after he had given them the liver samples from Peter Marsh, the most recent DIC death. She considered sending Calvin after him—then decided that they could wait a few more minutes. Although she wasn't experienced with the X-ray crystallography machine, she was pretty sure she had set up the sample correctly.

"Let's give it a little more time."

Brett settled back, her arms crossed against her chest. She could hear her own heart reverberating in her ears, and she guessed Calvin was feeling the same level of excitement. It was a moment they were sharing—and it felt good. At the same time, Brett couldn't help feeling a little guilty; this was the type of moment she had not shared with Jake in a long time. Right now, he was probably at home, napping, or packing for his trip to Chicago. She wouldn't see him again for a couple of days—and the truth was, they needed the break. The tension level at home had reached painful proportions.

In contrast, the past six hours in the autopsy lab with Calvin had been paradise. They worked extremely well together, and the rushed, exciting atmosphere reminded her of medical school. Calvin had such an easy way about him—and there was no question what he thought of Brett. They were friends, but she knew that deep down, his feelings for her ran deeper than he could admit.

In the back of Brett's mind, she also felt the attraction—
and she wasn't sure whether or not that bothered her. It
definitely bothered Jake. And perhaps, unconsciously,
that's why she had let herself get so close to Calvin: there
was something karmic about Jake's jealousy.

Six years ago—a month after she and Jake had gotten
engaged—he had run off for two weeks with a former college girlfriend. He returned on hands and knees, begging
Brett to take him back; and though she had eventually for-
given him, she had never forgotten.

Working close to Calvin in the lab, shoulder to shoulder,
she had felt almost conspiratorial—and that only added to
the thrill. The scientific procedures of the past six hours
had been tedious—but the environment was tinged with
energy.

"Another minute and I'm going to put my foot through
the screen," Calvin hissed through his teeth. "Seriously, I
think something's wrong—"

He stopped in midsentence as the screen changed colors.
Suddenly, Brett found herself staring at a beautifully rendered X-ray photograph of a microscopic protein structure.
The atoms were colored light blue, the connecting electric
forces orange.

"Damn," Calvin whispered. "Ain't she beautiful."

"Six amino groups," Brett said, tracing the molecule
with her fingers. "Wrapped around a hydrocarbon. I don't
remember ever seeing anything like this before. Is it something you recognize?"

Calvin shook his head. "No, but I haven't studied my bio
books in a long time. You think it could be something new?"

Brett shrugged, staring at the protein. "I have no idea. We need to run it through the GenBank at the National Center for Biotechnology Information. See if they have a match on file."

"And if they don't?" Calvin asked. "Does that mean we get to be famous?"

Brett laughed. "I don't know about famous. But we would make some headlines. If we can show that some previously unknown protein has caused the deaths of four people from uncontrolled bleeding—we'd certainly raise some chaos."

"At the very least, it would get those bastards from the CDC down here mighty quick," Calvin said. "All right, let's dial up the NIH."

He reached past Brett's shoulder and began plucking keys. In a matter of seconds, he had saved the photograph as an image file and activated the computer's Internet connection. Brett watched his progress in awe. "You're pretty handy with this thing. What you just did would have taken me two hours."

"Boys' Club of Detroit," Calvin said, still hitting keys. The sound of the modem dialing reverberated in Brett's ears. "Boxing on Wednesdays, computers on Fridays. You rich kids missed out on all the good stuff."

Brett smiled, as the screen turned blue, the modem connecting with the NIH mainframe. She watched as Calvin entered his Central ID number at the prompt, then found the menu for the GenBank database. He used the mouse to reopen the image file, then he hit the space bar, sending the file spinning through the database. If there was a match, it would come up in a matter of seconds—

"What the hell?"

Calvin's hand had frozen over the space bar. The screen had begun flickering rapidly, shifting through a rainbow of colors.

"Are we losing the connection?" Brett asked.

"I don't think so—whoa, what the hell is this?"

The screen had turned bright red, so bright that Brett had to blink to keep her eyes from watering. Then a black-bordered box appeared in the center of the red. A second later, Brett found herself staring into what looked to be the interior of a small animal cage. The cage jerked slightly to the left, and Brett realized it wasn't a photograph—it was some sort of high-definition video image, playing right on her computer screen.

"How is this possible?" she asked.

"It's some sort of download," Calvin answered, staring, shocked, at the animal cage. "It's coming right off of the NIH database. Christ, is that a fucking monkey?"

The video shot had widened, showing a primate with reddish fur and long arms squatting in a corner of the cage. Brett felt as if she was about to start laughing.

"A chimpanzee," she said, stunned. Jake had worked with chimps during his Ph.D. "And look, on the other side of the cage—those look like golf balls."

They *were* golf balls. Eight of them, shiny white, sitting five feet away from the chimp. The animal was staring at the balls, a strange expression on his elongated face. Slowly, he rose to his haunches and crept across the cage. He grabbed one of the balls and carried it back to his corner.

"This has to be some kind of a joke," Calvin said. "We should reboot—"

"Hold on a second," Brett said, genuinely curious. "Someone must have gone through a lot of trouble to put this together—and to somehow stick it into the NIH database. We may as well watch."

Brett leaned closer, concentrating on the video image. The screen flickered once, then the image changed—slightly. It was still the same cage, the same chimp. But the row of golf balls had been replaced by a row of small boxes, about the size of cigarette packages. Again, the chimp rose and crossed the cage, grabbing one of the boxes. He returned to his corner and placed it next to the golf ball.

Over the next few minutes, the scene was replayed at least a dozen times—and each time, the chimp faced a different row of objects. Indistinguishable plastic toys, colored pencils, baseballs, ceramic plates. Each time, the chimp crossed the cage, picked up one of the items, and brought it back to his corner. Soon there was a fair-sized pile of objects in the chimpanzee's corner.

"We're zooming in," Brett commented, as the camera angle suddenly changed. The chimpanzee disappeared, replaced by a close-up of the pile of chosen items. Then a gloved hand appeared from above. One by one, the gloved hand turned over the items and held them up to the camera. Brett saw that each item had a tiny letter stenciled somewhere on its surface: G.

And suddenly, the video feed ended, replaced by a screenful of double-spaced type. Brett read the words quickly, realizing they might disappear any second. The copy was an extremely technical description of some sort of organic molecular structure. Brett's cheeks warmed as the screen scrolled down to a black-and-white photograph of the molecule; it was the exact same protein that she and Calvin had extracted from Peter Marsh's liver. Beneath the black-and-white photo was a single line of text:

```
Compound G. Proprietary rights, Dr.
Eric Heidlinger, Alaxon Industries.
Compound was designed specifically to
```

And there, the screen went blank. The type continued to scroll upward until Brett was left staring at a sea of unbroken red pixels.

She turned toward Calvin, and saw that he looked as confused as she felt. He reached for the keyboard and began hitting keys—but the screen was locked. He glanced toward the processor, then shook his head.

"The connection broke off. We'll have to link up again."

"What the hell was that?" Brett asked.

"I think it was some sort of plant. A Trojan horse, they call it. A computer program set to download information into someone else's unsuspecting computer. We must have set it off by searching for that protein."

"Compound G," Brett said. A shiver moved through her shoulders, as she tried to remember the exact words of the text. The molecular description hadn't told her anything she didn't already know—it was just a text description of the photograph itself. But the last line of type, the text that had ended midsentence—it had mentioned someone by name. *Dr. Eric Heidlinger.*

"Proprietary rights," she repeated from memory. "Does

that mean he *created* the protein? That it isn't naturally occurring—that he synthesized it himself, and named it Compound G?"

"That's what it sounds like," Calvin responded. "Ever heard of the guy? This Dr. Heidlinger?"

Brett shook her head. She had never heard of Alaxon Industries, either. This was getting stranger by the second. "Calvin, pull up our protein image again and make me a printout. Then reconnect to the NIH database. I want to make sure the photos match. And I want to watch that video again."

The video was confusing as hell—but Brett was determined to try and figure it out. Because somehow, it was related to the DIC deaths. The common factor was the protein itself—*Compound G*. It was a strange name for a protein—and it made Brett think that it had been developed with some goal in mind. The video she had just seen had something to do with that goal—of that she was convinced. Certainly, it was more than a practical joke.

Four people had bled to death in her ER. And somehow, Eric Heidlinger and Alaxon Industries were involved. Brett's head spun, a single question rising to surface of her thoughts.

What the hell *was* Compound G?

9

The enormous television screen rose like a space-age monolith out of the floor, turning the dark room cobalt blue. Ten feet away, Simon Scole shivered as an orchestral fugue cascaded out of the massive twin speakers set on either side of the long leather couch. The froglike man sitting next to him responded with the appropriate combination of awe and disdain, and Simon smiled, sipping from his crystal snifter filled with eighteenth-century brandy. He noticed that the snifter set in front of the man next to him was still untouched. The two inches of brick-red liquid sitting dejectedly at the bottom of the glass could have paid for the massive television screen *and* the speaker system. Of course, the money meant nothing to Tucker Grant.

Simon turned his gaze back toward the rising screen, pangs of jealousy erupting in his chest. His entire fortune—everything he had built in the past twenty years—was pocket change to his friend. The magnificent penthouse office perched on the top of the fifty-fourth floor of the Prudential Building was a maid's quarters, compared to Grant's Dallas headquarters—from which he ran his multibillion-dollar empire.

Simon tempered his feelings of inferiority with a quick glance at the aging billionaire. He had never met a more shriveled man in his life. He knew it wasn't Tucker's fault; age, combined with two years of intense chemotherapy, had accelerated the natural processes of life. Still, it was a difficult sight; in college, Tucker had been an athlete, handsome and fit. Now he looked minutes from the grave.

Simon quickly turned away, running a manicured hand through his immaculately coiffed blond hair. He could not bear the thought of his own body deteriorating so thoroughly. He prayed he had the strength to kill himself before he let that happen.

"Is the music part of the demonstration?" Grant croaked, breaking the silence. "Or are you just testing the limits of my hearing aid, Simon?"

Simon quickly reached forward and grabbed the remote control off the glass table. He hit a button, and the music softened, barely louder than the whir of the pneumatic gears beneath the television. "I'm sorry, Tucker. Sometimes my techs get a little overenthusiastic."

"Indeed," Grant huffed, settling back in the couch. His gnarled hand wiped spittle from his puffy lower lip. "Reminds me of my grandkids. Playing their damn music so loud I think blood's going to spray out of my ears."

Simon pretended to laugh. "In another moment, you'll forget about the music, Tucker. Just watch the screen."

He settled back in the couch, his muscles clenching with anticipation. At this point, everything hinged on the froggish Grant—on his ability to perceive what Simon had achieved. Simon prayed that he had not overestimated his former roommate's intelligence.

The television screen finally reached the top of its ascension, stopping four feet above the raised marble dais in the center of the circular room. Simon leaned forward, his blue eyes glowing as the oversized screen went ivory white.

A second later, he was staring at a supermarket checkout line, filmed from above in startlingly defined color. A time code ran in the bottom right corner of the screen, showing that the video image was in real time—that it was being filmed at that moment, by a tiny fiber-optic camera hidden above the checkout line. Simon had supervised the installation of the camera himself, dressed in blackout fatigues his son had purchased from a U.S. Army purveyor in New Hampshire. Simon had considered wearing his own night-camouflage from his tour of Korea—but had decided that his body had changed just enough in the past forty-five years to make the uniform a tight fit. Not bad changes, of course. But a natural loosening in his stomach and chest, a few centimeters beyond the state of physical perfection he had once maintained.

"Grand Market," Grant commented, correctly identifying the supermarket chain from the color scheme of the checkout lane and the light blue uniform of the young black girl standing at the cash register. "In the Prudential mall. I'm surprised they allowed you to use them for your demonstration. Bob Gannett, their CEO, is a tough little bastard. He raped me on twelve million units this year—charged me ten percent more for shelf space than last year."

Simon shrugged. Of course, he had never met Bob Gannett—had never even thought about getting permission for his demonstration. That would have required a breach in the secrecy of the project.

"Just keep watching, Tucker. You'll forget about that ten percent charge soon enough."

"I *am* impressed by the definition," Grant said. "Microwave transmission? I think I saw the satellite dish on your roof from the window of my helicopter."

Simon nodded. The tiny, hair-thin fiber-optic camera with the spherical, three-hundred-and-sixty-degree lens had a microchip built into its base that instantly converted the filmed image into microwave packets. The packets were relayed by satellite to the dish twenty yards above Simon's office, just beyond the helipad where Grant's McDonnell Douglas Sprite had landed barely thirty minutes ago.

"The camera itself is quite unobtrusive. The size of a human hair follicle, with a crystal lens—here we are, Tucker. Our first customer. Watch carefully."

Simon sucked in a breath as he watched a woman push an overflowing metal shopping cart into the checkout lane.

The woman looked to be in her mid-thirties, wearing a bright yellow sundress, a purse hanging from her left shoulder. She was plump, perhaps five-four, with frizzy dark hair. The perfect specimen, Simon thought, smiling to himself as he glanced at Grant. He could see the saliva pooling in his friend's partially open mouth. It wasn't the vicarious nature of the demonstration that was exciting the old man—it was the woman, *what she represented*. She was the stock and trade of Grant's fortune. A housewife, a homemaker, probably with two point five kids and a dog and a station wagon and floral-print curtains and eight thousand dollars in credit-card debt. She *was* the American Consumer.

Tucker Grant knew everything there was to know about her. His multibillion-dollar empire depended on that knowledge. Her wants, her needs, most of all, her pocketbook. What made it open and close, what motivated her to reach inside and grab for that credit card.

As Simon and Grant watched, the woman began pulling items out of her cart and placing them on the conveyor belt. The checkout girl rang them up, utter indifference on her face. The scene became robotic, the two women working in silent concert, the conveyor belt connecting their isolated worlds in a stream of frictionless black rubber. Item after item after item, out of the cart and onto the belt, off the belt and into a brown paper bag. Every two seconds, like clockwork, the woman in the sundress bent into her cart for another item. Every two seconds, like clockwork, the woman at the cash register flicked an item over the bright red laser, while the computer added the price to the rising total. Soon, there were three paper bags full of items standing at the end of the conveyor belt, and still the rhythmic performance continued. As it continued in checkout lanes all over the country, a million times a day. Pouring dollar after dollar into the wide pockets of froggish men like Tucker Grant.

"I don't see any brand loyalty," Grant said, his trance finally broken as he turned to face Simon. "The products in her cart seem to have been chosen at random. Only about a quarter of them are Tucker products. The rest are divided among a dozen of our competitors—Kraft, Tyson, Premium, Post, et cetera. So what the hell is this supposed to demonstrate, Simon?"

Simon smiled; he was enjoying Grant's impatience. The CEO and founder of Tucker National, the third largest manufacturer of household goods, was not used to being toyed with. "Take another look. Through the infrared receiver."

Simon leaned forward and hit a button on the remote control. The vast television screen shivered, then turned a light red color. A chemically infused shield inside the fiber-optic camera was now reading the infrared light reflecting through its lens. The woman in the sundress and the woman at the cash register both glowed a dark shade of magenta. The red price-laser next to the conveyor belt was like a sunburst, nearly overpowering the television's pixels.

"Look closely," Simon said, rising from the couch and circling around the glass table toward the television screen. "At the items in the cart and on the conveyor belt."

Grant leaned over the glass table, his rheumatic eyes glistening. Then his mouth opened. There was a tiny red mark on more than eighty percent of the items. Simon reached the screen, focusing on a pair of cereal boxes moving down the conveyor belt. One was some sugary children's concoction. The other was a bran mix, obviously geared toward health-conscious adults.

Both boxes had the same tiny red infrared mark in the top corner of their packaging. The mark glowed clear under the specialized lens. It was a tiny letter, written in computerized script.

A tiny imprinted G.

Grant coughed, and for a moment Simon thought he was choking on his own phlegm. Then the shriveled CEO took a handkerchief out of his front suit pocket and wiped it across his lips. "My God. Absolutely amazing."

"As you read in the specs," Simon said, standing in the glow of the television screen, reveling in the moment. "This demonstration is being conducted without the customer's knowledge. The infrared marking is completely undetectable. The marked products were picked by my scientists at random—blind choices, Tucker, without regard for packaging or quality."

Grant was rising from the couch, his feet planted heavily in the thick white shag rug that covered the floor. "And you're sure there are no side effects?"

Simon paused, swallowing. Then he quickly recovered. "The compound is perfectly safe. And, as you can see, incredibly effective. In half a dozen test markets, we've achieved an eighty to eighty-five percent domination."

He reached forward and hit a button on the top of the television. The screen immediately went dark, and the ceiling lights flashed on. The television screen began to descend into its raised marble housing. Simon's eyes flickered across his office, making sure that everything was in its perfect, proper place—reflecting his internal obsession with order. The white shag rug was stunningly clean, and the cream marble-lined walls had been polished just ten minutes before the meeting. The spiral stone staircase just behind the leather couch that led up to the building's glass skywalk glowed under the circular halogen lights hanging from the twenty-foot-high ceiling. And behind the staircase, running the entire length of the rounded back wall of the office—the twelve-foot-tall, three-inch-thick glass tank positively gleamed. Simon's chest heaved as he gazed at his pride and joy. The terrarium had cost him close to thirty thousand dollars. He was certain that there was nothing else like it in the world.

"Are you with me, Tucker?" he asked, moving across his office toward the terrarium. "Together we will change the future of market capitalism. We're going to redefine brand loyalty."

As he moved closer to the tank, he could see his reflection in the glass. He cast a striking figure. Six feet tall, his body robust, his hair perfect, his jaw and cheeks prominent and tanned—he did not look like a sixty-eight-year-old man. Even without the thick makeup powder that covered his face and the tops of his hands—he looked just as he had when he returned home from Korea. A strapping young man ready to take on the world, ready to build an empire.

"Eighty to eighty-five percent," Tucker said, awed. "Near total market domination—because of a chemical on the packaging. A chemical that can't be seen, smelled, tasted, or felt. Christ, Simon. Do you know what this is worth?"

Simon peered through the glass wall of his tank. The tiny black silicon beads—each no bigger than a grain of sand— that filled the tank blended together, creating an amazing visual effect. More than a work of art, it was a living tapestry, a microcosmic, vital world trapped between two sheets of centimeter-thick glass.

He shifted his eyes, quickly searching out the maze of tiny tunnels that ran through the tank, the nearly infinite branches of the lilliputian empire that he had watched grow from a single, freeze-dried specimen imported from the dirt-crusted mountains of North Korea. He followed one of the tunnels back toward the center—the lair of the queen ant herself. He bent close to the glass, his eyes quickly finding the tiny empress. The queen ant was bright red, less than a centimeter long, her dark wings folded on her back, her six legs tucked under the bulbous curves of her thorax and abdomen. An inch in front of her long anten- nae sat two of her guards, their sharp mandibles curving from their mouths like scimitars. The specially evolved guard ants would protect their queen with their lives. Unthinking, unrelenting, uncompromising.

Simon could not help thinking of Malthus when he looked at the queen's thoughtless guards. Protecting Alaxon and Compound G with his obsessive brand of loy- alty. Like the guard ants, he would die before admitting fail- ure.

"I know exactly what Compound G is worth, Tucker. To

both of us. That's why I have taken every precaution to keep it a secret until now."

Simon shifted his eyes away from the queen's chamber, following one of the tunnels toward the top of the tank. Near the very surface, where the black silicon beads became a moonscape of mountains and valleys, he saw that one of the tiny tunnels had collapsed in on itself, trapping a tiny worker ant. The dying insect helplessly flailed its forelegs, its antennae spinning in frantic circles as it tried, hopelessly, to dig its way to the surface.

A shadow crossed Simon's face. The sight was a reminder of how quickly things could go wrong. How quickly tragedy could strike.

Already, the project had almost been compromised. Though Malthus had tried to keep it a secret—Simon knew all about the leak involving Dr. Heidlinger. He also knew about his son's overzealous—and murderous—response. At first, he had reacted in horror; his son had crossed a line with the killing, and the blood was on his own hands. But the horror quickly faded. Malthus had acted correctly; the project was more important than an old scientist's life.

Simon barely noticed as Tucker Grant ambled next to him. "We'll announce the buyout at our stockholder's meeting in the Hynes Convention Center on Friday morning. Five hundred million dollars will be moved to your corporate account by that afternoon. How soon can you begin to ship the compound to my packaging plants?"

Simon kept his voice firm. "As soon as the buyout is announced, my trucks will leave for Dallas."

"Tucker National is going to take over the household

goods market," Grant said, his voice dripping with excitement. We're going to dominate the entire industry. It's foolproof. A sure thing."

Simon watched the tiny drone ant still desperately trying to dig its way out of the collapsed tunnel. Then he sighed.

In business, there was no such thing as a sure thing.

10

The defender went down in a spray of wet mud as Jake leapt over him, his cleats cutting through the damp morning air. Jake's body twisted three hundred and sixty degrees and he landed hard, his knees swallowing the impact. He saw the checkered ball in front of him, glowing in the bright morning light, and he stormed toward it, his lips curled back in an intense snarl.

The goal was ten yards away, wide open, its bright red, spherical posts obscenely swollen. The goalie was nowhere to be seen. Jake picked up the dribble with the inside of his left foot, keeping the ball tightly in control. He executed a perfect crossover, cutting the distance to the goal by half, then slowed, readying for the shot. He knew, inside, that this was the most important moment of his life.

He could see Brett in the stands up above the goal. Her mouth was open and she was trying to tell him something, but the sound was lost in the cheers from the crowd. Then her arm came up and she pointed, and suddenly Jake saw a flash of movement out of the corner of his left eye. Something was coming toward him at an immense speed. He didn't have time to change course, he had no choice but barrel ahead. His right foot cocked back for the shot and he focused every ounce of energy and determination and hope on the checkered ball—

With a sickening crack, something slammed into him, hitting Jake with immense force. Jake felt his spine shattering. His upper body twisted unnaturally with the impact, his hips seeming to snap right in half. Jake screamed, toppling to the side, his eyes whirling toward the thing that had hit him—and then his stomach dropped. He was staring at himself, naked and bleeding, teetering over the ball and then collapsing in a ruined, shattered heap—

Jake's eyes came open and he sat up, gasping. For a brief second he had no idea where he was—and then the soft light of his study chased the last images of the nightmare out of his mind. He was lying on the suede couch behind his desk, a thin fleece quilt pulled over his chest. The shades on the small window above the couch were drawn, but he could see through the crack at the bottom that the sky had turned a dull gray. He rubbed his eyes, trying to guess what time it was. Alex would kill him if he was late to the airport; worse yet, if he didn't get there soon enough, he would find the big fool passed out in the airport lounge, reeking of Scotch.

First, he had to stop by his lab and pick up his viewing device and the stack of photographic ASD evidence from all the tested samples. He had left both the device and his photographs locked in the cabinet in his office—

Midthought, he noticed an incessant beeping coming from the pile of clothes next to the couch; he realized that his pager was going off. He sat up quickly, searching the pile of clothes for his pants. He finally found the beeper still attached to his belt, and looked at the small alphanumeric display. It was Bernard Stoller's cellular phone. Jake raised his eyebrows, wondering why the hell the security guard was paging him. The pager was for emergencies—which meant it had to be something about the lab.

Jake crawled across the couch and leaned over the edge, reaching for the phone on the corner of his desk. A second later he had the receiver up and against his ear as he dialed Bernard's number with quick flicks of his index finger.

Bernard picked up on the second ring. The connection was bad, and Jake could barely make out the guard's voice.

"Is that you, Jake?"

Jake cleared his throat. "Tell me this is a social call, Bernard."

There was a brief pause, silence peppered with the heavy grate of satellite feedback. Then Bernard was back on the phone. "You better get down here, Jake. Right away."

Jake's stomach dropped as he realized he could hear sirens in the background. "Bernard, I'm supposed to be on my way to Chicago. Tell me what's happened."

"Just get down here, Jake."

The connection died, and Jake stared at the phone. Then he sighed, reaching for his clothes.

The parking lot at the Sandler Wing was lit up like New Year's Eve, red and blue flashing lights bouncing off the glass entrance and casting bright pinwheels of color into the darkening sky. Jake had never seen so many emergency vehicles. His eyes traced the side of the building—and his heart nearly stopped. The second floor window was missing; in its place was a gaping black maw, spitting curls of dark smoke.

"Oh my God," Jake whispered. "My lab."

He slammed on the brakes, narrowly missing a fire engine that was pulling to a stop in front of his reserved parking spot. In a second he was out of his Buick and diving across the lot, heading for the glass doors. There was a group of uniformed police officers milling about the entrance, joined by at least a half dozen fire marshals in yellow slickers. As Jake approached, one of the officers separated from the group, waving him aside. The man was heavyset, in his mid-fifties, and there was dark soot on his cheeks.

"Hold on, sir. This is an accident scene."

"That's my lab," Jake said, trying to push past him. "I have to get up there."

"Let me check with the fire marshals," the man started to say. Then there was a shout of recognition, and Bernard Stoller jogged up, patting the officer on the shoulder.

"It's okay, Clyde. I'll look after him."

The officer shrugged as Bernard grabbed Jake by the arm and walked him through the front entrance. The lobby was filled with nearly two dozen emergency personnel. Jake recognized a few BPD bomb-squad uniforms, as well as a fair mix of paramedics, firefighters, and regular police officers. Over by the reception desk he caught sight of a tall, handsome man with silver hair and a jutting, cleft jaw—Arthur Sandler himself. The wealthy attorney general was holding court in front of camera-wielding reporters from the local media.

Jake let Bernard lead him along the other side of the lobby. There was the thick smell of smoke in the air, and the carpeted floor was covered in dark, sooty footprints. A loud, metallic alarm chimed from up ahead, and orange emergency lights ran the length of the ceiling.

"What the hell happened?" Jake finally asked, his face pale. Bernard was leading him at breakneck pace. Jake saw that some joker had wrapped a fire-department slicker over the shoulders of the statue of the nude pregnant woman, which had been unharmed by the blast. Then they were past the statue and Jake saw firemen wearing gas masks propping open the electronic security doors at the back of the room. He could hear the metal detector going off—but nobody seemed to notice.

"They're not sure yet," Bernard finally answered, pushing past a pair of paramedics. "But the fire marshals think it started as an electrical fire in the fire-safety control panel. Then some sparks must have hit the compressed oxygen containers in the equipment closet at the back of your lab. The extinguishers didn't go off, because the electrical fire burned out all the detectors. It was a major malfunction, Doc. And a hell of a fire. Took out your entire lab. Thankfully, the initial eruption was so hot, it burned itself out before the fire department got here. They didn't even have to break out the hoses."

They passed through the security doors and turned a corner, heading in the opposite direction of the elevators. The emergency stairwell was open, and there was a young fireman leaning against the wall, coughing hard. Another firefighter held a wet rag to his forehead. Jake hurried up to the young man.

"I'm a doctor. You okay?"

"I'm fine," the young man coughed. Jake saw that his cheeks were pale, and there were flecks of vomit on his lower lip. "Just never seen anything like that before."

Jake's chest constricted. He shoved past the kid and bounded up the stairs. Bernard rushed to catch up.

"Doc, listen, you might want to take this slow."

Jake reached the second floor and burst through the doorway. His feet skidded against black ash and he nearly fell, grabbing a charred countertop. The countertop was hot, and he cursed, pulling his hand away. Then his eyes adjusted to the darkness, and his head began to spin.

He had never seen such devastation. Every surface had been scorched to near blackness. The air was acrid, and heat pressed into him from every angle like enormous, open palms. The floor seemed warped, bulging upward, and Jake could imagine the flames rolling through the lab, beakers and test tubes shattering from the heat. He turned his head toward the destroyed picture window and stared out the gaping hole, momentarily too stunned to move. Then he remembered the vomiting fireman at the base of the stair-well and he started forward.

As he got closer to the computer room, the smell of smoke grew stronger. Mixed with the smell was something else; something sickly sweet—something that made Jake retch as he stumbled the last few steps to the open doorway. He stepped over a melted chunk of plastic that he thought was one of the speakers from the ceiling—and then he froze. There were two paramedics in the far corner of the room, standing next to an opaque plastic coroner's sheet. Behind them, the computer screens were all melted, the processors completely destroyed. An entire section of the wall behind the mainframe was missing, and there were streaks of black spiraling out from the open hole.

Jake started forward again—and then his gaze settled on a twisted object lying on its side next to the coroner's sheet. It was the ergonomic stool, melted almost beyond recognition.

Jake swayed, catching himself on the charred doorframe. Bernard came up behind him, putting a heavy hand on his shoulder.

"Doc, you sure you want to do this?"

"It's okay, Bernard." Jake was a doctor—he was supposed to be able to handle this sort of thing. But then again, he wasn't that kind of doctor. This was Brett's department, not his.

He walked slowly across the room. The paramedics looked at him, and he could tell by their eyes that it was bad—even for them. Both were wearing sterile masks and thick latex gloves. They moved aside, and Jake knelt, reaching for the plastic sheet.

He held his breath as he drew back the sheet. The shape beneath the sheet was horribly twisted into an anguished fetal position. Every inch of skin had been burned to a curdled, red crisp. The hair was gone, the skull visible in places, and the eye sockets were empty, burned out. There were no clothes left on the body, not even a thread of the MIT Chess Team sweatshirt or a strand of the tattered green shorts. Jake pulled the sheet back over Daniel Golden's head, and rocked back on his feet. He leaned against the wall, his arms crooked over his knees.

"From what we can tell," one of the paramedics said. "He was working on the computer when the equipment closet on the other side of this wall went up. He was caught in a burst of oxygenated flame. He must have died instantly."

Jake rubbed his eyes with his hands. Daniel was just a kid, a smart, cocky kid. His whole life ahead of him. Jake suddenly felt sick.

"Jake," a voice interrupted from the other end of the computer room. "Are you okay?"

Jake looked up as Brett rushed across the room. She dropped down next to him, putting her hands on his cheeks. She was wearing scrubs, her stethoscope wrapped around her shoulders. Her chest was heaving, her hair soaked with sweat. She looked as if she had just run a marathon.

"I'm fine," Jake managed, not really knowing what he was saying. "There was an accident—"

"I know, my God, I came as soon as I heard. Are you hurt?"

"No, I wasn't here. But Daniel—"

Brett's gaze found the coroner's sheet. "Jesus," she said, her face assuming the unemotional veneer of a trauma specialist. She reached for the edge of the sheet and pulled it down, revealing the charred body.

"He was working on the computer," Jake said. "Compressed oxygen blew through the wall. He never had a chance."

Brett reached forward and pulled Jake's head to her chest. Jake could feel her tears dripping down onto his face, and he wrapped his arms around her, holding her tight.

"I thought maybe it was you," she said, shaking. "They told me someone was killed, but they wouldn't give me details over the phone. I thought it was you."

Jake felt his own eyes tearing up. They sat like that, holding one another, until her shaking subsided. Then she stepped back, helping him stand. He looked around the computer room, trying to digest the level of destruction. The place looked surreal, almost like an alien landscape—

His thoughts were interrupted by a familiar beeping.

"Is that yours?" Brett asked, reaching for her waist. Jake nodded, pulling his beeper off his belt for the second time that night. This time, he recognized the number immediately.

"Shit. Alex. I was supposed to meet him at the airport."

Jake's head spun as he suddenly remembered: ASD. Chicago. His groundbreaking discovery. Next to the charred body on the floor, it seemed insignificant. But rationally, he knew it wasn't. ASD affected thousands of people.

He turned toward Bernard, who was standing awkwardly in the doorway. "Bernard, can I borrow your phone?"

He took the phone from Bernard and stepped out into the lab. Brett remained next to Daniel's body, talking to the paramedics.

As Jake dialed Alex's cell phone, he walked toward his office. He passed the area directly in front of the equipment closet where the fire had started, stepping gingerly over the dark crater dug a few inches into the thick cement floor. A light fixture was hanging precariously from the ceiling, exposed wires spitting sparks at the blackened wall. Jake reached the entrance to his office by the second ring, and he paused. The door was hanging by one hinge, the knob melted into a silvery glob. The explosion had packed one hell of a punch, blowing outward in two directions—into the computer room, and out here, through his office door. He hadn't realized there was so much compressed oxygen stored in the closet. He wondered how many canisters the lab architects had considered a safe quantity. If someone had fucked up, Daniel's family had a right to know.

Daniel's family. Jake's shoulders drooped as he thought about the phone call he would have to make—if the police hadn't already notified them. Sorrow hit him as he realized he didn't even know where Daniel grew up. They had never really had a conversation; they certainly hadn't been friends. Teacher-student didn't really sum up their relationship, either; basically, they had worked in the same lab. But that didn't make Daniel's death any easier to stomach—

"Jake," a slurred voice erupted in Jake's ear. "Where the fuck are you?"

Jake stepped past the hanging door into his office. He spoke as quickly as possible, not wanting to give Alex a chance to rant. "Alex, there's been a horrible accident. A fire in my lab. Daniel Golden was killed."

There was a clatter on the other end. "Shit. Are you serious?"

Alex had an amazing capacity to sober up in the face of tragedy. "It's pretty bad. There's no way I can make the conference. You'll have to give the presentation without me."

"Are you sure? I don't have any of the data. Or your viewing device."

The viewing device. Jake closed his eyes, cursing. Then he rushed forward across his burned office. The leather couches were nothing more than frames, the cushions having disintegrated in the fire. His desk had cracked down the center and had turned the color of old charcoal. His computer was melted into a mass of gray plastic, and the bookshelf by the window had collapsed. Wisps of smoke still rose from the pile of burned books.

"Jake?" Alex called through the phone. "You still there?"

Jake had reached the back of his office. He stopped in front of the normally locked bookshelf—and cursed. The bookshelf doors were wide open, the interior blackened by flame. He bent to his knees, his heart sinking. His viewing device was completely destroyed. He could no longer see the copper wires in the base, and the lenses were gone, shattered by the heat. It would take months to rebuild another device.

Despondent, he searched for the photographs. His heart fell as he saw the melted and charred mass. "Ruined. It's all ruined. The viewing prototype and the photographs."

Shit. Well, at least they still had the printed data. It wasn't the same—a lecture without photos, a theory without proof—but maybe it would be enough. It would still turn heads, even as a theory. They could follow up with the data when Jake managed to put together another viewing scope.

"Alex," he said finally. "You'll just have to present the syndrome with our printed data. I've got that at home—I'll overnight it tomorrow to the hotel suite. You'll have it for the last day of the conference. The effect won't be the same, but it will still get the point across."

Alex was silent on the other end. Jake could picture him swirling his Scotch. Perhaps he was contemplating skipping the conference altogether. Presenting a syndrome like ASD without any proof wasn't the most wonderful prospect—especially considering that Alex was an obstetrician, not a fertility expert. But Jake didn't see what choice they had. The fertility community had to be told about ASD. Tens of thousands of men in Boston were suffering from infertility, and the experts needed to turn their attention toward finding a cure. The conference was the best place to reach them en masse.

"I guess that's the way it has to be," Alex said at last. "I'm sorry about Daniel, Jake. I wish I hadn't given the kid a hard time. I feel like such a damn bully."

"Nobody could have expected this," Jake said, looking around his destroyed office. His gaze settled again on the burnt interior of the normally locked shelf, and a thought hit him. Why were the doors open? Had the blast somehow opened the lock? He carefully pushed one of the metal doors shut. The lock didn't look damaged at all. *Strange.*

Perhaps he had left the shelf open when he headed home

from the office late last night? No, he remembered closing them. He hadn't wanted Daniel to find the photographs—because he wasn't sure what Daniel would have done with such groundbreaking information. Daniel had a network of Internet colleagues with whom he had constantly shared information; his group of ambitious cohorts would have salivated at the sight of ASD, and Jake doubted Daniel could have contained himself.

Jake had never trusted Daniel—and maybe his mistrust had been well deserved. Maybe Daniel had broken into the cabinet before the fire and left the doors open. Perhaps Daniel had seen the photographs—and e-mailed them to his cohorts on the Internet. If so, the photographic data was still out there, somewhere. A long shot, but perhaps a lead worth following.

"Alex," Jake said into the phone, crossing toward the hanging office door. "I'll overnight the print data first thing tomorrow morning. Try not to get kicked out of the hotel before then."

Alex responded with a muted laugh, then broke the connection. Jake shut the phone and moved from the office to the lab. He almost ran into Brett, and they paused near the crater in front of the equipment cabinet. Jake slid his arm around Brett's waist, and she leaned into him, her head near his shoulder. For the first time in ages, the closeness didn't feel awkward or forced.

"Brett," he said, quietly. "Let's go home."

11

"Ain't it just the way of the world. They're gonna make us wait here all night. If we were healthy enough to wait, we wouldn't be in the emergency room."

Malthus forced himself to smile at the old woman sitting in the cushioned chair next to him. She was short, stocky, with curly gray hair and bright red cheeks. She waved a handful of perfumed tissues in front of her lips, one hand held against her generous breasts. There was a slight wheeze in her voice, and Malthus guessed she was asthmatic. He didn't think the perfumed tissues were helping, but he refrained from comment. He didn't want to say too much—because he had an unfortunate tendency to say exactly what he was thinking.

He shifted his eyes away from the woman, gazing at the doors that led out of the small waiting area into the main hall of the emergency room. He couldn't see much through the small circular glass windows halfway up the double doors, but from the gathering in the cubic walk-in area, he guessed that the ER itself was crowded. The main hall had a separate entrance, where the ambulances pulled up. The walk-in area was low priority, staffed by a triage intern in blue scrubs and two trauma nurses. The two nurses were sitting at the reception desk by the doors, hidden behind huge stacks of patient charts. Ahead of them, eight rows of occupied cushioned chairs took up most of the white-walled room.

A constant, frustrated din rose above the chairs, an almost liquid sound composed of whiny complaints, coughing, crying, retching, and a backbeat of full-out vomiting. An interesting symphony, Malthus thought, probably common to ER waiting rooms across the country. *Maybe someday someone will cut a CD.*

"Next time I'm calling an ambulance," the old woman suddenly sputtered. "They treat you much better if you come in by ambulance. That's because Medicare pays for the paramedics. They lose money on the walk-ins."

Malthus wished the woman *had* called an ambulance. She had started bothering him the moment he walked into the ER. It had taken fairly intense concentration to ignore her while he filled out a patient chart for the trauma nurses. He wanted to shove the sharpened pencil through the asthmatic woman's vocal chords. But the Air Force had taught him to control such impulses. There was a time and place for everything. The same logic held true now that he was a member of the corporate world.

His present outfit was a perfect example. He was wearing khaki pants and a loose-fitting white-collared shirt. Business casual—because it was close to eight P.M. on a Friday night. If he had showed up at the ER in his suit, he might have raised eyebrows. And if he had worn the blue janitorial coveralls he used four hours ago to breach the security of the fertility lab, he certainly would have drawn attention to himself. The coveralls were covered in blood—because it had taken a good seven minutes to torture the necessary information out of Daniel Golden, the young man who had unknowingly accessed Heidlinger's information.

Malthus felt a warm tingle as he remembered the terrified look on the little nerd's face when he asked him about the Trojan horse. The poor kid had pretended to know nothing about Compound G—until Malthus used the butane torch from the lab's equipment cabinet on his eyeballs, melting the orbs into useless, jellied blobs. Then Daniel told him the truth. He had accessed the information on Compound G completely by accident; and he had told no one else about his discovery. He did not think anyone else who worked in the lab knew anything about the protein— the arrogant nerd did not believe anyone else was smart enough to follow his footsteps.

Satisfied, Malthus had shoved the tip of the butane torch down his throat, cauterizing his esophagus and thereby silencing his screams. Then he had attached a tiny C–4 charge with a three-minute timing mechanism to twelve canisters of compressed oxygen he'd found in the lab's equipment cabinet. Since compressed oxygen had an incredibly high flash point, Malthus knew the explosion would destroy every trace of the timing mechanism. He doubted the local police would find the tiny amount of C–4, and even if they did, it would be traced to a radical antiabortion group in South Carolina, from whom Malthus had purchased the explosives two years ago.

A clean mission, with a fairly low level of difficulty. Certainly not a test of Malthus's abilities. But still, his father would have been proud. He had stifled the leak with no risk to the corporation. It would have been a time for celebration—had not a second leak suddenly come to Malthus's attention.

He sighed, throwing another glance at the doors that led to the ER. He hoped this mission would go as smoothly as the last.

"So tell me, young man," the woman next to him croaked, almost simultaneous with his thoughts. "What brings you to the ER?"

Malthus pointed to his right arm. "I cut myself. I think I might need stitches."

The woman glanced at his arm, but couldn't see anything beneath his oversized white sleeve. Then she shrugged. "Doesn't look like there's much blood."

Malthus raised his eyebrows, looking at his sleeve. "You're right. It doesn't look so bad."

The woman turned away, coughing into her tissues. Malthus shifted his body toward the wall, shielding himself from the woman's view. Then he quickly pulled back his sleeve. He turned his arm over, revealing the long tattoo that ran up the soft white skin of his forearm. He grimaced as he read the curling black letters: PROPERTY OF THE U.S. AIR FORCE.

He reached into the pocket of his khaki slacks and pulled out a short, pearl-handled boot knife with a serrated, razor-sharp edge. He had carried the knife during Desert Storm, and the sight of it brought back sad memories. He shook the memories away, holding the knife tightly in his palm, so only the tip of the sharp blade showed between his fingers.

With a swift motion, he slashed the blade down his forearm, slicing the tattoo directly in half. His skin separated easily, and a sheet of blood spilled out, splattering toward the floor. He held his arm out, trying to avoid ruining his khakis.

"Excuse me," he said to the asthmatic woman. "Could I borrow one of your tissues? I think my cut just got worse."

The woman stared at the wound, her eyes round as saucers. She quickly handed him all her tissues, and he held them against his forearm, trying to slow the bleeding. The pain sharpened his mind. He had learned the value of self-inflicted pain during his basic training. He had often carried razor blades into combat—not for self-defense, but to cut himself right before an engagement, to give an edge to his thoughts.

"Mr. Hamlin," a female voice chirped from somewhere near the ceiling. "Mr. David Hamlin. A doctor is ready to see you."

Malthus rose from the seat, holding his arm up, crooked at the elbow. It was one of his standard aliases—and came complete with a driver's license, passport, and falsified medical records. He smiled thinly at the asthmatic old woman. "Well, nice chatting with you. Hope your lungs clear up."

She continued staring at his arm. Malthus turned and headed to the reception desk. A young man in stained scrubs stood by the desk, chatting up one of the nurses. He looked about five-six, with dark curly hair and a puggish face. There was something snide and arrogant about his look—something that reminded Malthus of Daniel Golden. He smiled inwardly, remembering how Daniel's eyeballs had popped in the blue flame from the butane torch.

"Well," the young intern said, watching him approach. "That looks like a nasty cut. How'd it happen?"

Malthus had the sudden urge to wipe the confident smirk off the intern's face. *I was cutting up your wife with a razor blade. She screamed as I removed both her breasts.*

"I was cutting a mango and the knife slipped," Malthus answered out loud. "I can be so clumsy sometimes. Especially after a hard day at the office. You know how it is."

The intern nodded and then held the double doors open with his palm. "Third curtain on the right. I'll stitch you right up."

Malthus walked past him into the ER. As he had assumed, the room was crowded. Stretchers rolled across the tiled floor, pushed by orderlies in dark uniforms. Nurses dragged equipment carts after the stretchers, while doctors in scrubs shouted orders. The room seemed chaotic, but of course there was a logic, a stiff chain of command.

Malthus saw the ER as just another kind of corporation, with its own set of rules. Like any corporation, it had a dress code, a shared vernacular, and a clear consumer policy. Perhaps it also employed men like Malthus Scole, men whose job it was to keep things running smoothly, to deal with obstacles as they arose. *To plug the leaks.*

Malthus paused a few feet from the curtained exam room, staring toward the back of the ER. The target was unmistakable; tall, muscular, black, with a perfectly shaved head and friendly, boyish features. His scrubs and high-top basketball sneakers were splotched with blood, and there was a stethoscope slung over his wide shoulders. At the moment, he leaned over a stretcher, speaking quietly to a patient, a young boy with tubes in his nostrils. When the boy responded, the target laughed, raising his head. Malthus got a clearer look at the man's features, and a warm, anticipatory feeling moved through him.

Calvin Johnson, age twenty-eight, born in Detroit, trained at Duke, a crack ER doctor and an amateur boxer with twelve KOs in six months. Malthus had studied the file prepared by his research team on the way over to the hospital. It had taken Malthus's specialists less than twelve minutes to compile the data once the tracking program had identified the second download from the NIH mainframe. Calvin Johnson had used his ID to access the GenBank database—and that ID had marked him indelibly.

Malthus had no idea why an ER doctor would be interested in Compound G; but he intended to find out. He was, after all, the VP of Research and Development. By corporate rules, that made him responsible.

"Right in here," the brash intern from the waiting room interrupted, pulling the curtain aside to reveal a small, well-lit area containing an exam table and an equipment cart. "Up on the table."

Malthus finally shifted his eyes away from Calvin Johnson and allowed the intern to guide him into the exam cubicle. He sat on the table, watching as the intern shut the curtain, closing off the rest of the ER. The intern quickly crossed to the equipment cart, gloved up, wiped the wound down with Betadine, then retrieved a syringe and a vial of clear liquid. He was about to fill the syringe with the liquid when Malthus raised his good arm.

"No anesthesia."

The intern raised his eyebrows. "I checked your chart. You're not allergic."

Malthus smiled grimly. "It's a spiritual matter, doctor. I believe in experiencing every second of life."

The intern rolled his eyes and then shrugged. He dropped the syringe back onto the cart and grabbed a thin needle and a spool of antiseptic thread. "Okay, Gandhi. Hold out your arm."

Malthus clenched his teeth as the needle went into his skin. The sharp pain ricocheted all the way to the top of his spine, but he made no sound. The intern looked at him, his face slightly pale. "That religion of yours must be pretty tough. I'd be sobbing by now."

Malthus stared at him, releasing his jaw. "We like to call it a corporation, not a religion. And please keep the stitching tight, doctor. I don't want a jagged scar."

The intern finished the stitching in silence, keeping his

eyes on his work. When he was done, he wiped the injury with a cotton ball covered in alcohol. The burning sting was almost erotic, and Malthus blinked, accepting the pain. The intern tossed the bloody cotton ball toward the floor and then wrapped a sterile white bandage over the stitched wound. Satisfied that the bandage was tightly clipped below Malthus' elbow, the intern clapped his gloved hands together. "Okay, good as new. If there's nothing else, I'll escort you back to the waiting area—"

"Actually, there is something else, doctor. A rather embarrassing problem."

The intern paused, obviously annoyed but trying to remain professional. Malthus had rehearsed his part, and made sure he sounded as believable as possible. "Two nights ago I was at a bachelor party. I drank a little too much—and woke up next to a woman in garters with dyed blond hair. This morning, when I went to pee—"

"Burning and itching," the intern finished for him.

"That's right, doctor. I was wondering if there was something you could give me."

The intern nodded, the superior smirk back on his face. "First, we've got to get you checked out. I'll need to grab an STD kit, so just drop your trousers and I'll be right back."

The intern headed for the curtain. Malthus' research department have given him detailed maps of Central's ER, including geographically correct laundry lists of all its stored medical equipment. He knew the STD kits were kept in a supply room around the corner—just far enough to give him the necessary few minutes to acquire the target.

At the count of twelve, he quickly rose from the exam

table and crossed to the curtain. He pulled the curtain back, his eyes flickering across the ER. *There.* By the back doors that led out of the ER, speaking to a nurse. As he watched, the young black doctor patted the nurse on the shoulder, then stepped through the doors.

Malthus was out of the exam room and moving like a gazelle through the ER. As he had assumed, nobody looked twice at a bandaged patient in the ER; his entry strategy had been fairly elaborate, but necessary. Central's policy of having doctors escort patients into the ER meant he couldn't have just walked in through the front doors; but once inside the ER, it was his doctor's responsibility to keep an eye on him. The nurses at reception were concerned only with unattended patients moving through the front doors.

Not the back doors. Malthus slipped through the double doors and out into a white, sterile hallway. Calvin Johnson was five yards ahead, pushing through another doorway marked with a bright red ONE. Malthus erased the distance in three long steps, then slid in after him.

The room was brightly lit by two halogen spots hanging from the high ceiling. There was a metal table in the center, raised on a hydraulic pedestal. Blood and fluid gutters ran around the edges of the table; attached to an articulated arm coming out of the table's side, a tray brimmed with surgical equipment. Calvin was standing at the back of the room, reaching into a wooden cabinet.

Malthus quietly shut the double doors behind him. His fingers found a metal lever midway down the wood, and he flicked it hard to the right. He knew that on the outside of the doors, beneath the surgical room's numerical label, a small red bar had appeared. The bar would warn the hospital's trauma staff that a delicate procedure was in progress, that they were not to disturb except in an emergency. Assuredly, a bright nurse or intern would realize that the room was not supposed to be occupied—but ERs were notoriously chaotic, especially on Friday nights. Malthus would have at least a few moments alone with the young doctor.

He moved into the room, stopping next to the raised metal table. He saw Velcro restraint straps hanging below the blood gutters and articulated stirrups at the bottom of the table. His eyes shifted to the tray of surgical instruments. Scalpels, forceps, different shaped scissors, antiseptic gauze, bandages, and various sizes of syringes. He turned back toward the young doctor, whose back was still toward him. He cleared his throat.

Calvin Johnson grabbed a box of wooden tongue depressors from the cabinet and then turned, seeing Malthus for the first time. A look of impatience slipped across his dark eyes. "Sir, this is a restricted area. You shouldn't be in here."

"Actually," Malthus answered, his voice slow. "I was hoping to have a little conversation with you, Dr. Johnson. Take a meeting, in corporate speak."

Calvin stared at him, obviously wondering how some patient he had never seen before knew his name. "I'm sorry, sir. I'm in the middle of my shift. I don't have much time. Let me direct you to reception, and they'll find someone—"

"I don't think you understand, Dr. Johnson. We *need* to interface. It's a matter of corporate relations."

Malthus grinned, taking a menacing step forward. Calvin's face changed, anger moving into his cheeks. He was a doctor—but he wasn't going to take crap from an obvious maniac. "Look, either go back into the ER, or I'm going to call security."

Malthus reached out and grabbed a handful of cotton from the surgical tray. "You can make this easy or hard, Dr. Johnson. I'm going to ask questions—and you're going to give answers."

Calvin stared at the handful of cotton and then put the box of tongue depressors down. His muscular body shifted into a boxer's stance. "I'm warning you, sir. You need to go back into the ER."

"And you need to *listen*, Dr. Johnson. I'm going to ask questions. You're going to give answers. Beginning with everything you know about Compound G."

Calvin's eyes widened. Before he could say anything Malthus swept forward, cutting the distance in the blink of an eye. Calvin's hands came up, balling into fists. A boxer's confidence, gleaned from years of training, flitted across his dark face. His right arm shot forward—but Malthus was much too quick. He feinted left, striking out with a specially designed steel-toed leather shoe. His foot connected with the doctor's kneecap, and there was a sickening crunch. Calvin's mouth opened but before the scream could emerge, Malthus shoved the handful of cotton between his teeth. Malthus's other hand grasped the doctor by the throat, and he half lifted him into the air. The doctor's cheeks bulged, his eyes rolling back in pain. Malthus tightened his grip until he could feel the walls of Johnson's esophagus through his black skin. "In business, it's very important not to underestimate the competition. You might very well be a competent boxer. But your primary talent is in the emergency room. This, however, *is* my primary talent."

Malthus spun on his heels and then slammed the doctor backward onto the metal exam table. With his left hand, he quickly strapped the Velcro restraints around the doctor's chest and waist. He moved close to the young man's face, looking at his dazed eyes, at the trickle of blood that ran from the corner of his lips. He hoped he had not squeezed the man's throat too tightly.

"Dr. Johnson? Still with me?" Malthus pulled the cotton out of the man's mouth, letting him breathe. "Are you ready for our meeting?"

Calvin gasped, struggling vainly against the Velcro straps. Then a thin whisper slipped out from between his lips. "Who are you?"

Malthus exhaled. "You still don't seem to understand. *I* ask the questions."

"Who the fuck are you!"

Malthus sighed. The target was being difficult. A tough kid from the tough side of Detroit. Malthus glanced at the closed double doors leading out of the exam room and decided this would have to be brutal and quick.

He walked down the length of the exam table to the base and grabbed Calvin's ankles, one in each hand. Then he yanked the doctor's legs apart, placing an ankle in each of the gynecological stirrups. Calvin screamed at the motion, and Malthus could see blood soaking through his scrubs where the shattered kneecap was tearing through his skin.

"Each question will be asked only once," Malthus said,

speaking quietly as he grabbed a sharp pair of scissors off the surgical tray. He carefully snipped away a section of the young doctor's loose scrubs, revealing his white underwear, focusing on the dark bulge of the man's genitalia beneath the thin material. "If you hesitate in any way, if you cry out or resist—well, I think you'll quickly figure out the rest."

Calvin's eyes had gone wide, his face pale. His lips quivered as he stared up at Malthus from between his spread legs. "Please. I don't know anything."

Malthus let the first infraction slide, as he gently cut away the man's underwear. Calvin's penis looked abnormally shriveled from fear, resting against his bulbous scrotum like the trunk of a geriatric elephant. Malthus held the sharp point of the scissors against the sensitive tip, and cleared his throat.

"Tell me, Dr. Johnson. *Who else knows about Compound G?*"

12

Jake watched Brett's breasts rise and fall, the reddish tips of her small nipples trembling as some unconscious dream fluttered behind her eyelids. He wondered if the dream had anything to do with the incredible night of passion they had both just experienced. The night began with a quiet dinner, then a slow dance in front of the unlit fireplace in the living room. There had been no talk of basal body charts, cervical mucus, or fertility statistics. No mention of Daniel Golden, ASD, or Jake's destroyed lab. Only hands touching cheeks, gentle kisses, eyes full of understanding.

Jake cupped his palm over Brett's breast, feeling the nipple harden at his touch. They had let things get so close to the breaking point—but now everything was going to be okay. After the tragedy in the lab, something had rekindled. For the first time in more than six months, they had made love like lovers. And even though Jake knew—for a scientific fact—that his sperm had gotten nowhere near the swollen blister slumbering in her fallopian tube, it had felt right.

He leaned forward, kissing her lips. Then he carefully slid his other arm out from under her head, trying his best not to wake her. She had been working insane hours for days, and she needed the extra time in bed. Besides, judging from the light trickling through the window shades, it was still sometime around six A.M.

Jake crossed to the window, looking down at the quiet, tree-lined street. A young couple strolled by in jogging shorts. A newspaper truck chugged to a stop at the corner, the driver lifting a cup of coffee off the dashboard. The heat had finally broken, and it looked as though it was going to be a beautiful day.

Then Jake closed his eyes and pictured Daniel's charred body lying in a fetal position on the floor of the computer room. His stomach clenched and he headed for the dresser, searching for his clothes. He wished he could stay hidden in his bedroom forever. But the world didn't work that way. He had a destroyed laboratory to deal with—and an epidemic to expose.

An hour later—after a stop at the FedEx office near Government Center to mail Alex the ASD folders—Jake arrived at the rear entrance to the Sandler Wing. He eased off the gas as he parked the Buick next to a delivery van that bore a painting of an armored Roman soldier across its exterior. Two burly men stood next to the open back doors of the van, arguing in loud voices. A broken crate lay next to an overturned dolly on the ground between them, a sea of brightly colored condoms strewn across the asphalt.

Jake skirted the condom spill, heading for the rear door to the wing. The door responded to his ID card and clicked open, and he found himself in a warren of well-lit corridors. In contrast to the opulence of the front lobby, this entrance had a utilitarian simplicity: sheer cement walls, unlabeled wooden doors, and fluorescent strips that lined the curved ceilings. This was the operations department: janitorial services, stationery supplies, mail sorting and delivery, computer services. Ops was the spinal infrastructure beneath the smoothly running Wing.

Jake turned a corner, then stopped in front of one of the doors. He could hear the beeps and buzzes of a dozen computer processors slipping through the wood, and he imagined the engineering bay of a spaceship, something out of a science fiction movie. He had never visited the Wing's tech-services department before—usually leaving the dirty work to Daniel or his other graduate students.

He opened the door without knocking and entered a small, carpeted entry room, furnished with a desk and two potted plants.

He vaguely recognized the man behind the desk; short, rotund, balding, with glasses perched high on his nose and a poorly knotted tie hanging beneath oversized jowls. Albert Finsey, Director of Computer Operations, had installed the computers in Jake's lab six months ago and had given a short seminar on the Wing's Internet-access system.

Finsey looked up as he entered the room, his lips pursing in annoyance. Then his look changed as he recognized Jake.

"Dr. Foster. Everyone's very shaken up about what happened in your lab. Daniel was a great kid. It's just so awful, I don't know what to say."

"Actually, Daniel's what I want to talk about. He spent a lot of time on the computer, e-mailing to a circuit of colleagues. I'm trying to reconstruct what he was doing yesterday. I think he might have sent some important data through the Internet, and I'm hoping there's some way to track it down."

Jake felt slightly irreverent, focusing on something that seemed so unimportant compared to Daniel's death. But Finsey didn't seem to notice. To him, there was nothing more important than the computer system—and perhaps, in a way, reconstructing Daniel's last day was a way of honoring him.

"Well, if he accessed the Internet, we'll have a record on our main system. We don't keep tabs on individual e-mails— that would be an unfair breach of privacy. But if he made an upload from the computers in your lab, our system would have made a backup."

Jake nodded. If Daniel had found the photographs of the ASD sperm and had uploaded them to friends on the Internet—then Jake could get the backups, reprint the photos, and send them to Alex in Chicago.

He followed Finsey out through a door at the back of the

room and into another white hallway. He passed an alcove filled with AV equipment: video cameras, tripods, portable TVs, VCRs. Finsey noticed his interest and smiled. "We just got a new shipment of DVD cameras from Japan. Absolutely fabulous technology. One of the cameras fits in the palm of my hand."

Finsey held up a fatty paw, and Jake raised his eyebrows. He couldn't imagine what use a Wing dedicated to human fertility and pregnancy would have with a palm-sized video camera. But that was par for the course with Arthur Sandler; his foundation had money to burn, and he knew how to burn it.

Finsey turned an abrupt corner, and they entered a vast, circular room lined with computer terminals. A massive mainframe stood by the door, the front open, computer boards standing in vertical rows. Finsey crossed to one of the terminals and shoved his rotund frame into a cushioned chair. He beckoned Jake to his side and began punching keys.

"Okay," he said, his thick fingers moving at near light speed. "Let's punch up yesterday's Internet-access schedule. Function out the other labs—here we go. This is Daniel's packet ID—and his handle, Hobbit3. Okay, Hobbit3 was e-mailing all morning, hits to the mainframes at UCAL, Harvard, Microsoft, then a JPG upload to the NIH—"

"A JPG," Jake asked. "An image file, right?"

"That's right. Want me to bring it up from backup?"

Jake nodded, excited. He stared at the screen, praying that it would soon be filled with suicidal sperm. The pixels flashed—and suddenly he was staring at a red-and-blue photograph of some sort of protein. The colors were incredibly bright, and Jake squinted, trying to figure out what the hell it was.

"It's an X-ray crystallography," he said. "But I've never seen that structure before."

"According to the time code," Finsey said, "he uploaded this picture to the NIH GenBank Database at three forty-five. If I remember right, the fire alarms went off at four-fifteen. Thirty minutes later."

Jake glanced at him, then back at the screen. The upload was probably one of the last things Daniel did before the fire.

"The NIH GenBank," he said, thinking out loud. "It's a database, used to match proteins. Daniel must have been trying to figure out if this structure was something brand-new."

A thought hit him—could Daniel have found the chemotaxin he'd been looking for? Was he looking at the Holy Grail of fertility studies?

Jake shook the unlikely thought away. But what was this protein? Where did it come from?

"Can you print this up for me?" he asked.

Finsey nodded. As Jake waited, his thoughts unintentionally turned to the phone call he had made last night, before he and Brett returned home. Daniel's parents were devastated by the news of their son's death—and Jake had had nothing reassuring to say to them.

He wished he'd spent more time with his graduate student; at the very least, he should have followed Daniel's work more closely. As Finsey handed him the printed page, he stared down at the colorful molecule, tracing the electrical connections, wondering what secrets they held.

He thanked Finsey and exited the computer room. As he moved through the Ops hallways, he decided that Daniel's protein was worth investigating. His thoughts shifted through possible research trails as he slipped out the back door and into the parking lot

Halfway across the lot, he noticed that the condom van was no longer parked next to his Buick. In its place was a metallic blue Jaguar. Jake immediately recognized the car—and the man stepping out of the driver's side. Arthur Sandler caught sight of Jake and a sad smile broke above his square, protruding jaw. His blue eyes looked tired, his silvery hair uncharacteristically unkempt. He straightened the rumpled lapels of his tailored blue suit and started forward.

Jake felt a bit nervous as he met the attorney general halfway across the lot. Sandler was one of the most powerful men in Boston—as well as Jake's unofficial boss. Despite his outward fatherly charm, he was intensely driven, with well-documented aspirations. Soon, he would probably be governor. Perhaps, one day, even president.

"Dr. Foster," Sandler said, shaking hands. "I'm sorry I didn't get a chance to speak to you last night at the scene. Things were pretty crazy. How are you holding up?"

Jake exhaled. "It's been difficult."

"A horrible tragedy," Sandler continued. "I was up most of last night dealing with the press, the fire department, and the insurance companies. Not that I'd have been able to sleep. I've got a son about Daniel Golden's age. I can imagine the horror his parents are going through."

A shadow swept across Sandler's weathered cheeks. Jake nodded, again thinking of the phone call to Daniel's parents. "There's no way to prepare for something like this."

Sandler sighed. "True. But I promise you, I'm going to make damn sure this sort of thing doesn't happen again in my Wing. I don't care if I have to tear down every lab and rebuild. That's why I'm here this morning—to go over the building specs with a representative from the fire department."

"About my lab—"

"We'll relocate you by the end of next week," Sandler answered, his eyes kind. He paused, then placed a hand on Jake's shoulder. His voice changed, his tone low and filled with real sorrow. "This is going to be very difficult for all of us. I keep thinking, what if it were my own son dying like that. It was an accident—but even so, I want someone to blame."

Sandler paused, breathing deep. Then he sighed. "Anyway, Jake, if there's anything else I can do, please let me know. Anything at all."

Jake thanked the attorney general, then continued across the lot toward his car. As he slid into the front seat, he unfolded the printout from Finsey's computer and studied Daniel's strange protein once again. Sandler had said Jake wouldn't have a new lab until the end of next week. That left plenty of time to chase the brightly colored molecule.

The protein might have nothing to do with ASD—but Jake didn't like mysteries. Daniel had run this protein through the NIH database shortly before his death. Jake intended to find out why.

13

Brett squinted as a ray of reflected sunlight flashed off the back window of an ambulance pulling into the circular drop-off bay in front of her. The lilt of the sirens echoed through the headphones of her Walkman, punctuating the last few bars of the Beatles song that had carried her the last quarter mile of her brisk jog through Beacon Hill. Even the sirens and the ambulance made her smile, because the sound and sight both seemed so normal. She felt better than she had in nearly a year. It had taken a horrible incident to knock sense into her—but she had been so focused on what

Jake couldn't give her, she had forgotten how much he already *had* given her. Last night was proof; Jake was the constant in her life. She could not allow herself to take him for granted—despite the mistakes he had made in the past.

She slowed to a walk as she passed the lit-up ambulance and shoved open the double doors that led into the ER. The familiar, antiseptic scent wafted out at her, and she breathed deeply, mentally preparing herself for the day ahead.

The second she passed through the double doors into the ER, she could tell that something was wrong. Her spine tingled as she took note of the muted atmosphere, the lack of the normal, usually off-color banter of the trauma nurses, interns, residents, and med students. Then her gaze settled on the group of uniformed police officers by the back doors, and her heart jumped. The presence of police officers in the ER was common; but standing in the center of the group, talking in heated tones to a tall officer with gray hair and wire-rimmed glasses, Brett saw a familiar, roosterlike figure. Six feet tall, with thinning brown hair, an oblong nose, almost no jaw, spindly arms, and a curved spine from an incorrectly treated childhood bout of scoliosis: Maxwell Cross. Cross wore his white doctor's coat over a light green golf outfit, and it was obvious the chief had been interrupted midway through his morning off. But even from a distance, Brett could tell something was different about Cross's usually vicious demeanor. As he lit into the police officer, there was a tinge of real distress in his beady green eyes—and that scared Brett much more than the sight of the officers themselves. Cross had a heart of pure stone.

The chief looked up as Brett crossed the ER, then waved at her. She hurriedly pushed through the group of officers, arriving next to the tall cop with the glasses and gray hair. The officer glanced at her. "Is this her?"

Brett did not like the officer's tone. But before she could say anything, Cross was speaking for her, his eyes avoiding her face.

"Yes, this is Dr. Foster. She was the attending scheduled to head up the ER last night. But she signed out at eight P.M. to Dr. Kressle, one of our veteran attendings. He was covering the ER in her absence."

"But he wasn't present at eight P.M.," the officer said, his lips pursed. "He was in his office on the fourth floor."

Cross's head crooked angrily to the side. "Both he and Dr. Foster were on beeper last night. And it wouldn't have made any difference if they *had* been here."

Brett looked back and forth between the two men. *What the hell are they talking about?* She felt that she was being blamed for something, but she had no idea what it could be. "Dr. Cross, I'm sorry I had to leave early last night, but I had a personal emergency. My husband's lab—"

"Brett," Cross interrupted, his voice softer, "there was a homicide here last night. One of the doctors under your charge."

Brett stared at him. "A *homicide?*"

"A butcher job, actually," the officer grunted. "Must have been some brand of psycho, from the looks of things."

Brett's mouth had gone bone dry. *One of my people is dead.* Her ears rang as she heard her mouth ask the necessary question. "Who?"

Cross couldn't look her in the eyes. Her stomach dropped as she watched his thin lips shape the words.

"Calvin Johnson."

Tears streamed down Brett's face as she gripped the metal frame of the autopsy table. Her body rocked back and forth with the force of her sobs as she gently pulled back the white sheet. His eyes were open and slightly bulged, his cheeks swollen and mottled, his lips dark purple and curled back, locked in anguish. Brett paused, trying to catch her breath, her fingers turning white against the cold table frame. Why Calvin? *Why?*

She opened her mouth and the question echoed through the empty autopsy room. If Dr. Kelly had been there, he would have looked at her sadly, shaking his head. The pathologist could tell her how—but not why.

Brett pulled the sheet a few inches farther, revealing the dark blue bruises around Calvin's throat, where the rubber IV wire had strangled him. Dr. Kelly could have told her the exact force of the wire, the exact amount of time it had taken for Calvin's brain to run out of oxygen. He could have diagrammed each bruise, calculating the assailant's height, weight, and musculature—but he couldn't have explained what had been going on in the assailant's head.

The sheet drifted farther, revealing Calvin's chest and the purplish marks left by the Velcro restraint straps. Then his stomach, the abdominal muscles clenched beneath his paled, oxygen-deprived skin. Brett's entire body started to shake as she pulled the sheet the last few inches. Cross and the police officer had begged her not to look—but she was a trauma doctor, and Calvin was her friend. *More than a friend.*

"Calvin. My God, Calvin." Her throat constricted, trapping his name as she stared at the mutilated area between his thighs. What kind of monster could have done this?

It was so fucking unfair. Calvin had dedicated his life to helping others. He didn't deserve to die like this. *Nobody deserves to die like this.*

Brett yanked the sheet back up. Her jaw clenched, anger rocketing through her. The police officer had called it a random, violent homicide, perpetrated by some psycho who had slipped into the ER unnoticed. A psycho who didn't need any motivation beyond his own psychosis to kill.

But that wasn't good enough for Brett. She was going to find out why this had happened. Why Calvin had to die in such a violent way.

Ten yards away, Malthus Scole pressed his face against the small round window perched halfway up the door to the autopsy lab. His cold blue eyes drifted down the beautiful doctor's body, from her trembling shoulders to her bent knees, to her fingers, long and narrow, clenched against the corpse's weathered skin. Her short black hair and porcelain skin reminded him of the whore, and he exhaled, overwhelmed by her anguish. He had watched the whore tremble like that as the embolism had moved through her circulatory system.

Malthus stepped back from the door to the autopsy lab, surprised by the sudden memory. He had not thought about the whore's death in years. He was struck by the realization that the memory had less to do with the physical similarities between the two women than with what they represented. Both seemed to be dilemmas without answers.

Based on his interrogation of Calvin Johnson, Malthus knew that the woman in the autopsy lab—Brett Foster—was to some degree aware of Heidlinger's leak. But Malthus couldn't simply kill her, because of the thorough investigation a second ER doctor's death would surely trigger. And the whore had once seemed equally difficult to erase—because she had somehow worked her way behind his walls. Made him briefly feel real emotions, for the first—and last—time in his life.

He leaned back against the basement hallway, breathing hard behind the sterile surgical mask he had found in an equipment cabinet after his meeting with Calvin Johnson. His dark green scrubs—also from the equipment cabinet—were soaked through with sweat, and he struggled to reclaim his nerves. The situation had suddenly become dangerous. Brett Foster had been working with Calvin Johnson, investigating some sort of deadly bleeding disease, when they stumbled onto Compound G. And she was married to Jake Foster—the head of the fertility lab where Daniel Golden had worked. From what Malthus had learned from Daniel Golden, he didn't think that Jake Foster knew anything about Compound G—*yet*. But once the husband and wife began to share information, there was no telling how much damage they could do.

Malthus had to eliminate them; but first, he had to find

out how much they knew, and whom they had told. He had already sent Pierce after the husband—chasing his credit-card transactions to Chicago. Malthus would shadow Brett, and soon he would know how badly the leak had expanded.

As per his father's orders, he wouldn't let anything stand in the project's way—just as he had prevented his own confusing feelings from interfering with his duty concerning the whore. Once his father had offered him the position at Alaxon, he knew that the whore would have to die.

He had killed her in a unique but fitting manner. He'd been planning the event for days—but the moment itself arose spontaneously. Kneeling between her legs in their small apartment in Marakesh, the sound of her euphoric moans lilting through the desert air, Malthus suddenly decided to try something he had read about in an ancient Persian assassin's text. An intriguing technique he had never really believed would work.

He had leaned forward, pressing his lips tightly around the whore's vagina, creating an airtight seal. Then he had blown as hard as he could, forcing the air directly into her body. Her body had begun to shudder as an air embolism entered her bloodstream, racing upward toward her heart. When the embolism hit the cardial sac she lurched forward, eyes wide, mouth frozen in terror. Then her face had turned ash white, and she had collapsed. Malthus had watched her die, almost as surprised as she was. *Death by cunnilingus.* A truly fitting end to a whore's life.

Malthus opened his eyes, suddenly calmed by the memory. Every problem had a resolution. It was just a matter of coming up with the appropriate strategy.

Malthus moved back to the window. He watched Brett
rub her hands over her eyes, finally controlling her tears.
She was a strong woman, and she would not give up easily.

Malthus could almost taste the whore on his lips.

Every problem has a resolution.

14

Red and blue splotches spun in front of Jake's eyes as he reached for his third cup of coffee in twenty minutes. It took him a few seconds to find the ceramic mug in the avalanche of textbooks, open magazines, printouts, and fertility manuals that covered every inch of the desk in front of him. Behind him, Brett's IBM computer screen glowed in radiant harmony with the open screen of his laptop on the floor by his feet, and the strange protein from Daniel's upload cast two sets of shadows across the wood-paneled study walls.

The screen on Jake's desk contained a different image. It

was the final frozen frame of the bizarre video that had spurted out of the NIH database the second he had tried to retrace Daniel's last known act. In the center of the screen, a gloved hand held a golf ball to the camera. The focus of the shot was a tiny mark in the center of the ball—an imprinted single letter: G.

Jake brought the mug to his lips, hoping the hot liquid would help clear the hazy splotches from his eyes. He had been staring at the protein all day. He'd made a dozen print-outs of the compound and then had gone to the Sandler Wing library and had checked out every molecular chemistry manual and textbook he could find. He'd spent the entire afternoon searching for anything that resembled a match. He had wanted to save the NIH database for last—because he didn't just need to know if the protein was something new, he needed to know how and where Daniel had found it. He had been hoping that the textbooks would lead him to some experiment Daniel might have conducted, in his search for the chemotaxin at the base of fertility. But the textbooks had gotten him nowhere. He had found nothing to match the image on the two computer screens.

So he had dialed up the NIH database. The strange video download had begun a few seconds after he started the match process. After the video ended, he had redialed the NIH and watched the bizarre show a second time. He had frozen the screen on the last frame of the video file, and had been staring at it ever since.

He wondered what Daniel had thought when he saw the chimpanzee crawling through the chain-link cage, choosing the marked items one at a time, building a strange collection of different-shaped objects. He wondered if the display had somehow made sense to Daniel—because maybe he knew where this protein came from. Daniel had crystallized Compound G in the fertility lab sometime before the fire, and had uploaded this very image barely an hour before he was scorched to death.

A slam reverberated through the townhouse, and Jake nearly dropped his coffee. He glanced at the window above the couch, and saw that it was still light out. He looked at his watch, confirming the time: not even five-thirty. Brett was supposed to be on call until midnight.

He listened to her footsteps moving through the first floor of the house. He didn't hear her car keys hit the glass table, but of course that made sense, because her sporty Toyota Coupe was still parked in one of their spots in the alley behind the house.

When her footsteps reached the stairs leading to the second floor, his back tensed; he could tell by the sound that something was very wrong. After the rekindling of last night, he would have expected her spirits to be high. But it sounded as if she was dragging herself up the steps.

"Brett?" he called, spinning his leather swivel chair to face the door. "I didn't expect you home until late. Is everything okay?"

She stopped in the doorway and Jake rose from the chair. The expression on her face scared him. "It's Calvin. He was murdered last night. Mutilated, strangled with an IV wire."

Jake felt the breath knocked out of him. "That's horrible."

He couldn't think of anything else to say. Two tragedies

in the space of twenty-four hours. Jake's grad student and Brett's senior resident. It was such an awful coincidence. Jake quickly crossed the room and hugged his wife, pulling her head against his chest. He felt stunned, unable to comprehend the tragedy. Mutilated? He wasn't sure he wanted to know what that meant.

"I've got to find out why this happened," Brett whispered. "I took the rest of the week off from the hospital."

Her voice was filled with anger, and Jake tried to quiet her, his hand in her hair. "Brett, I'm sure the police are handling things."

"The police aren't *handling* things," Brett said, pushing back from his chest. "They don't even have a description of the killer. They think someone must have wandered into the ER—but that's not possible. The reception nurses would have noticed an unattended visitor. That's their job."

There was venom in Brett's voice, and Jake knew from experience it was time to back off. But he didn't like the idea of her chasing after some murderer. "Friday nights are pretty crowded. Maybe some patient got away from one of the interns for a few minutes. Or maybe someone did slip by the reception nurses. Either way, it's the police's job."

"I know you never liked Calvin. I know you could never accept the fact that he and I were just friends. But I'm not going to let him become just another ER statistic."

Jake told himself to keep his mouth shut. Brett was in pain, and she was going to take it out on him unless he stayed silent. It wouldn't do him any good to say what he was thinking.

"Brett, you have to let it go. If you obsess over this, it's going to kill you."

Brett's eyes turned dark. "That's my problem, isn't it. I *obsess* over things. Like the fact we can't have a child. Like the fact that you went off and fucked some bitch because you didn't have the guts to marry me. And now—Calvin's murder. Another obsession, right Jake? *So fucking deal with it.*"

"Brett." Jake said quietly. His face was red, and he felt as though he had just been slapped. She hadn't mentioned the affair for a long time. He knew why she was bringing it up now. She was goading him into admitting his jealousy concerning Calvin. She wanted him to set their marriage on fire—once again. But he wasn't going to do that. For once he was going to be smart. *Jake, keep your DAMN MOUTH SHUT.*

He swallowed, waiting for the explosion he knew was still coming. But Brett's eyes had suddenly gone wide. She was staring at something behind him.

He turned—and saw her computer screen glowing red and blue. He turned back to Brett. She was pointing at the protein, her face a shade paler than before. "Where did you get that picture?"

"Daniel uploaded it from his computer an hour before he died. It's some sort of protein. I think it's something brand-new, but I'm not sure. When I tried to find a match on the GenBank database—"

"You got the monkey video," Brett whispered, her finger shifting toward the screen on Jake's desk. "This doesn't make any sense."

Jake stared at her. He was worried that Calvin's death was making her delirious. He reached out and took her wrist in his hand. Her pulse was racing. "Brett, what are you talking about?"

"Compound G," she said, looking at him. "Six amine functional groups wrapped around a cyclic hydrocarbon. Developed by someone named Eric Heidlinger at Alaxon Industries."

Jake let go of her wrist. "How do you know about it?"

Brett stepped past him into the study, moving closer to the glowing image of the protein. "Calvin and I found a large quantity of Compound G in the livers of our DIC patients."

Jake felt the air rush out of him. He remembered that Brett had been working on a mystery in the ER involving DIC. "Your four bleeders."

"That's right. We think the unknown protein induced the patients to bleed out, kind of like a toxic shock reaction. And when we tried to look it up on the GenBank, we got the same strange download. Calvin was going to make me a printout of the protein, but I never had a chance to get it from him. I got the call about your lab and rushed out of the ER. When I returned this morning, Calvin was dead."

She turned away from the screen, her eyes strange. Jake leaned back against the wood-paneled wall. He wondered if she was thinking that somehow, the two tragedies might be related. He shook his head, pushing the thought away. *Absurd*. Calvin Johnson was murdered, Daniel Golden died in an accident. A remarkable coincidence—but a coincidence nonetheless. "So Compound G is the cause of a fatal syndrome?"

Brett ran a hand through her hair. Her anger seemed to have subsided. "In a sense. The patients actually succumbed to an allergic-type reaction by their immune systems. The protein would only cause DIC in patients with a genetic predisposition, a specific matrix of immune system cells. Probably a very rare reaction. Calvin and I were stumped on why these four patients had the protein in their blood. The odds that four men with such a predisposition would come in contact to the protein seem astronomical."

"Unless this protein was all over the place," Jake said, half joking. "Brett, why the hell would a fertility Ph.D. have crystallized this protein? Daniel couldn't have known anything about your DICs. He had to have come upon it independently."

Brett dropped onto the leather couch. "Jake, we have to figure this out."

Jake dropped onto the couch next to her. "Daniel was researching fertility, you were investigating a devastating syndrome. Somehow you both stumbled onto the same unknown protein. There has to be a link."

Brett took his hand and held it between hers. They sat like that, in silence, thinking. Finally Brett spoke. "We've got a couple of clues. Eric Heidlinger and Alaxon Industries."

Jake nodded. Inside, he was becoming consumed by the new mystery. Then his mind drifted—and he pictured Alex Stern at the Excelsior Hotel in Chicago, preparing for the speech he was going to give at the Fertility Conference tomorrow morning. He realized he still hadn't told Brett anything about ASD.

But for the moment, ASD seemed overshadowed by the

connection between Daniel's protein and Brett's DIC cause. Jake quickly forgot about Alex Stern and the Fertility Conference. He and Brett were going to solve the new mystery together.

Because we're partners.

15

"Whatever happened to the good old-fashioned sports bar?" Alex Stern sighed, waving his fifth glass of Scotch at the bartender, a young, mustached man dressed in a bright medieval page's outfit. "I mean, this is Chicago. Home of the fucking Cubs. You should be dressed like an umpire, not goddamn Prince Valiant."

Alex rocked his head back, pouring the Scotch down his throat. He had stopped ordering ice three drinks ago because it was just slowing him down. He slammed the empty glass on the bar, blinking rapidly to keep the room from spinning. He knew he was pushing it—even for him—but damn if he was going to stop at five drinks. It was only ten P.M., and the first lecture of the conference didn't begin until eleven in the morning. His speech wasn't scheduled until two—which would give him more than enough time to go over the data Jake had sent him.

Tonight, he was on his own. So far, his trip to Chicago had been a dream vacation. He had started the afternoon with a private tour of Wrigley Field, given by one of his wife's second cousins, a VP of marketing for the Cubs. The tour had been followed by dinner at Michael Jordan's new restaurant. He had shaken hands with two Blackhawks and a Bear, and had ordered an oversized steak from a menu that Michael Jordan probably had never touched.

After the steak he took a short nap in his suite on the top floor of the elegant, if antiquated, Excelsior Hotel. A quick shower, and he was ready for a night on the town.

He decided to start off the evening with a short stop in the hotel bar. Tragically, the bar had been redecorated since his last stay at the Excelsior. The place was now done up like a medieval pub, all wood tones and dark, weathered iron. The long bar that ran down the center of the room had been carved from a single, enormous oak tree, and the stools were actually old-fashioned saddles, complete with iron stirrups. On the back wall hung green and blue tapestries showing maidens in billowy skirts frolicking with what had to be eunuchs in monklike habits. The ceiling was cluttered with raw wooden beams, and there was a shiny suit of armor standing by the door, beneath an enormous triangular coat of arms. Next to the suit of armor, red velvet drapes dripped down over the large picture window that looked out onto the street.

The total effect ranked somewhere between a museum and a brothel. Alex grimaced as he watched the bartender pour another Scotch out of a bejeweled chalice, the wide-mouthed rim encrusted with fake rubies.

"Admit it," Alex said, as the bartender handed him the Scotch. "You feel like an idiot in that outfit. You've lost all sense of dignity. You're a shell of a man."

The bartender shrugged, walking back toward the other end of the bar. He had been avoiding conversation since the second Scotch—when Alex had asked if they'd consider renting out the suit of armor. Alex smiled, shaking his head. Some people didn't know how to have fun. He wished Jake were with him; it would have been like old times.

A sad feeling moved through him as he thought about Jake's ruined lab, and the poor dead nerd. He knew he was drinking extra hard because of the kid; he wished he hadn't been such a jerk the few times they had met. But Daniel Golden *had* been one hell of a geek. The kind of kid he had pushed around back in high school. He sighed, raising his glass. *To you, Daniel Golden. And all the other nerds out there. May you one day all gang up, and kiss my fat ass—*

"Hope you're not toasting the decor," a voice bounced at him from his right. "I grew up just outside of Las Vegas, and even I think this place is garish."

Alex set his glass down and turned toward the voice. A man was sitting two stools down, hunched slightly forward over what looked to be a gin and tonic. The tall, well-built

man had a Cubs baseball cap pulled down low over his forehead. He was wearing a blue sports coat and khaki slacks,
and a name tag pinned on his lapel. Alex recognized the tag
from the conference reception desk in the lobby of the
hotel.

"You here for the fertility conference?" he asked. He
noticed that his words were slightly slurred, his vision the
tiniest bit blurry. Good, familiar signs. "My name's Alex.
From Boston. I do obstetrics."

The man didn't look up. His hands were cupped together
over his drink, and he was twirling a stirring stick from his
gin and tonic. Alex realized the stick was actually a miniature lance—stiff, thick plastic about eight inches long,
tapered to a fairly sharp point.

"If I'm not mistaken," the man said, still twirling the
lance. "You're signed up to give a lecture tomorrow afternoon. You and Jake Foster. I met Jake two years ago at the
Repro Conference in San Francisco, and was hoping to
catch up with him—maybe share a few drinks."

Alex squinted, trying to make out the man's face. He
didn't think he recognized him, but then he had never been
big on conferences. *Bunch of eggheads sitting around talking shop.*

"Unfortunately, Jake couldn't make it. I'm staying under
his name and giving the lecture on my own. But you're not
going to want to miss it. It's gonna blow the roof off this
place."

Alex slapped the bar for emphasis. He knew he was getting
drunk—but the mention of tomorrow's lecture reminded
him how wild things were going to get when he described

ASD to the gathered specialists. Even without hard proof, it was going to cause an uproar.

"Sounds interesting," the man at the bar said. "Care to give me a preview?"

Alex waved his finger. "Sorry, can't give away the punch line before I tell the joke. But it's going to be well worth the wait. It's the biggest thing to hit the fertility world since the Paris sperm-rate study. Hey—you still didn't tell me your name."

The man paused, then lifted his head, looking right at Alex. Alex unintentionally drew back; the stranger's face was covered in raised scars. "The name's Pierce. As I said, from Las Vegas. Nice to meet you, Alex from Boston."

Alex swallowed, tasting Scotch. He shifted against the saddle-stool, aligning his posture. He knew he was being rude by staring at the man's face, but he couldn't help himself. Sober, he didn't have much tact. Drunk—he was a complete bastard. "Those are some nasty scars, Pierce. Some sort of childhood accident?"

Pierce didn't seem to mind the attention. He shrugged his muscular shoulders. "Desert Storm, actually."

Alex raised his eyebrows, surprised. "You were in the Army?"

"Airborne Ranger. A second lieutenant. Ran eight sorties into Iraq during the engagement."

Alex whistled. He didn't know much about the military—but he knew the Airborne Rangers were usually the first units deployed. Real hardcore soldiers. Certainly as tough as any football player out there. "So your face got bashed up during the war? Must be a hell of a story."

Pierce nodded, turning back to his drink. "A hell of a sad story. I'd tell it, but I wouldn't want to bring you down."

Alex leaned toward him, his interest piqued. This was the sort of conversation you wanted to have in a bar. "Hey, I like sad stories. I've been a Red Sox fan since birth."

Pierce smiled. Then he shrugged. "Happened the last day of the war, actually. It was a recon mission, nothing serious. My eight-man unit was dropped twenty miles inside the Iraqi border, fully armed, in desert gear. I was second in command behind the major—the toughest bastard you'd ever want to meet. He had trained me—and the rest of the unit—himself."

Pierce took a deep breath and sipped his drink. "Anyway, we were sent in to check out a bunker that was supposedly being used to hide a couple of Scud missiles. When we got to the bunker, we were met by six Iraqi soldiers carrying white flags. By this point in the war, the Iraqis were surrendering in droves, so we didn't think anything of it. The major and I were joking back and forth as the Iraqis led us into the bunker. The war was almost over, and we'd be heading home in just a few days. Spirits were fuckin' high as a kite."

Alex leaned heavily against the bar, listening intently. Pierce's voice had gone soft, and Alex had to strain to hear every word.

"Turned out," Pierce continued, "the whole thing was an ambush. There were a dozen more Iraqis inside the bunker, armed to the teeth. The minute we were through the door, they opened up on us. Bullets flying everywhere, grenades going off, the major screaming in my ear. Before I could get off a single shot I took a burst from an AK–47 in the direct center of my body armor. Luckily, the armor held, or I'd have died on the spot. As it was, the shells shattered on impact, splintering upward into my face. I went down nearly blind from the blood. Lay there on the floor, waiting to die. But the major pulled me out. He pulled all of us out. We only lost two men in that bunker, because of him."

"Christ," Alex said. This was better than an old Red Sox war story. "What happened next?"

"Well, we radioed in for a helicopter and some relief troops. When the troops arrived, the six original Iraqis came out of the bunker—waving the same damn white flags. This time, they were surrendering for real. Two of them ended up riding in the same helicopter as me. The major couldn't fucking believe it. He wanted to shoot 'em all right there, but the relief commander wanted to play it by the book. The Iraqis were dropped off in a POW camp inside Kuwait, and we headed back to base."

Alex shook his head. The entire bar spun with the motion. "You guys must have been pretty pissed off."

Pierce shrugged, lifting his face in Alex's direction. The scars seemed even more pronounced now that Alex could picture the moment, the flash of the shells as they had exploded against Pierce's body armor.

"Things got even worse. A week later, it turned out that those same fuckin' Iraqis who had tricked us were going to be handed back—some sort of goodwill gesture on the part of the Allies. My unit was royally fucked over, two of us dead, me with a face full of shrapnel—and the Iraqis were going home."

Alex could feel the man's anger, could see the veins popping in his overly muscled neck. "Well, I guess there was nothing you could do about it, was there?"

Pierce looked at him. His eyes seemed almost glazed. "The night before the Iraqis were supposed to be handed back, the major slipped into their holding cells with his commando knife and carved 'em up. Slit three of their throats, gutted the rest. Left 'em naked and dead in their cells. Took their ring fingers as mementos."

Alex gasped, nearly falling off his stool. He stared at the scarred man, not quite knowing what to say. Finally, he managed an unsure grunt. "Sounds like your major was a real, uh—patriot."

Pierce nodded, his expression completely serious.

"The Air Force didn't think so. We all got discharged after that. They wanted us to testify against the major, but we'd have died for him—still would. The major had to stand charges; ended up serving six months hard time. A raw deal, if you ask me. Major Scole was only looking out for his men."

Pierce turned back to his drink, stirring it with the miniature lance. Alex stared at him, sweat dripping down his bald head. He decided it was time to get the hell out of this bar—and away from Scarface. He glanced down toward the end of the room, spotting the door to the restroom. Keeping with the decor, the door was marked KNAVES. "I think I need to hit the bathroom. I'll be right back."

"Take your time," Pierce responded, reaching into the inside pocket of his blazer and pulling out a small cellular phone. "I have to make a phone call. I think I need to make a little adjustment to my night's schedule."

Alex quickly moved away from the man, crossing toward the restroom, his legs wobbly. His heart was beating a little too fast, and he shook his head, trying to clear his mind. It was just a story. Nobody was that violent in real life. *Not even linebackers.*

He smiled as he shoved open the door to the restroom and crossed to the bank of shining white urinals that ran along the far wall. At least the bathroom hadn't been decorated like a medieval outhouse. He could urinate in twentieth-century luxury.

He chose the farthest urinal from the door and assumed the position. His mind wandered as the familiar sound echoed through the restroom, and he found himself thinking about ASD, about the tiny, foolish, suicidal sperm and the fortune they were going to make both him and Jake—

There was a cough from just a few feet away and Alex turned, startled. To his utter shock, Pierce was standing next to him, using the adjacent urinal. Alex hadn't even heard the man enter the restroom. Even in his drunken state, he felt instantly uncomfortable—there were five empty urinals, and Pierce had chosen the one right next to him. He glanced at the man's horribly scarred face, and a sudden question entered his mind.

"Hold on a minute, Pierce. You were an Airborne Ranger during Desert Storm—and now you're a fertility doctor?"

Pierce smiled. "Not exactly. I was an Airborne Ranger. Now I *kill* fertility doctors."

With a sudden motion, he brought his right arm up from below his waist. Alex saw a flash of color and realized Pierce was still gripping the miniature stirring lance with the sharpened point. Alex tried to move out of the way, but his reactions were slowed by the Scotch. The lance arced toward him—the sharp point catching the side of his throat, the stiff plastic piercing his esophagus, tearing a hole in the surface of his carotid artery. There was a splash of bright red blood and Alex staggered back from the urinal, his hands flailing through the air. Pierce leapt after him, his other hand sweeping forward. Alex felt an incredibly sharp pain in the center of his chest, and he slammed back against the far wall of the bathroom. He looked down, and saw the black hilt of a serrated commando knife sticking out of his sternum.

He gasped, his knees giving out. He hit the floor, and his back sprawled against the wall, his chest jerking as he struggled for air. Pierce knelt in front of him and grasped the black hilt with both hands. He twisted hard to the right, then yanked the blade free. A fountain of blood spurted out into the restroom, and Alex groaned, the sound mangled by the miniature lance sticking into his throat. His vision swam as he felt Pierce grab his right hand, stretching out his fingers against the floor. He watched in shock as the scarred man lifted the commando knife high into the air.

"A souvenir for the major's collection," Pierce said, his voice echoing through the deserted restroom. "In the corporate world, it's the little things that help you get ahead."

Alex's eyes rolled back as the serrated blade slashed downward, severing his ring finger between the first and second knuckles.

16

Jake stood, shifting his weight back and forth, as he watched the long helicopter blades spinning in slow motion. His shoulders were hunched forward, his hands gripping tightly around the rubberized handle of his miniature putter. The ten feet of green between his golf ball and the crashed helicopter was curved slightly to the left, designed to look like a stream of oil leaking from the shattered fuselage of the chopper. Halfway down the green sat a bright yellow golf ball, and a few feet beyond that, nearly blocking the tiny hole that led through the helicopter to the flat, circular glade on the other side, a bright red ball with purple stripes. Jake grunted as he brought his club down in a perfect arc, catching his ball in the direct center. The ball spun down the green, heading at breakneck speed for the chopper. It passed both of the other balls, straight on course—but a second before it disappeared into the chopper, the helicopter blade swept down, catching it with full metallic force. The ball hopped into the air, smacked the mangled fuselage, then bounced back down the green, landing just a few feet from the tee.

Jake cursed, stepping back. The two middle-aged men in white shirts and suspenders standing behind him applauded. The taller of the two men—blond-haired, blue-eyed, with gray herringbone slacks, gold cuff links, and a sizable gut pressing out against his leather belt—took a cigar out of his mouth and waved it toward the green. "Hey, don't worry about it, Jake. This is the toughest hole on the course. Par three. Took me three weeks to master the bastard."

The other man—short, stumpy, nearly bald, with dark rimmed glasses and acne scars across his bulbous forehead—laughed as he wobbled toward the green, shaking his putter back and forth. "Don't let Stan fuck with your head. He hasn't come near par three on the helicopter. The windmill, maybe. But not the goddamn helicopter."

As the stumpy man took position over the yellow ball, Jake leaned back against the chopper's tail, smiling. The two men were an absurd sight, dressed as they were in Wall Street business attire and smoking cigars in the middle of a miniature golf course. But in truth, Jake had only been mildly surprised when Stan Humphrey had set up the meeting at the Putt Putt Course on I–93. Stan was almost as crazy as Alex Stern. Back in college, Stan had been the clown of the group, playing elaborate practical jokes on everyone from Nobel Laureate professors to the janitors who cleaned the dorm toilets.

The idea of calling Stan had come to Jake the minute he and Brett had decided to divide the clues from the videotape—Jake taking the Alaxon lead, while Brett followed up on Eric Heidlinger himself. Jake had realized that if he wanted to research a science-based corporation, Stan Humphrey was the best place to start. He knew everything there was to know about Boston's corporate scene. And more than that—Stan Humphrey owed him.

Two years ago, Stan had shown up in his office asking for advice about fertility drugs. He had just graduated from Harvard Business School, and had gone to work for Fidelity as a VP in charge of a relatively small biotech fund. He was looking for stock bargains—and fertility was just getting hot.

A year later, based partly on Jake's advice, Stan had doubled the size of the fund to a net value of close to three hundred million dollars. Most of that money had come from a single stock buy: Pfizer, the company behind Viagra, the instant-erection drug. Because of his success, Stan had immediately been promoted to executive VP.

"The key," Stan said, as he pointed his cigar at his stumpy friend. "Is to ignore the helicopter blades. Get a sort of Zen thing going in your head, function out everything but you and the ball—bingo, Chad. Perfect swing."

The putter sliced gently through the air, just touching the edge of the yellow ball. The ball whizzed across the green, dodging the helicopter blades by a millimeter. It disappeared into the helicopter, then rolled out the other side, stopping inches from the hole. Chad Roberts—Stan's associate at Fidelity, an expert on computer companies—clapped his fat hands together. "Now this beats real golf any day. Immediate gratification, eh Stanley?"

Stan crossed toward the purple striped ball, eyeing Jake. "Bet you thought I'd gone crazy when I told you to meet us here. But we realized months ago that we were just wasting our time on the big courses. It's all about putting anyway. I'd like to see Tiger Woods go up against the dinosaur at hole three."

Jake laughed, glancing at his watch out of the corner of his eyes. He had promised to meet Brett back at the house by noon. He needed to get Stan talking about Alaxon as soon as possible. "Listen, Stan, about the company I asked you about—"

"Alaxon Industries," Stan said, dropping to one knee on the green, sighting through the helicopter to the glade on the other side. "Chad, sounds like our friend Jake here's interested in chem companies. How's that strike you?"

Chad pulled at his suspenders, rocking on his heels. "Ugly. Chems have been a bust since Dow went belly up on the tit parade. What kind of idiot thought it was a good idea to put silicone inside people's bodies? Where was the R and D on that little fiasco?"

Jake cleared his throat. He knew from experience that Stan and his investment-banker friend could go on like this for hours. "I'm not interested in chem companies per se, Stan. Just Alaxon Industries. Do you know anything about it?"

Stan rose, scraping his shoes against the green. "They make pesticides, mainly. Some commercial bug repellents. A few types of tick and flea collars. For a while, they even got into suntan lotions that were supposed to repel mosquitoes—but the line never took. Caused eczema in every third consumer. Not good for business."

Chad stretched his arms, catching Jake's attention. "The bottom line on Alaxon is that they've got a bit of a cash-flow problem. Low reserves, heavy fixed debt. Still, eight months ago they moved their offices to the top floor of the Prudential Building. Maybe it's just posturing—but it looks like they expect flush times ahead. Maybe they've got something new in the works."

Jake had not expected this much information, and he was surprised the two men seemed to know so much about Alaxon. "Pesticides and insect repellents. Is the company privately owned or public?"

Stan lined up behind his ball. "Sixty percent ownership resides with the CEO and founder, a guy named Simon Scole. I met with him two years ago in their old offices, down by South Station. I was looking into adding the company to my domestic fund. After a little interface with the guy, I decided it wasn't such a good idea."

Jake raised his eyebrows. "Why not? You didn't like the CEO?"

Stan snorted, shaking his putter. "The guy's a nutcase. Wears makeup and dyes his hair platinum blond. But that's not the worst part. He's got what you'd call a—fixation."

Jake waited for Stan to continue, but he seemed more interested in his putter. Jake coughed, frustrated. "A fixation?"

"Ants, Jake. The guy's obsessed with them. He has a massive ant farm in his office. Not just any ants. Korean little fuckers. Like red ants, but more vicious. He told me the story during our meeting."

Stan tapped the putter against his left shoe as he continued. "Scole was a GI during the Korean War. Ended up spending the night in a foxhole full of the little buggers. Got bit like a thousand times. Almost died from the poison. When he got to the hospital, a doctor asked him why he didn't get out of the foxhole. His response? His commanding officer had given him a direct order. Like that was good enough reason to sleep in a hole full of poisonous, biting insects."

Jake exhaled. "So after the war, he founded a company that makes pesticides. I guess that makes sense."

"Did pretty well for himself over the next two decades," Chad added. "Expanded to close to a hundred employees, with trucking distribution across the U.S. Didn't start having cash problems until the fiasco with the suntan lotion in eighty-nine."

Jake glanced at him. "You seem to know a lot about Alaxon, too."

"Everyone's watching the company now," Stan interrupted. "As of two weeks ago, a big rumor sprang up about an upcoming buyout. A pretty massive deal, involving Tucker National. You've heard of them, right?"

Jake nodded. Tucker was one of the biggest companies in the country. He'd seen their logo a thousand times—on TV, in the supermarket, in the cupboards of his home. "They make cereal and soup, right?"

"They make everything," Chad answered. "They're the third-largest manufacturer of household goods in the world. Cereals, detergents, soups, pretty much everything you see on the supermarket shelves. So now everyone's asking: Why the hell is Tucker interested in a shit-ass pesticide company?"

Jake didn't have an answer, either. He watched as Stan finally lowered his head, his putter right next to his ball. "The truth will come out soon enough. Tucker is holding a huge stockholders' meeting in the Hynes Convention Center tomorrow morning. My sources say it's going to be covered by CNN *and* MSNBC. Either Tucker's going to put the rumors to bed—or give 'em body. And since the Hynes is located right next to the Prudential Building, a stone's throw from Simon Scole's office—I'd put my money on a buyout."

He swung his putter, chipping the striped ball. It slipped past the spinning chopper blades and raced through the fuselage. Out of steam, it slowed to a stop an inch behind Chad's ball, and Stan cursed, tossing his club to the green. "Fucking green needs to be returfed. Your shot, Jake."

As Jake stepped over Stan's putter, his mind whirled through everything he had just learned. What did it all have to do with Compound G? Was the protein somehow related to a pesticide? Or a flea collar? Jake wasn't sure he had made any progress at all. He hoped Brett was having better luck in her search for Eric Heidlinger.

He was about to swing at his ball when Stan clapped his hands together, a bright look on his face. "I almost forgot, Jake. Hold on a minute."

Jake watched as Stan pulled something out of his pocket. It was one of those snow-globe paperweights, the kind that you shook up to make the synthetic snow fall over the plastic landscape inside.

"I never properly thanked you for the Viagra tip," Stan said. "Their PR people sent these out to all their major stockholders last week. I thought you'd get a kick out of it."

Stan tossed the paperweight at Jake, and he caught it in midair. It was heavier than he had thought—about two pounds—and made out of thick glass. The liquid inside was thick with the tiny flakes of snow, and Jake shook it harder, watching the blizzard rain down on two plastic figures attached to the base.

"Look more closely, Jake. Look at the flakes."

Jake held the paperweight close to his face, squinting. The tiny flakes were shaped like little tadpoles. And the two figures were a naked man and women, lying on a bed. Jake laughed out loud. But even as he laughed, the stupid toy nipped at his thoughts. At that very moment, Alex was probably picking up the ASD package from the Excelsior front desk. Jake had tried to put the epidemic out of his thoughts while he joined Brett in trying to figure out the mystery concerning Compound G—but every moment he spent away from ASD was a moment away from looking for a cure. Certainly, he didn't have any more time to waste on a miniature golf course.

Jake shoved the paperweight into his pocket, then swung his putter with one hand, hitting his ball dead center. The ball rifled past the spinning helicopter blades and entered the helicopter at full pace. A second later it erupted out the other side, skidding past both of the other balls, and plopped straight into the hole.

As the two businessmen stared at him, Jake leaned his putter against the helicopter. "Guess that puts me one below par. Thanks for your help, guys."

He headed toward his Buick waiting in the Putt Putt parking lot, already thinking about Brett. Hopefully, she was on her way to meet with Eric Heidlinger at Alaxon's headquarters. Maybe Heidlinger could explain how a fertility Ph.D. student and a pair of ER doctors had stumbled onto the same unknown protein. Or what a company that made pesticides had to do with the monkey video Jake had downloaded from the NIH database.

Maybe Heidlinger can explain what an upcoming corporate buyout has to do with four dead bleeders lying in the morgue at Boston Central.

17

Brett paused in front of the three-story Victorian, wondering if she had gotten the address right. Her Toyota was parked two blocks away, in front of the Harvard biology labs where she had spent most of her four years at college. Two blocks in the other direction were the low buildings that housed the chemistry department, and another quarter mile beyond that, the Harvard Science Center, where most of the undergraduate science lectures were held. But the building directly in front of Brett looked like it had sprung out of some sort of time machine.

Brett looked from the arched windows of the first and

second floors to the shuttered third floor, partially covered in shadows cast by the high, triangular turrets that rose from all four corners of the building. The walls were painted hunter green, the shutters lime. Brett guessed the building dated back to the late nineteenth century, perhaps even earlier. In Harvard terms, that wasn't unusual; but in this three-block area where most of the university's science departments were housed, it made less sense.

Brett started up the gravel path that led to the pillared front porch. Less than an hour ago, she had called the switchboard at Alaxon Industries, asking to speak to Dr. Eric Heidlinger. A few long minutes later, a receptionist sadly informed her that Heidlinger had passed away just a few days ago, the victim of a sudden heart attack. Shocked by the timing of Heidlinger's death, Brett had used her computer to perform an obit search, hoping to find out more.

According to a short piece printed in the *Boston Globe*, Heidlinger had gone into cardiac arrest while visiting the New England Aquarium. Heidlinger had left behind family in Indiana—but no real trail in the Boston area. Brett had been about to give up hope when she reached the last sentence of the article, a brief, journalistic laundry list of the man's professional accomplishments. Most of the data was unremarkable: graduation with honors from Yale, a Ph.D. from Stanford, a number of awards along the way. Then Brett had found something interesting.

According to the *Globe*, up until three years ago, Heidlinger had been a professor of biology at Harvard. Brett still knew many people at the bio labs, and she had never heard Heidlinger's name.

A call to one of her old mentors had quickly cleared up her confusion. As it turned out, the *Globe* had not gotten their information correct. Heidlinger *had* been a professor at Harvard, *affiliated* with the biology department; but he had not been a professor of biology. He had been a professor of entomology. *An insect expert.*

Brett had immediately hopped in her car and headed over the bridge to Cambridge. The truth was, she hadn't even known that Harvard *had* an Entomology Department. She had no idea how an insect expert could be involved with a protein found in four dead patients' livers, but she intended to find out.

She reached the porch and grabbed the oversized brass door handle. The door swung inward with a resounding creak, and Brett smelled the distinct scent of formaldehyde. She stepped inside, finding herself in a vast front hall with hardwood floors and high ceilings. A crystal chandelier hung directly over her head, casting soft orange light against the freshly painted walls. She saw a high bookshelf to her left and a set of creaky-looking wooden steps ascending to the open second floor on her right. Directly ahead sat a small wooden reception desk, staffed by a matronly woman with curly gray hair and too much lipstick. The woman was leafing through a copy of *Scientific American*, angry lines cracking her thickly applied makeup.

"This is not good at all," the woman mumbled, loud enough so Brett could hear. "Dr. Tanner is going to have a fit when he sees this."

Brett approached the desk, recognizing the name from her conversation with her mentor. Tanner was the head of the entomology department, and Heidlinger's former boss. According to Brett's contact, Tanner was a legend in the Harvard community, a wily octogenarian who had earned international acclaim in the late seventies for his work on ant colonies.

Brett reached the reception desk, and the matronly woman waved the open magazine at her. A black-and-white drawing of an ant took up most of the two-page spread.

"This is an abomination. You see the elongated gaster region? The flattened alitrunk?"

Brett stared at the picture, seeing nothing but a creepy little insect. But she nodded politely.

"Clearly," the woman continued. "This is a *Paraponera clavata*. But here in the caption, they say this species is indigenous to New Guinea. *Paraponera clavata* is indigenous to Costa Rica. Tanner will have an absolute fit."

Brett tried not to smile. "Maybe you shouldn't show it to him."

The woman winked at Brett conspiratorially. "My dear, that's a very good idea."

She folded up the magazine and shoved it under her desk. Then she looked Brett over. "You don't look like a visiting entomologist. So you must be lost. Can I direct you somewhere?"

Brett smiled, glancing around the old building. There was a ceramic bust of a bee's head sitting on the middle bookshelf to her left, and a photograph of a butterfly hanging behind the woman's desk. "Actually, I'm here to speak with Dr. Tanner. I tried to call to make an appointment, but nobody answered the phone."

The woman nodded, pointing to an empty space on the desk in front of her. "Dr. Tanner got rid of the phones two weeks ago. He said the ringing disturbed his colonies."

Brett swallowed, unsettled by the image. She didn't like bugs. She especially didn't like ants. As a child, she had once inadvertently sat on a fire-ant hill.

"Must be pretty lonely here without a phone."

The woman nodded. "And Dr. Tanner isn't much help. He spends all his time upstairs, with his collection."

"Is he up there now?"

"I believe so. Go right on up and check. He'll be pleased to have a visitor. But don't mention the *Paraponera clavata*."

Brett started up the stairs and glanced from the chandelier to the wooden balcony that lined the second floor. Chipped paint covered the wooden posts of the balcony, and the wood itself didn't look too sturdy. She glanced down at the creaking steps beneath her feet. There were cracks in some of the boards, and Brett took the last few yards as lightly as possible.

There was an open doorway at the top of the stairs beneath an oil painting of what must have been some sort of prehistoric ant. The insect looked to be nearly a foot long, with oversized, serrated mandibles. Brett shivered as she passed through the doorway into a large rectangular room lined on three sides by brightly lit glass cases. The third wall contained another arched, open doorway, leading to a similar room. Brett could see more glass cases in the second room.

As she stepped into the room, Brett's eyes were drawn to

the nearest glass case. Beneath the glass were five parallel rows of ants, pinned to a white background by tiny black pushpins. Beneath each ant was its scientific name, followed by the area to which it was indigenous. Brett moved her gaze slowly across the case, counting the different species. The first case alone contained twenty different species of ants.

She moved to the second case; here, the ants seemed larger, with longer legs and antennae. The next case contained row after row of bright red ants, the sight stirring Brett's memory, causing her to scratch at a sudden tickle on the back of her neck. She quickly moved on to the next case—and here the ants seemed mutated, with jutting heads and long, dark mandibles. Brett was amazed at the diversity of the ant species—a quick estimate gave her more than a thousand different representatives on this side of the room alone. She hadn't realized there were that many different types of ants.

She moved away from the cases, searching the room for any sign of Dr. Tanner. Then her gaze paused on a circular case next to the arched doorway in the far wall. The case seemed different from the rest—raised a few feet off the ground beneath an oversized light blue spotlight.

Brett crossed to the circular case. She noticed a tiny warning label on the side of the case, alerting her to the fact that the case was alarmed and contained a seismograph meter. Brett wondered what could be so valuable in a place like this.

Her eyes widened as she stared through the glass. There was a single ant inside—but it was like no ant she had seen before, except in some childhood nightmare. The ant was huge, almost a foot long. Its exoskeleton was jet black, and a barbed, four-inch-long stinger jutted out of its elliptical tail section. "Christ, that's one big fucking ant."

"Eloquently put."

Brett turned to see an excruciatingly thin man in a white lab coat. He had white, wiry hair and wore thick plastic glasses.

"Formicium giganteum," the man continued. "That fossil comes from the Middle Eocene in England. It's the largest undamaged fossilized specimen ever found—of the largest species of ant that ever existed. The stinger and sagittal section alone are close to five inches."

Brett swallowed, glancing back at the huge ant in the case. She was glad it was just a prehistoric fossil. She'd hate to find one of those crawling up her leg. She turned back to the thin old man. "Dr. Tanner? I'm Brett Foster. I used to be a student in the biology department. Now I'm an attending at Boston Central. I was wondering if I could have a moment of your time."

Tanner's eyes flashed, and his smile grew even wider. "A lovely woman like you visiting my museum. Doesn't happen everyday. You can have all the time you want."

"It's quite a display," Brett said, waving toward the cases. "I didn't realize there were so many different types of ants."

Tanner beamed proudly. "This is the biggest single collection in the world. But it doesn't begin to do justice to the diversity of the ant population. There are eight thousand eight hundred documented species."

Tanner was rocking on the balls of his feet, his enthusiasm for the insects bleeding out of every pore. Brett decided it wouldn't hurt to play to his obsession. "That's spectacular."

"Everything about ants is spectacular. They are the predominant soil turners in the world, responsible for a vast proportion of the Earth's energy. They have the most complex form of communication of any animal. One third of the entire biomass of the Amazon rain forest is composed of ants. And do you know what? Not one biologist in a thousand could describe for you the life cycle of an ant. Not one biologist in a thousand could tell you how an ant lives."

"That's certainly a shame." Brett tried to keep her face serious. "Perhaps there should be more courses at the undergraduate level. Get more people interested. I know I would have signed up for a lecture series on the social lives of ants."

Tanner eyed her, his smile coming back. "If only I were fifty years younger. So, Dr. Foster, what brings you to my doorstep?"

"Actually, I'm interested in a former colleague of yours. Dr. Eric Heidlinger."

Tanner's cheeks sagged, his lips turning down. He sighed dramatically. "I heard he passed away last week. It's a sad thing when a student dies before his teacher."

Looking at the man's wrinkled face, Brett guessed he had outlived many of his students. But he seemed especially saddened by Heidlinger's passing. She sensed something telling in his demeanor. "Dr. Heidlinger worked with you until a few years ago, correct?"

Tanner's lips curled even farther down. "He had such a

promising future. He was so close to a breakthrough—and then the poor fool had to go and sell out. It was a shame. More so, now that he's dead."

"Sell out? How do you mean?"

"To industry, my dear. Some company threw money at him and he jumped. They threw the same money at me— but I'm way too old to jump."

Brett raised her eyebrows at the thought of a company seeking out two Harvard insect specialists. "Can I ask what Heidlinger was working on that had piqued corporate interest?"

Tanner shrugged and then abruptly spun on his heels and headed through the arched doorway that connected the two case-filled rooms. Brett hurried after him. "Dr. Tanner?"

"It's my colony," he called over his shoulder. "I can't leave them alone this long, not now. It's an integral stage in the colony's history. I've recently added a hostile subgroup to their environment, and I'm interested to see how they deal with the situation. Genocide? Slavery? Or will they allow the new group to incorporate within the hive—"

"Dr. Tanner," Brett called, frustrated as she followed him at a near sprint across the second museum-styled room. She wasn't sure if he was avoiding her question, or just reacting to some mental imbalance due to his age or his absent-mindedness. "Please, Dr. Tanner. If there's anything you can tell me about Heidlinger's work—"

"Pheromones," Tanner suddenly said, stopping in front of a metal door in the back of the room. "Eric was studying pheromones. The chemicals at the core of ant communication."

Brett watched Tanner unlock the metal door with a key from his pocket. *Pheromones*. Chemicals released by insects to attract or communicate with other insects. Recently, it had been proven that other animal species also used pheromones to attract mates or to warn other individuals of impending danger. Traces of pheromone-like compounds had been found in human sweat, and perfume companies had spent millions researching the chemicals, hoping to stumble onto something with aphrodisiac qualities. According to the literature, the search had proved fruitless. Though in recent months, Brett remembered seeing something about the discovery of pheromone receptor sites in the mammalian endocrine system, which might open up an entirely new line of research—

"Try and be quiet," Tanner interrupted, as he beckoned her past the metal door. "The colony must not be disturbed."

Brett's mind was still working as she stepped into a cold, windowless cube, specially reinforced with aluminum-plated walls. The decor looked like the interior of a boxcar, lit by a pair of operating-room spotlights hanging from the ceiling. Directly beneath the spotlights was an enormous, three-foot-high steel tank. The tank took up most of the room, and was filled halfway with shiny white sand. A conic hill in the far corner of the tank stood a foot tall, and Brett could see thousands of tiny shapes racing up and down the slanted sand. As she gazed across the tank, she realized that the tiny shapes covered much of the sand's surface, a constant sea of motion. Her stomach clenched and her skin crawled as she fought the urge to turn and run out of the room.

"I know," Tanner whispered, walking right to the edge of the tank. "It's beautiful. An entire civilization for us to study. Three hundred queens, close to forty thousand individual ants. Infrared sensors attached to the bottom of the sandbox are linked to a computer system, giving us a constant, fluctuating model of the ant's developing social structure."

Tanner moved around the side of the tank, toward a high cabinet standing against the far wall. Next to the cabinet was another door, and Brett could hear the quiet whir of a computer mainframe. She took a deep breath, trying to forget that there were forty thousand ants just a few feet away. "Dr. Tanner, you say Heidlinger was working with ant pheromones. Is that what Alaxon was interested in?"

Tanner shrugged, pausing to lean over the side of the tank, focusing on an area of intense activity. "I'm not sure, but I assume so. Pheromones are big money right now. And Heidlinger was working on a particularly interesting ant secretion. A *releaser-effect* chemical. You've heard the term?"

Brett shook her head, looking more carefully at the area of the sandbox in front of Tanner. She realized she was watching an ant war; thousands upon thousands of the tiny creatures rolling together, tearing at each other with their mandibles. This must have been the territory of the sub-group Tanner had added to the colony. "Not that I remember."

"Releaser-effects are pheromones that induce the classic stimulus response, mediated entirely by the nervous system. In other words, a chemical secreted by one ant stimulates the nervous system of another, setting off an involuntary response. In the case of the chemical Heidlinger was study-ing, it set off a pleasure-response—an endorphin kick simi-lar to a minor orgasm. Queen ants use it to attract mates and to draw workers in for protection."

Brett squinted her eyes, digesting the information. Heidlinger had been studying chemicals that ants used to attract one another. Alaxon had paid him a lot of money, presumably because of that research. "And Heidlinger's research was valuable, in corporate terms?"

Tanner nodded vigorously. "Eric wasn't simply studying the pheromone—he was trying to synthesize it, create a chemical that could be used cross-species. He hoped to come up with a version that would cause similar stimulus response in mammals. Such a discovery would be worth an unbelievable amount of money."

Brett felt her face growing warm. A pheromone that could affect mammals. A chemical that could attract a person.

"A golf ball that could attract a chimp," Brett whispered.

Tanner glanced at her. "Sorry?"

Brett blinked. She didn't quite know what it meant—but the chimp video could be explained by Eric Heidlinger's mammalian pheromone. The objects the chimpanzee had grabbed all been labeled with a tiny *G*. Perhaps they had all been treated with Heidlinger's compound—*his mammalian pheromone.*

Compound G.

Brett stared at the tiny ants swarming across the surface of the sandbox. "Dr. Tanner, is it possible Heidlinger com-pleted his research and created the mammalian version of the ant pheromone he was studying?"

Tanner smiled, shaking his head. "Doubtful. If he had really succeeded, there would have been an enormous uproar in the news. It would have generated a massive ethical dilemma for Heidlinger and the company that hoped to patent such a chemical; pheromones are extremely powerful—they play *the* central role in the organization of ant societies. Imagine what the world would be like if human beings were suddenly affected by similar chemical processes. The concepts of free choice and of independent thought would suddenly be rendered extinct. My God, think of it. *What if we were guided, like ants, by our nervous systems?*"

Brett's face paled. It was an impossible thought. And she had no idea how it was connected to Compound G—or her four DIC patients. But she felt sure that Heidlinger's work on pheromones was connected to the chimp video. The objects must have been coated with Compound G, a pheromone, and the synthesized protein had *attracted* the chimp.

Still, that didn't explain why she had found the compound in the livers of her DIC patients. Unless they, too, had somehow come in contact with the pheromone—and because of their genetic setup, the pheromone set off an allergic reaction.

"Dr. Tanner," she said, her voice suddenly tight. "Can you describe the molecular structure of the pheromone Heidlinger was studying?"

Tanner smiled at her. "I can do better than that. I can show you the pheromone itself."

Tanner turned toward the cabinet behind him. He rummaged through the shelves, searching with both hands. When he turned around, he was holding a small plastic spray bottle in one hand and a rectangular metal device in the other. Brett recognized the device; it was a handheld, battery powered ultraviolet lamp. She had used such a device during her bio days to look at bacteria with fluorescent properties.

"Originally, this was Eric's idea, though I've found it extremely useful in my own study of the colony's social interaction. Basically, we attached a harmless, fluorescing bacteria to the antibody for the pheromone, which we found in worker ants past their mating prime. We made a spray out of the fluorescing serum—which acts as a fluorescent tag to the chemical, attaching itself whenever it comes in direct contact. The serum will allow us to *see* the pheromone itself."

Tanner moved to the corner of the tank containing the anthill, and leaned over the edge, the spray bottle held tightly in his hand. He pulled the handle twice, spraying a thin dew over a section of the hill. The ants beneath him seemed to barely notice the gently falling liquid.

"Don't worry," Tanner whispered back at Brett. "The serum won't disturb them at all. The bacteria was specifically designed to be as unobtrusive as possible. And the serum lasts only for a few moments—the bacteria have been implanted with a suicide gene, which causes them to die off very shortly after coming in contact with an oxygenated atmosphere."

Brett wished Jake had come with her to Tanner's office— as a Ph.D., he'd have been more familiar with Tanner's vocabulary. She held her breath as Tanner held the fluorescing lamp out over the tank and flicked the switch with his thumb.

Bright, blue glowing splotches undulated up and down the anthill, in sync with the constant motion of the tiny creatures. The blue glow was more concentrated near the mouth of the hill, more scattered as the ants moved farther away from the lair of their queens. "As you can see, the workers who have recently been close to the queens are covered with the attracting chemical. The pheromone itself works through the air—attracting by means of both scent and taste—but the compound shows up only where it is tactually concentrated, where it has been affixed by direct contact."

Brett watched as the blue spots slowly dissipated and then disappeared. Tanner turned off the fluorescing lamp, and Brett took a step toward him. Her body was filled with excitement. Tanner had just given her the key she was looking for—a mechanism to seek out the compound itself.

If her instincts were correct, if Compound G really was Heidlinger's pheromone, then her path was clear. Somehow, her four geographically distinct DIC patients had come into contact with the compound. The serum spray and fluorescing lamp could show her—in glowing Technicolor—how that was possible. The serum would let her *see* Compound G.

"Dr. Tanner," she said, her eyes intense. "I need to ask a favor."

As she briefly told him about her four DIC patients, the chimp video, and Compound G, her eyes settled on the swarming surface of the sandbox and her mind drifted back to something Tanner had said: *What if we were guided, like ants, by our nervous systems?* She pictured the chimpanzee reaching for the marked items, and her face went cold.

She was beginning to think that she and Jake were chasing something much more ominous than a syndrome that had caused four young men to bleed to death in her ER.

18

Stan Humphrey's metallic-gray BMW rolled the last few yards to the edge of the steep, shrub-pocked embankment. The engine coughed once and then went silent, the sound replaced by the soft crunch of gravel beneath the BMW's tires. Inside the sedan, Stan hunched over the steering wheel, squinting through the windshield. He could just make out the warehouse at the bottom of the embankment, two hundred yards below; a long, rectangular structure with twin aluminum bay doors leading out to a paved parking lot. A pair of sixteen-wheeled trucks dozed in front of the bay doors, and groups of men in strange white jumpsuits scurried between the massive vehicles. The men looked remarkably like insects; at first, Stan thought it was just the distance playing tricks on him. Then one of the men paused at the edge of the parking lot, and the late afternoon sunlight flashed off his bulbous, insect-eyes. Stan jerked back, startled—before the realization hit him: the men were wearing gas masks.

Stan relaxed, tapping his stubby fingers against the steering wheel. He considered lighting a cigarette, but decided to give his lungs a break. He'd smoked two cigars before lunch and had spent the entire afternoon breathing the cramped air of Fidelity's corporate library. His body felt wired, his muscles abnormally tense. It had been a long time since he had last followed one of his hunches.

He quietly pushed open the car door and stepped out onto the gravel road. Except for the warehouse, the area seemed deserted; he guessed the access road had led him at least twenty miles from Route 128. It seemed an odd place to build a warehouse—but then, everything about Alaxon Industries seemed odd.

Stan hooked his thumbs under his suspenders, squinting down the embankment. From the moment Jake had first asked him to look into the chemical company, he had become absorbed by Alaxon's incongruities. First, there were the rumors concerning the upcoming buyout: Why the hell would Tucker National want to purchase a cash-poor pesticide manufacturer run by a nutcase like Simon Scole? Then there was the recent shift of Alaxon's headquarters: Why would a failing company move offices to the posh Prudential? Unless, of course, it expected a huge influx of business.

The more Stan researched Alaxon, the more the mystery deepened. Over the past few years, Alaxon had diminished into a state of near dormancy. Despite its monetary problems, R&D expenditures had grown at a remarkable rate, with the purchase of state-of-the-art laboratories and the hiring of new high-level staffers. Stranger still, most of the new hires were not chemists. Simon Scole had been scouring the local universities for biologists and geneticists, offering huge signing incentives and promises of continuing compensation.

Obviously, Scole had his labs working on something he believed would turn the company around. Genetic biology was a hot ticket—and hell if Stan was going to sit back and wait for Wall Street to discover Scole's secret. Jake Foster had led him into millions once before—and Stan had a hunch lightning was about to strike a second time.

He carefully started down the slope, his meaty arms waving at his sides as he fought to keep his balance. He kept his knees bent as he moved, partially shielding himself behind a bank of young pine trees that rose up from the edge of the warehouse parking lot. He wasn't sure what would happen if he was discovered snooping around the warehouse—at worst, he guessed he would get some sort of fine for trespassing. It was definitely a risk worth taking, considering the possible payoff. At least, that was what he had been telling himself since he had discovered the warehouse's address in a trucking register in Fidelity's Alaxon file.

He reached the cluster of pine trees and dropped into a low crouch. His chest was heaving, and drops of sweat ran down the sides of his face. He crawled forward, his belly sagging against his damp shirt. He knew how absurd he looked, worming his way between the low pine trunks, his fingers digging into a blanket of moist needles. But he also knew that it was moments like these that separated the merely successful from the true giants in his profession.

He poked his head out from behind one of the larger trees, brushing pine needles from his sleeves. Directly across from him lay the trucks and the twin bay doors. Beyond the open doors, the interior of the warehouse was lit by bright fluorescent ceiling panels. Groups of suited men moving in and out of the far door pushed steel-framed dollies. The dollies carried huge cylindrical canisters, about four feet high and three feet in diameter. More men loaded the canisters into the back of the farthest truck.

Stan watched the closer warehouse door. The warehouse contained at least five hundred of the cylinders, aligned in tidy rows. The warehouse was divided by an interior wall, and the suited men gathered on the far side. He wondered if he could make it inside the closer bay door without being seen.

He was about to make his move when he heard voices coming from his left. Near the edge of the parking lot, two men stood next to a pair of hooded trash cans, their gas masks under their arms. Stan immediately recognized the taller of the two: Malthus Scole, Simon's gangly son and Alaxon's VP of research and development. Stan had met him two years ago on his one visit to Alaxon's old headquarters. Malthus had just returned from serving in the Air Force, somewhere in the Mideast.

Stan crawled a few feet closer. Malthus's voice became

barely audible over the din coming from the other side of the parking lot.

"We're going to need a third truck, maybe even a fourth. This has to go out as a single shipment. And you've got to be ready to roll as soon as the announcement is made."

The second man nodded. "There won't be any problems on our end. I can't vouch for the packaging plant in Texas—"

"Tucker's plant is already production-ready," Malthus responded sharply. "The minute you arrive, the chemical will be loaded into their assembly line."

"Then everything will go as planned. As soon as the stockholders' meeting ends, the compound will be on its way to Texas."

The two men moved back across the parking lot. Stan watched them go, his face growing warm with excitement. It sounded like the coming buyout was more than a rumor—and that the canisters in the warehouse were at the center of the merger. If Stan moved a large portion of his fund into Tucker and Alaxon stock, he was sure to make a killing. Maybe even as much as he had made on the Viagra deal. He rubbed his hand across his lips, glancing back toward the warehouse—and the nearer of the two open bay doors. Curiosity burned inside him like a bonfire. He glanced at the second bay door and the men with the dollies, measuring the distance, searching out a clear path along the edge of the parking lot.

He rose and started forward, concentrating on the millions he was going to make. His heart pounded in his chest, and he could barely feel the pavement beneath his feet. He expected someone to call out any second—and then he would have to race back up the embankment. But as the bay door loomed closer, he realized he was going to make it.

He skirted around one of the tractor trailers, passed through the bay door, and found himself in a cement-floored cavern. This side of the warehouse was a hundred yards across, with cinder-block walls and a slanted ceiling. A line of gas masks hung from pegs drilled into the cinder blocks; he took one and strapped it over his head. The glass eye-shield made the room look yellowish, and the filtered air tasted bitter against his tongue. He adjusted the straps, feeling the tight rubber digging into his forehead and the skin behind his ears.

The mask was uncomfortable but safe—and the perfect disguise. He crossed to the row of canisters, which were unlabeled and molded out of steel. He paused in front of one of the containers, his gaze gliding over the rounded cover. There was a panel directly in the center of the cover, containing a single black button.

Stan glanced over his shoulder, making sure he was alone. Then he reached forward and hit the button. There was a series of clicks—and the cover jutted upward. His pulse racing, Stan gently placed his hands on the edge of the rounded steel and gave it a slight shove. The cover slid forward as if on ball bearings.

Stan peered into the container. His eyes widened as he saw his masked face reflected across the surface of a shimmery, silvery liquid. The liquid was like nothing he had ever seen before—a cross between melted glass and metallic paint. It was like looking into a viscous mirror.

Stan took a deep breath, wondering what the hell the

chemical was. He realized he'd need to take a sample to a chemist to know for sure. He wondered if it was dangerous to touch. He held his hand out over the liquid—and a strange heat rose through his body. His eyes widened as the feeling intensified. His breathing became quick, and saliva dripped from the corners of his mouth. His hand began to shake—slightly at first, then harder—as the warmth moved from his chest, down through his stomach, to his groin.

My God, it feels good. Stan laughed out loud, pulling his hand back. It was the strangest thing he had ever experienced. An almost erotic sense of well-being. Christ, what the hell was this stuff?

"Euphoric," a voice stabbed at him from a few feet away. "Isn't that how you'd describe the feeling?"

Stan whirled on his heels. There was a man standing just a few feet away. Tall, gangly, with long arms clasped behind his back. The man's round face was hidden behind a gas mask, but Malthus Scole's angled build was unmistakable.

"You want to touch it," Malthus continued softly. "You want to put your hands into the liquid, you want to feel it against your skin. More than anything, you just want to be near it."

Even through his sudden burst of fear, Stan realized that Malthus was right. He could not ignore the pull of the silvery liquid. His muscles twitched, his body begging to turn back to the open canister. He coughed, trying to regain his composure. "I, uh, missed a turn on Route 128. I was heading back to Boston, but I guess I got lost—"

"The explanation isn't necessary Mr. Humphrey," Malthus interrupted amiably. "My employees discovered your car a few minutes ago, and we've already run your plates. You're an investment banker—and you're here checking out a possible investment. Isn't that right?"

Stan swallowed, staring at Malthus's cold blue eyes. Finally, he shrugged. "Well, yes. I guess I was a bit curious. There's been a lot of fuss about your company—"

"And now you know what all the fuss is about. You've seen the compound—you can feel it working on your body right now. But you still don't really understand, do you?"

Stan glanced back toward the canister. His fear dwindled slightly as his curiosity rose. "It's some sort of drug, right? Something that affects you through the air. That makes you feel good?"

Malthus nodded, his gas mask jerking up and down with the motion. "The liquid in the canister is the compound in its most concentrated form. As a vapor, the chemical is actually invisible—and its effects are much less conspicuous. But the idea is still the same."

Stan's eyes widened. He turned back toward Malthus. "It's an aphrodisiac. But why is Tucker National adding an aphrodisiac to its production line?"

Malthus shrugged—and suddenly rushed forward, erasing the distance between them. His arms whipped out and Stan felt his gas mask rip free from his face. Then he was spinning around, his ankles tangling together. He crashed to his knees in front of the canister. He felt Malthus's hands land heavily on his shoulders, and he gasped, terror splitting his thoughts. "Jesus—what are you doing?"

"Quenching your curiosity." Malthus answered simply.

Stan felt weight against the small of his back, bending

him forward. His chest hit the edge of the canister, and he stared down at his own reflection, shimmering in the glassy surface of the strange liquid. A burning sensation burst through his nostrils and his muscles went slack, his entire body gripped by an overwhelming sense of pleasure. His reflection moved closer and closer and closer—and suddenly his face burst through, and an enveloping cold engulfed his head.

His mouth filled with the thick, syrupy liquid and his lungs clamped shut. His brain screamed out but his muscles remained slack, his body succumbing to the incessant waves of pleasure. He could no longer feel Malthus's hands against his shoulders. There was only the silvery liquid against his skin, the wonderful heat within his veins. His lungs surrendered and the thick liquid streamed down his throat, filling his chest.

And even as he drowned, he realized that he didn't want to pull away. . . .

19

Brett watched as Jake grabbed the accordion-style elevator cage with both hands. A metallic squeal echoed through the marble hallway when the cage folded back to reveal the tiny interior of the two-person elevator. It was lined in red velvet, with orange lighting and a thick shag carpet. Brett's fingers tightened against the fluorescing lamp and the spray bottle as she squeezed in next to Jake. He closed the cage and then searched the bank of buttons for the penthouse.

As the elevator jerked upward, Brett leaned back against the velvet wall, cradling the fluorescing lamp and the spray bottle in her arms. The elevator reminded her of her mother's mansion on Beacon Hill: expense for the sake of expense, a tasteless display of wealth. Her mother would also have approved of the Commonwealth Street address, one block from the Commons and the base of the Hill, but still part of the posh, jaunty section of the Back Bay.

Peter Marsh—her most recent DIC patient, who had died on a park bench in the Public Garden—had done well for himself. When Brett had spoken to his widow from her car phone on the way to the address, she felt a tug in her chest at the tragic nature of his young death. Married two years, a high paying job at one of the finance firms downtown, and the Commonwealth apartment—his life had been something worth envying. *And his death is all the more tragic.*

Now Brett was determined to track down the source of that death. With the spray bottle and the fluorescing lamp, she would search Marsh's home for any signs of Compound G. Now that she could actually *see* the tailored pheromone, she hoped she could find the link that connected her four DICs—and use that link to figure out the connection to Alaxon Industries. If her plan worked, she would owe an enormous debt to Dr. Tanner.

As the elevator bumped to a stop on the penthouse floor, she glanced at Jake, noting the pensive look on his face, the worried lines above his dark eyes. Something about the information she had learned at Tanner's lab—combined with what he had learned from Stan Humphrey that morning—was bothering him. As was his way, Jake was going to keep it to himself. It was almost amusing, the way the faults in their marriage seemed to spring up no matter how bizarre their circumstances or how removed they were from ordinary concerns. Even when things were going smoothly, they had a major problem with communication. It went well beyond the man-woman paradigm; at least Mars and Venus were in the same solar system. Sometimes, Brett wondered if Jake was even carbon-based.

"This thing is a bitch," Jake grunted, pulling the accordion cage aside. "I guess it's supposed to be elegant. But there's a reason it went out of style. Torn rotator cuffs."

He stepped out into a marble-lined hallway. In front of the single door at the end, a homey, beaded mat sprawled across the floor. As Brett approached, she saw that the beads were actually balls of amber and pearl, intertwined together to spell out the names Celia and Peter Marsh. Brett felt a tug in her chest as she gently knocked on the door.

Celia Marsh beckoned them inside the opulent penthouse apartment. Tall, blond, statuesque, her hair tied back in a complex series of knots, she was wearing a black gown that had obviously been designed for her body. Her makeup was flawlessly applied—though no amount of cosmetic skill could hide the puffy bags beneath her eyes. She looked as if she had stepped out of the pages of a magazine; watching her, Brett tried to picture Peter Marsh as he had looked without the blood or the EKG leads or the endo tube. The Marshes had been a striking couple.

"I was surprised by your call," Celia said, pointing Brett and Jake toward a plush leather divan. "The medical examiner's office already sent people by a few days ago. Has there been a new development?"

Brett could hear the hopefulness in Celia's voice. The

ME's inconclusive findings must have torn at the poor woman's heart.

"We're investigating the possibility of a chemical contamination," Brett said, choosing her words carefully. "If it's okay with you, we'd like to test for trace elements of a protein that might have had something to do with your husband's death."

Celia glanced apprehensively around the living room. "Contamination? In the apartment?"

"We'd like to start here, then move to his place of work. If this protein is responsible, we don't believe it's dangerous except to a very small number of individuals." Brett showed Celia the spray bottle. "This liquid will help us conduct our search. It's a harmless serum that will evaporate shortly after it leaves the bottle."

Celia paused, her eyes leaving the bottle of serum to measure the brooding look on Jake's face. "If you think this will tell me what happened to my husband—yes, of course, go ahead. Do you want to start here, in the living room?"

Brett nodded, crossing to the entertainment center. She didn't know where the most likely connection between Alaxon—a chemical company that made pesticides and bug spray—and a young investment banker might lie, but she intended to be thorough. His home, his car, his office, his gym.

She handed the fluorescing lamp to Jake, then opened the glass doors and carefully sprayed a fine mist over the knick-knacks inside. Jake waited for her to step aside and then flicked on the high powered light. Celia Marsh peered over Jake's shoulder, clearing her throat. "I don't see anything at all."

Brett nodded, moving deeper into the shelves with the spray can. "I don't expect much more than trace elements, something he might have inadvertently picked up sometime close to his death."

The next ten minutes passed in silence as they carefully moved through the living room, checking every shelf, corner, and item of furniture. Then they began to move through the rest of the apartment. By the time they had reached the second bathroom located behind a small television room near the back of the apartment, Celia had retired to her bedroom, where she had curled up with a photo album from her wedding. Brett did her best to ignore the muffled crying drifting through the wood-paneled hallways as she sprayed a porcelain-seated toilet. Jake sighed, perhaps equally moved, and cast the blue light across the surface of the bowl. Again, there was no trace of the protein. Brett moved to the glass-faced medicine cabinet, the first inklings of frustration evident in her reflection.

"Maybe this is a shot in the dark," she said. "We don't know when—or where—Marsh picked up Compound G. He could have come into contact with the pheromone anywhere; he didn't necessarily bring it home with him."

Jake shrugged. "Short of going through Alaxon itself, we don't have much of a choice. And we can't hit the company until we know exactly what we're dealing with. They're not going to want to talk to doctors investigating a series of possible contaminations."

"I'm not so sure," Brett responded, pulling the medicine cabinet open. "If they're making a product that has such a vicious side effect—"

"They won't want to know about it. Look at the cigarette companies, Brett. Fifty years ago they realized their product had a thirty percent death rate—one hell of a side effect. They've done their best to cover it up for half a century."

Brett contemplated this, spraying the serum over the contents of the medicine cabinet. The tiny drops glistened on brightly colored plastic containers of aspirin, toothpaste, facial and shaving cream—a dozen different brands, many of which Brett recognized from her own medicine cabinet. After they checked the packages themselves—probably overkill, but again, Brett intended to be thorough—she would test samples of each product. "Well, maybe the contamination didn't come from a product—maybe it was some sort of chemical dumping, or a factory leak. Maybe all four victims were in the vicinity of a spill—"

"And Alaxon's going to want to admit that, a day before a huge, multimillion-dollar buyout?"

Brett was surprised by the tone of Jake's voice. "This isn't an argument, Jake."

"I'm just trying to think this through—because it doesn't make a whole lot of sense. A chemical company manufacturing a pheromone derived from ants. Four men somehow come into contact with that pheromone—and end up dying in your ER. At the same time, my grad student—a *fertility researcher*—independently crystallizes the same damn chemotaxin. The odds against anything in my lab containing the same protein that caused the death of your four DICs are astronomical. For that to be possible, we'd be finding traces all over the place. Everywhere I shined this damn light."

He flicked on the fluorescing lamp—and suddenly his face froze. Brett turned—and saw that almost all of the items in the medicine cabinet were glowing bright blue. Her heart collided with her rib cage and she gripped the edge of the sink. Then she looked more closely at the glowing objects. All looked to be normal containers of brand-name products; two bottles of contact-lens solution, a bottle of Tylenol, a tube of Crest toothpaste, a bottle of skin lotion, even a box of tampons. "Christ."

"The packages," Jake whispered. "It's on the packages. Almost all of them."

Brett swallowed, trying to understand. Had the compound been sprayed into the medicine cabinet? Or had the packages picked up the protein somewhere else? Brett watched as the blue glow slowly dimmed, the bacteria in the serum killing themselves off. She lifted the spray bottle and doused the items again. Beneath the fluorescing lamp, the cabinet looked like a dying star.

"My God. The level of contamination is completely uniform. This isn't haphazard—these packages were doused with Compound G."

She reached toward the box of tampons—and Jake grabbed her wrist. She gently pushed him away. "Jake, the DIC was caused by a genetic matrix of MHC Class II molecules. An inherited, unlucky error in Peter Marsh's immune system. Only people with that same random, genetic matrix are affected by the protein. And besides, Heidlinger wasn't working on a *contact* pheromone. Just being this close to the packages has the same effect as touching them."

She lifted the box of tampons out of the medicine cabinet. It was the same brand that she used, the same colorful red package she had in her medicine cabinet at home. But this box had been doused with Compound G. The questions sprang through her head. How? Where? *Why?*

"Mrs. Marsh," she called out, "Where do you buy your toiletries? Your tampons, contact-lens gear, et cetera?"

There was a quiet cough, then Celia's voice lifted through the apartment. "Grand Market, in the Prudential Mall. The same place I buy all my groceries. Why?"

Brett didn't answer. She dropped the box of tampons into the sink and headed out of the bathroom. A moment later, she and Jake burst into the kitchen—a modern, open area with tiled white floors and stainless-steel cabinets. Brett brushed past the shiny conventional oven and the microwave, heading straight for the refrigerator. She yanked open the door, feeling the cool air against her face. The refrigerator was half full; two cartons of milk, a bottle of juice, various Tupperware containers, a twelve-pack of Coke, a carton of eggs, a few bags of vegetables. Brett stepped back, glancing behind her, watching as Jake threw open the steel-faced cabinet doors above the microwave, revealing shelf after shelf of cereal boxes, peanut butter jars, bags of chips, rolls of paper towels. An average American kitchen stocked with average American goods.

Brett took a deep breath, then began spraying the items in the refrigerator. She carefully moved from shelf to shelf, covering everything within view. Then she started across the kitchen, aiming the spray bottle into the stainless steel shelves, drenching the packages, showering everything she could reach until the spray bottle was nearly half empty. Finished, she stepped back, nodding at Jake.

He held up the fluorescing lamp and flicked the switch. The entire kitchen seemed to light up, a dazzling shade of blue. Brett stepped forward, her eyes shifting from glowing item to glowing item. Nearly nine out of ten objects in the shelves were coated with Compound G. In the refrigerator, the blue glow covered everything but the Tupperware containers and the carton of eggs. Brett leaned back against her husband, staggered by the sight.

Celia Marsh stepped quietly into the kitchen. "Christ," she whispered. "Why is everything glowing?"

Celia had a handkerchief clutched against her chest, and her eyes were red and puffy. Brett wasn't sure what to say. The woman's kitchen was completely contaminated with the protein that had killed her husband. Objects she had brought home from the supermarket. It seemed impossible. Grand Market was one of the largest supermarkets in Boston. Half the city bought groceries there—it was located in the heart of the Prudential Mall, at the base of the towering Prudential building. She and Jake had been shopping there for years.

"Mrs. Marsh, you bought all these items at Grand Market? Did you and your husband do the shopping yourselves?"

"Yes," Celia whispered, still staring at the fading blue glow. "We were going to use a service, but Peter hated the idea of someone else touching our produce. He always said that's the best way to catch something."

Brett glanced at Jake, who looked as if he was about to be

sick. He was staring at the boxes of cereal in the steel cabinet in front of him. Cheerios, the exact same brand he ate every morning.

"Jake," she said, quietly. "We might have just found the link between my four bleeders."

Twenty minutes later they were standing in the front lobby of an apartment complex in Cambridge. Brett's fingers trembled as she hit the buzzer for an apartment on the fifth floor. The short drive over the river had been silent; as scientists, neither she nor Jake wanted to jump to conclusions without more evidence. But in her heart, Brett knew they were onto something. Something big.

An irritating buzz let them into the building. A door halfway down the hallway was partially open, and there was a short blond woman in a terry-cloth bathrobe leaning around the wooden frame. Her kinky hair was pulled back in a tight ponytail, and freckles covered her round cheeks.

"Sandy Butler?" Brett asked, as she and Jake approached. "I'm sorry about the short notice—"

"It's no problem," Sandy answered, ushering them into the apartment. "Does this have anything to do with what happened to Ted on that bus?"

"We believe it might," Brett said. "If it's okay with you, we'd like to check out your kitchen cabinets."

Sandy raised her eyebrows. She was a pretty girl, probably twenty-three, twenty-four years old. Her bathrobe was open a few inches at her throat, revealing more freckled skin and a bright green jade necklace that matched her eyes. "My kitchen cabinets?"

Brett nodded, shifting the spray bottle of fluorescing serum from one hand to the other. She glanced at Jake, but he was already heading toward the doorway at the other end of the living room, the ultraviolet lamp tucked under his right arm.

"That's right, Ms. Butler. As I told you on the phone, my husband and I have been investigating your boyfriend's death, as well as three other similar tragedies. There's a possible link we need to investigate."

The young woman watched Jake moving across her living room, then shrugged her small shoulders. "Please—whatever you have to do."

She stopped, clutching her bathrobe tightly shut at the invasive thought. Brett followed Jake out of the living room and through a small alcove that led to the kitchen. There were pictures stuck to the refrigerator door, mostly of Sandy and her deceased boyfriend. Brett focused on one taken in front of the Eiffel Tower. Ted Conners had been tall, well built, with wavy blond hair and a bright smile. But when Brett blinked, she saw him as he had appeared in her ER a little over a week ago—his skin yellow, blood caked across his face, more running in streams out of his nose, mouth, and ears. Ted Conners had been her first DIC patient since medical school, and she would always remember the choking sense of panic she had felt when he died in front of her.

She watched Jake pull open the refrigerator door, and then she moved to the cabinets. Brett began spraying the various packages, cans, cartons, and bags of produce. As in the Marshes' kitchen, she recognized many of the brand names and colorful, trademarked images. She tried not to let her mind roam as she coated the package surfaces with a fine mist of serum. She knew a terrifying thought was building inside of her—but for the moment, she had to remain a scientist and a skeptic.

She stepped back into the center of the kitchen. Sandy Butler stood a few feet behind her, still clutching the front of her bathrobe. They both watched Jake as he held the ultraviolet lamp ahead of him and hit the switch.

"Christ," Jake whispered. "It's everywhere."

The cabinets and refrigerator glowed a brilliant blue. Brett blinked, her chest heaving. Now there was no doubt. Compound G covered most of the products in two of the four DIC victims' cabinets. This was the link she and Calvin had been looking for. Both Ted Conners and Peter Marsh had been exposed to Compound G, which had somehow contaminated ordinary household goods. Both had been unlucky enough to have immune systems that overreacted to the protein—like the random sample of women who had died from using tampons in the late seventies. Sandy Butler and Celia Marsh had been exposed to the same product packaging—but their immune systems had not misinterpreted the antigen as a threat.

"Ms. Butler, where did you buy these products?"

Sandy was staring at the fading blue glow, her face frozen in confusion. Brett cleared her throat. "Ms. Butler?"

"Grand Market," Sandy finally said, her gaze breaking away from her cabinets. "Right across the Mass Ave. Bridge, in the Prudential Building."

Brett felt her cheeks growing pale. She looked at Jake. He

leaned back against the breakfast table. "A chemical pheromone applied to product packaging. Those products sitting on the shelves of a major supermarket."

Brett looked back at the packages in the refrigerator and the cabinets. The blue glow had faded almost completely—but she knew the compound was still there, covering every inch of the colorful objects. A pheromone. A chemical designed to set off an involuntarily response inside the body, a pleasurable signal—*an attraction.*

"I don't feel anything," she said, searching her own physiology for some sign or response. "I'm not overly attracted to anything in these shelves. Maybe Heidlinger never succeeded in tailoring the protein to the mammalian system."

Jake shook his head. "If Heidlinger's pheromone works, it's not something you would notice. Pheromones function on a delicate, internal level. You're drawn without *knowing* you're drawn. You might think it's the color of the packaging, or the shape of the objects, or the contents themselves—and to a large extent, you'd be right. But somewhere deep inside your body, the decision is being biased by a pleasure response. You choose these items, and you think it's an individual, free choice. But it's not."

Brett shook her head. This was too much to accept. But the evidence was difficult to ignore. Both Peter Marsh and Ted Conners had refrigerators full of Compound G. Both had shopped at the same supermarket. They couldn't have chosen the coated products by accident.

Nor were they the only people who shopped at Grand Market. How many thousands of people had come into contact with the compound? How long had this been going on?

"Jesus, Jake. Where do we even begin?"

"First thing," Jake responded. "We need to go to Grand Market and test the items on the shelves. Then we need to try to figure out how many other supermarkets have been contaminated."

"And what about the possibility of other side effects?" Brett asked. "This is an unresearched chemical—"

She paused, noticing that Jake's face had turned ash white. His eyes widened—and suddenly he was pushing past Sandy Butler, moving out of the kitchen at a near run.

"Jake?" Brett rushed after him, "What is it?"

Jake didn't answer. He stopped in the center of the living room, shouting back over his shoulder. "Ms. Butler, where is the bathroom?"

"To your right," Sandy answered from the kitchen. "Second door down."

Jake continued forward, Brett a few feet behind him. He entered the small bathroom, then turned to face her.

"Jake?" Brett repeated, shocked. "God damn it, tell me what's going on!"

Jake shut the bathroom door and turned back toward his wife. For the first time, he told her about ASD, painting a vivid picture of the self-destructive sperm in visual terms only he would think to use.

"I believed I had stumbled on a syndrome that might explain much of the local fertility crisis," Jake finished, leaning back against the sink. "And I hadn't yet begun searching for a cause. But what if ASD isn't a syndrome? What if it's a *side effect*?"

Brett realized immediately where he was going. "You

mean Compound G. Are you suggesting that my DICs and your ASD patients are related?"

Jake nodded. "It's not as far-fetched as it seems. The male reproductive system is incredibly fine-tuned—especially the glands associated with the production of sperm. A pervasive chemical—like a pheromone that's designed to affect the glandular system— could easily find its way into the testes."

"And once there?" Brett asked.

"Well, we're talking about a chemical designed to attract. On a microcosmic level, isn't that exactly ASD? Sperm attracted to *one another*—instead of to the egg. Perhaps because each sperm contains within it a pheromone—Compound G."

"Jake—" Brett started.

"It's a theory," Jake interrupted. "One we can test, right here. Right now." Jake undid his belt and then unzipped his pants and pulled them down to his knees. Brett stared at him, standing in the middle of Sandy Butler's bathroom in a pair of boxers. Her face reddened as she realized what he intended to do.

"Jake—"

"This can't wait. This could be the key to a disease affecting thousands of couples."

Brett's hands clenched involuntarily against the spray bottle. She thought of the past two years of hell—and the many other couples who had experienced the same brand of torture. Then she thought of the bewildered woman standing not twenty feet away, wondering what two doctors were doing at this very moment in her bathroom. It was an absurd situation. But Brett knew Jake's mind was already made up.

"Okay, doctor. But let me help you."

She placed her hands on the waistband of her husband's boxers and drew them down his legs. She glanced over her shoulder, making sure the door was tightly shut—then she dropped to her knees, placing the spray bottle next to Jake's shoes. The tiled floor felt cool through her thin stockings, and she leaned forward, placing her hands between Jake's muscled thighs.

Jake came quickly, and Brett carefully collected the specimen in her palm. Jake retrieved the spray bottle from the floor and unleashed a fine mist of serum over her palm. He then raised the fluorescing lamp and hit the switch.

Brett's palm glowed bright blue. *Jake's sperm is saturated with Compound G.*

"This still doesn't prove causality," Brett said, quietly. "We don't know for sure that the protein is causing your ASD."

Jake dropped back onto the toilet, the fluorescing lamp on his knees. "At the very least, now we know where Daniel got his Compound G. He must have fractionated sperm cells from one of my ASD patients. He had no reason to guess it was a synthetic compound, created by a chemical company. And when he tried to plug the protein into the NIH database—"

Jake paused, looking at Brett. Brett felt a strange heaviness in her chest. She remembered the moment when she and Calvin had first watched the chimpanzee video. A Trojan horse, Calvin had called it, a sort of computer virus.

A download of information, aimed at whoever set off the trigger—whoever searched the GenBank database for Compound G.

"A warning, Jake? Some sort of info leak from inside the company?"

"Possibly. Like the memos leaked from inside the cigarette companies, documenting executive knowledge of the side effects and addictiveness of smoking. And remember, the information attached to the monkey video identified Eric Heidlinger—the man who synthesized Compound G. You can't get any more inside than that."

There was a moment of silence as they both digested the idea. Brett felt something tick at the back of her thoughts—something dangerous, something she didn't want to bring out in the open. But Jake was already ahead of her.

"Brett, what if Alaxon knew about the Trojan horse—and had some way of tracing it?"

Brett had the sudden memory of Calvin's fingers flying over the computer keyboard as he plugged in his Central ID number. Then the image changed—to Calvin lying on an autopsy table, his body mutilated, his neck bruised from the IV wire. She shook her head. It was unthinkable.

"Even if they didn't know about the side effects," Jake continued, rising from the toilet seat, "they'd have a hell of an incentive to keep Compound G secret. And if someone tried to blow the whistle on them—like Eric Heidlinger, who probably knew more about the chemical than anyone else—who knows how far they'd be willing to go? Would they murder Daniel?"

Brett stared at her husband. "What about Eric Heidlinger,

Jake? The newspaper said he died of a heart attack just two days ago. Do you think that was murder, too?"

Jake shrugged, heading for the bathroom door. "Calvin Johnson died of respiratory failure. It just so happened there was an IV tube tied around his throat."

20

Jake's head spun as he pressed Brett's car phone against his ear. The young pathology clerk on the other end was still speaking, but Jake had already stopped listening. He had heard everything he needed to hear.

He thanked the woman, then flicked off the phone and placed it in his lap. He stared out through the windshield past Ted Conners's apartment complex, toward the river that separated Cambridge from Boston. Up above, the sky had gone orange—another day ending—and shadows clawed at the tree-lined sidewalk to his right.

"Well?" Brett asked.

"According to the autopsy report from the path labs at Central, there was a high level of potassium found in Eric Heidlinger's bloodstream around the time of his death. The pathologist wrote the finding off to natural biodegradation and to Heidlinger's advanced age."

Brett tapped her fingers against the steering wheel. "But you don't agree."

"Potassium chloride, injected anywhere into the bloodstream, will set off a cardiac seizure. On autopsy it will look very much like a heart attack. And aside from elevated potassium levels, there isn't any real evidence left behind. It's a wonderful murder weapon."

Brett didn't look convinced. "What about puncture wounds from an injection?"

"If you were a pathologist checking out a sixty-three-year-old cardiac arrest, would you be looking for puncture wounds? Brett, the coincidences are piling up. Calvin, Daniel, and Eric Heidlinger all died under abnormal circumstances. And all three were linked to the Trojan horse program—and to Compound G."

Jake shivered at the enormity of what they had uncovered. They had found Compound G in the cabinets of two disparate DIC victims. And they had found the compound in Jake's own sperm. Compound G was widespread—and the supermarket shelves were the obvious link.

Jake could only think of one reason to spray packages in a supermarket with a pheromone like Compound G. *Money.* He remembered what Stan Humphrey had told him about the rumors of the upcoming buyout involving Tucker National. Stan had wondered why Tucker—a maker of household products—would be interested in a chemical company like Alaxon Industries. Now Jake had a pretty good idea.

"If this pheromone really works," he finally said, breaking the silence, "and the chimp video seems to imply that it does—it would be an invention worth protecting. Worth killing for—"

Jake stopped, his eyes widening. "Shit. Alex. I completely forgot. He's going to blow the whistle on ASD this afternoon in Chicago at the National Fertility Conference. He doesn't know anything about Compound G."

Brett lifted her hands from the steering wheel. "You think Alex is in danger?"

Jake's cheeks went pale. "I don't know. But if someone's trying to cover up Compound G—"

Jake left the thought unfinished and grabbed for the cellular phone.

Jake felt hot tears on his cheeks as he listened to the heavily accented voice of a Chicago police officer describe the murder of his best friend.

Alex Stern, murdered in the bathroom of a bar in the Excelsior Hotel. Stabbed to death with a knife, then mutilated—one of his fingers cut off and taken from the crime scene.

Crazy, untamed, incorrigible Alex—dead on a bathroom floor. An anguished groan caught in Jake's throat as dozens of images flashed behind his eyes. Alex in school, Alex at his wedding, Alex playing with his kids . . .

The voice on the other end grew louder, as the Chicago

cop tried to regain his attention. "You got any idea why someone would want to kill Dr. Stern?"

Jake closed the phone, cutting the cop off in midsentence.

"I'm so sorry," Brett said, her hand touching his arm. "My God, this is horrible. We have to go straight to the police."

Jake didn't look at her. Every muscle in his body was throbbing, and white-hot shards of anger ripped up his chest. He wanted to fling the cell phone through the front windshield. He wanted to shove his fist through the dashboard, tear out the engine with his bare hands. He wanted to run through Cambridge screaming his rage, ripping the trees out of the ground, tearing up the sidewalk with his fingers.

I want revenge.

"We have to put a stop to this," Brett continued softly. "We have to expose them. They've killed Daniel, Calvin, and now Alex. They're going to come after us."

Jake knew she was right. The people behind Compound G were doing everything they could to eradicate the threat to their product. "It's got to be the upcoming buyout. Alaxon, maybe Tucker—protecting their interests."

Brett paled, her hand clenching against his arm. "Will the police believe two doctors over two multimillion dollar companies?"

Jake shook his head. "We don't have time to explain this to the police. We need to reach higher—someone with enough power to stop this on his own."

Jake glanced at the sky and then at his watch. It was

late—but hopefully, not too late. Jake knew it wouldn't be easy. Their story seemed insane: three violent murders, a pheromone derived from ants. But Jake had access to one of the few people in Boston powerful enough to do something about it—if only Jake and Brett could make him believe.

Jake slammed his fists against the car seat beneath him. Damn it, he would have to believe. They had killed his best friend.

Jake's anger would not subside until he had brought the fuckers down.

21

Simon Scole stood in front of the raised television screen in the center of his office, his bare right arm out in front of him, his fist clenched so tightly that his fingers had turned white. His teeth were clenched, too, his eyes wide open, every ounce of strength fighting to keep his arm still as the stinging pain rocketed through his nervous system. Each of the nine, bright red ants crawling across his forearm had bitten him a dozen times already, and his naturally pale skin was covered in purplish welts. But the pain still had not overcome his anger—and his anger was much, much worse than the pain. The pain he could compartmentalize and control. The anger controlled him, and as the CEO of a multimillion-dollar corporation, he could not allow himself to be run by emotion. *I have to set an example.*

There was a quiet knock on the door to his office, and he took a deep breath, swooning slightly from the heavy alkaloids contained in the North Korean fire ants' venom. Then he carefully brushed the ants into his palm, allowing them to continue sinking their tiny stingers into his skin, again and again. As he carried them toward their thin glass terrarium, he ran his tongue along the inside of his mouth, tasting the familiar bitter foam that had risen from his gums. The foam was another side effect of the venom, and it instantly sent his mind spinning backward to that awful night nearly forty-five years ago.

A moment later, Simon's eyes came open and he realized his hand had clenched shut, crushing the nine ants into a reddish paste. He cursed, flinging the remains to the floor. He heard the knocking again, more insistent this time. He looked at himself in the glass of the ant aquarium, making sure his age-concealing makeup was properly applied, that his hair was still perfect. Then he cleared his throat.

"Please come in."

His son slunk into the room. Malthus kept his round face turned downward, his eyes averted, an expression of pure deference and fear. Simon felt his eyes narrow as he watched a bead of sweat run down Malthus's puffy, childlike cheek. He remembered the day when he visited his son in the military stockade, right after the discharge trial. Malthus had exhibited the same fear—because the discharge and sentencing themselves had been meaningless to him. His father's disapproval was a thousand times worse.

"I brought you a belated Father's Day present," Malthus said, his voice weak. His right arm swung out from behind his back. He was holding a hockey stick, almost half his height in length. Even from the distance, Simon could see Wayne Gretsky's signature scrawled across the wood. "I found it in a memorabilia store downtown."

Simon's lips curled down at the corners. He knew where Malthus had actually gotten the hockey stick. He knew all about the obstetrician in Chicago—whose office Malthus had just returned from searching. He also knew about the young Ph.D. student in the fertility lab, the black ER doctor, and the investment banker at the distribution warehouse. He was not a fool. He had been watching his son closely since the episode with Heidlinger and the Trojan horse; electronic bugs in his office, a tap on his cellular phone, even a small tracking device sewn into the lining of his poorly tailored jacket.

But until now, he had allowed his son the illusion of independence, the delusion that he could keep the growing fiasco from his father's attention. Simon had hoped that his son could handle the situation on his own—to prove himself, rebuild his self-confidence after his failed military career. But Malthus had not handled the situation. Indeed, the situation had worsened astronomically, and now threatened everything Simon had worked so hard to achieve. He clenched his fists, his stung forearm throbbing as the blood coursed heavily through his body.

"Malthus," he said, evenly. "It's time for us to interface. Not as father and son, but as CEO and employee."

Malthus glanced up, a stricken look on his face. Simon waved him toward the leather couch in front of the television screen. Malthus carefully placed the hockey stick against the wall, then crossed to the couch. Simon waited until he was seated before he spoke.

"I know about the leak. I've known for some time."

Malthus's cheeks went pale. He coughed, crossing and recrossing his long legs. "I was going to tell you. And now that the situation's under control—"

"Don't lie to me, Malthus. The situation is *not* under control. When Heidlinger came to you in the first place, you should have sent him directly to me. None of this would have ever happened."

Malthus lowered his head. "I thought the side effect Heidlinger had reported—"

"Your job does not involve thought," Simon growled. "I knew all about Heidlinger's concerns involving the compound. The side effect was an acceptable cost. I could have explained that to him, perhaps made him see the light. Instead, you frightened him until he had no choice but to run."

Simon stepped forward, his shadow drifting over his son's cowering form. His anger swelled, as he thought about how close Heidlinger had come to ruining everything. He had inserted that damn Trojan horse into the NIH database, threatening to topple Simon's world. "Now we have a problem, Malthus. One day from the buyout, we've got a major snafu."

One day from the greatest moment in his life—the moment he had been planning since he had first read about

Heidlinger's research into cross-species pheromones in an obscure entomology journal. Consumers choosing products for reasons that had nothing to do with the products themselves. Consumers attracted, *involuntarily*, to the packages themselves. It was brilliant. The ultimate marketing strategy: *a product aphrodisiac.*

Like cigarettes, Compound G had its detrimental side effects. But surely the profits outweighed both the risk of discovery and the side effects themselves. As the cigarette companies had decided years ago—a certain level of liability was acceptable.

"After tomorrow," Simon continued, calming himself, his gaze focused on his son's bowed form. "The leaks won't matter. Because once the buyout happens—once the trucks leave for Dallas and the money is deposited in our account—it will take an act of God to keep Tucker from using the compound. And it will take months, if not years, of studies to prove the side effects in a court of law. By then, the profits will be so stupendous, so enormous, the liability won't matter."

The logic was clear—the exact same logic the cigarette companies had used. Corporate courts were notoriously slow. And Compound G was almost undetectable. If there had been no leak, if Heidlinger had never been allowed to insert his Trojan horse—no one would ever have known about Compound G. The side effects themselves would have been a tragedy without a known cause, like lung cancer in the forties. *An acceptable liability.*

But there *had* been a leak. And now that leak threatened everything. Simon reached forward and put his right hand on his son's shoulder. Malthus quivered under his touch.

"Malthus. This ER doctor and her fertility-expert husband. They cannot be allowed to expose the project. I brought you into this company because I believe in your skills."

He slipped his hand under Malthus's rounded chin and yanked his head up, locking their blue eyes for an intense moment.

"Don't you dare disappoint me."

22

Jake held Brett's hand as they moved up the cobbled sidewalk. Even the air seemed to taste different up here; there was a certain crispness, a palpable tang of history. This was the heart of Boston, Beacon Hill—a genteel maze of eighteenth-century townhouses and aristocratic mansions perched in the shadow of the golden-domed state house. The higher Jake moved up the slope of the famous neighborhood, the more overwhelming the sense of aristocracy. By the time he and Brett reached the three-story building near the peak of the hill, an electric charge sparked through his nerves. *This is serious. This is real.*

He tried to remain calm as he hit the doorbell halfway up the high oak door. A second passed in brutal silence, then the door swung inward. The first thing that caught Jake's focus was the jaw; square, symmetrical, jutting out a full three inches above the man's immaculately white dress shirt. With effort, Jake pulled his gaze upward, across the weathered cheeks, to the blue eyes and silver hair.

"Jake," Arthur Sandler said. "Welcome to campaign headquarters."

"Thank you for seeing us at such short notice," Jake responded, shaking the man's manicured hand. "I know you're extremely busy—but this couldn't wait until morning."

Sandler patted his shoulder, smiling. "Nothing ever can."

Jake thanked him and then introduced Brett. Sandler's smile widened as he shook Brett's hand. "I'm glad to get the opportunity to finally meet you. I've heard so many wonderful things from my friends in administration at Central."

Brett blushed, obviously charmed. Sandler was truly charismatic. Jake could easily see him winning a term in the Oval Office. He had looks, the right background, and an undeniable appeal. As attorney general, he had a stellar record. He was a man who knew how to get things done—exactly the sort of help Jake and Brett needed.

After letting go of Brett's hand, Sandler gestured for them to come inside. Jake followed Brett through the doorway and into a wide, rectangular room filled with three rows of computer desks. Between the desks, nearly every inch of the carpeted floor was cluttered with rolled up posters and bubble-wrapped cardboard signs. A few of the signs were partially revealed, and Jake saw Sandler's beaming visage, surrounded by a circle of bright blue lettering: SANDLER FOR GOVERNOR—A MAN WITH A MISSION.

Sandler pushed a few of the signs out of the way and sat on the edge of one of the desks, waving them toward a pair of chairs rising out of the sea of posters. "Please pardon the disorder—but we just got a shipment in from the printers. My night staff will be arriving in a few hours to take care of the ads—but for now, I'm stuck staring at myself wherever I look. It's like being trapped in a hall of mirrors."

Jake nodded politely. The posters made him slightly uncomfortable; although the election was still half a year away, the man sitting across from him was most likely going to be elected governor of Massachusetts. Jake felt out of place in the campaign headquarters, deeply out of his league.

Then he thought about Alex—and his reservations disappeared.

"Mr. Sandler," he said. "My wife and I have stumbled into something horrible. A conspiracy that has led to the murder of four people—including Daniel Golden."

Sandler's gray eyebrows arched, his jaw jutting an inch further below his lips. He looked from Jake to Brett, reading their expressions. He reached onto the desk beneath him and retrieved a pad of paper and a pen.

"Tell me," he said, stone serious and respectful.

Slowly, carefully, Jake told Sandler everything. From the moment he had discovered ASD to the phone call to Chicago barely an hour earlier. Halfway into the discussion he let Brett take over, and she deftly outlined her investigation into the DIC patients—and her discovery of the link to Heidlinger and Compound G. When she was finished speaking she looked at Jake, and he shifted against his chair, turning his attention back to Sandler.

Relief filled him as he looked into Sandler's eyes. There was no trace of disbelief. Sandler had taken it all at face value, and the notepad in his hands was covered in black scrawl. His eyes burned with the heat of a lawyer on the hunt for justice.

"This is certainly an amazing story. And—if what you say is true—an incredibly unethical, criminal situation. A chemical company disseminating a chemical pheromone. A cover-up involving murder—and the destruction of half of one of my own buildings."

"That's just the beginning," Jake said, his own anger igniting. "I believe this compound has caused a massive number of infertilities, affecting perhaps tens of thousands of people. And at least four people have died of DIC, a sort of rare allergic reaction to the compound."

Sandler was silent, staring down at his pad of paper. He tapped his jaw with his pen, then looked up. "You were right to come to me. We've got to figure out how widespread this is. And if it's really linked to the possible buyout of Alaxon by Tucker—then there's a chance the Texas company plans to use this pheromone on a national level."

"Exactly. We have to stop them before the stockholders' meeting tomorrow morning."

Sandler wrote something on the pad of paper. "Of course

we'll need cooperation from the FBI, the local police—but that's my problem, not yours. The only real concern I have at this point is proof; from what you say, the only evidence we have of the product tampering is in the two apartments you checked out."

Brett leaned forward, pushing a rolled up poster out of her way. "All of the products from both apartments were purchased at Grand Market on Boylston Street. Jake's system also shows traces of the compound—and we can assume he came in contact with it in the same manner. This would suggest that a large quantity of packages treated with the compound must be on the supermarket shelves."

Jake nodded. "Mr. Sandler, we've got a way of making the compound visible. All we need to do is go to the supermarket and spray the packages with our fluorescing agent. We can record the evidence in bright blue Technicolor."

Sandler was up off the desk. "This is going to be enormous, doctors. A major conspiracy brought down by my office—with your help. Just give me until tomorrow morning, and I'll have Alaxon swarming with federal agents. For now, the two of you must collect your evidence. I can get you any equipment you need."

Jake shook his head. He was already thinking ahead. "At the moment, my only real concern is our safety. These people are evidently willing to kill to keep this quiet."

Sandler paused as he reached the other side of the desk. His eyes were searching for the phone. "I'll have two of my best security people here in five minutes. They'll shadow you tonight—and accompany you to the supermarket when you're ready to collect your evidence."

He paused, drawing a small white card out of his shirt pocket and handing it across to Jake. "This is my private number. Call me as soon as you've got the evidence we need. In the mean time, I'll get the wheels of justice turning. As I told you earlier, Jake, I have a son Daniel's age. I won't rest until these crimes are redressed."

Jake's body trembled as he met the man's resolute gaze. It wasn't going to bring Alex Stern back to life—but at least, in the end, there would be justice.

Malthus Scole watched through the fogged windshield of his black Range Rover as the pretty couple started back down Mt. Vernon Street toward their waiting car. His blue eyes darted from the couple to their escort—two burly men in dark suits, most likely off-duty police officers, each at least six feet tall. The bodyguards had arrived at the Beacon Hill address just minutes earlier. Malthus could have killed them both before they had reached the front steps to Arthur Sandler's office—or better yet, wired their Chevy with the pound of C–4 plastique tucked in the glove compartment of the Range Rover. But the bodyguards were not a threat. They knew nothing about Compound G.

Malthus's hands trembled as he clenched the steering wheel in front of him. The woman still evoked memories of the whore; from behind, her long limbs, narrow waist, and short dark hair reminded him of the evening he had dragged the corpse to the ocean's edge, weighing it down with iron motorcycle chains and then gripping it by the hair, pulling it deep into the dark water. His legs had shivered, the water lapping at him as he watched the corpse sink, settling face-down in the sandy muck. He had looked out across the moonlit ocean—and felt nothing. But in the back of his mind, he had imagined his father watching him from somewhere in the black sky, nodding his approval. *For you, Father, I did this for you.*

Malthus blinked, his eyes burning at the corners, as he pinned his gaze to the tall man at the new whore's side— Jake Foster. He took in the man's athletic gait, his wavy dark hair, his muscular legs and arms. He did not look like a scientist; he looked like the men who had shown up on the first day of Airborne boot camp—confident, sauntering jocks who thought they could handle the world because they had so effortlessly handled high school. Malthus's lips curled back as he imagined what it would feel like to crack Jake Foster's spine with his bare hands. To tear his esophagus out through his throat, using it to strangle his screaming wife, gutting them both with his commando knife, watching the steam rise from their exposed entrails as they begged for mercy, mercy, mercy.

"For you father," Malthus whispered. "This also, I will do for you." He reached past the wheel to the ignition, and seconds later the Range Rover grumbled to life.

23

It was a few minutes before nine when Brett pulled her car to a stop on Boylston Street, miraculously finding a parking spot across from the college bars and mediocre restaurants that dotted this section of the Back Bay. Craning her neck to peer past Jake through the side window, she could see the base of the towering Prudential, the windows lit up in some flickering, indescribable pattern. Even at this late hour, she knew the building was swarming with businessmen in suits, corporate drones moving through the hallways and offices like the ants in Dr. Tanner's sandbox.

Her fingers clenched against the tiny camera strapped to her right palm. She quickly stopped herself, making sure she hadn't damaged the intricate piece of equipment. The video camera was a marvel of miniaturization, smaller than a package of cigarettes. The lens itself was no bigger than a dime, self-focusing and set to accept almost any level of light. The DVD tape inside had three hours of record time, and according to the slight, balding computer specialist in the basement of the Sandler Wing, it would capture the highest-quality image that technology allowed.

It had been Jake's idea to get the recording equipment from the computer department of his lab. The tiny camera would allow them to gather video evidence of the Compound G contamination—evidence Sandler could use to bring Alaxon down.

That thought had occupied Brett as she navigated the car through the mild Thursday-night traffic. Meanwhile, Jake had made sure the green Chevy remained visible in the rearview mirror; the presence of the two steroid-addled ex cops made Brett feel leagues more confident.

"Looks like Tweedledee and Tweedledum couldn't find a spot," Jake commented from the seat next to her. "They're double-parked across the street."

"That's good enough," Brett responded. "We won't be inside long—and you've got the panic button, right?"

Jake nodded, pointing at the white circle of plastic hanging against his shirt, suspended from a black string tied around his neck. Max Kendrick, the larger of the two security agents, had given Jake the shortwave alarm when he had described their plan in Sandler's campaign office. The security agents would wait outside in their car, watching the supermarket entrance while he and Brett gathered their evidence. The panic button would act as their security blanket; one quick press and the ex-cops would come running.

Brett threw a glance at the Chevy across the street, catching Kendrick's eyes. The man's square head waggled on his thick neck, and he held his radio receiver up to the window, signaling that everything was ready. Brett turned toward Jake. "Okay. Let's do this."

Jake nodded, firmly gripping the spray bottle and the fluorescing lamp. He would be in charge of the spraying, she would record the data with the miniature camera. *Partners.*

Brett pushed her way onto the sidewalk and followed Jake toward the glass front entrance to the massive supermarket. The supermarket was tucked into a corner of the enormous Prudential Mall, a low, modern structure that stretched all the way from the base of the Prudential Building to the Marriot Hotel behind Copley Square. On the other side of the Prudential—perhaps a hundred yards from the entrance to the supermarket—was the Hynes Convention Center, a three-story stone cube full of lecture halls, meeting rooms, and massive auditoriums. Tomorrow morning the convention center would be filled with Tucker stockholders from around the Northeast—not to mention a squadron of television and print reporters. Before Jake and Brett had left Sandler's office, the attorney general had verified that the meeting would be broadcast on CNN and MSNBC. He had also determined that the main convention hall—where the meeting would take place—had been wired for closed-circuit TV. Tucker's CEO had recently been diagnosed with lung cancer, and, because of his weakened state, he would speak to the gathered stockholders via television. Sandler had also verified that Simon Scole, CEO of Alaxon, was scheduled to be at his side at the head of the main hall; but Arthur had assured them that the schedule was about to change. With or without evidence, he intended to put a hold on any corporate buyout until the possibility of product tampering in the supermarket could be investigated.

Brett raised her right hand a few inches as she and Jake reached the electronic glass doors that led into the brightly lit supermarket. She used her thumb to start the camera recording, catching the bright blue Grand Market sign above the entrance with the Prudential Building looming up above the curled, neon lettering.

A second later, she was through the electronic door and into the front entrance to the vast supermarket. A mountain of bright blue stacked baskets was to her left, row after row of parallel checkout counters were to her right. All of the counters were busy, the black conveyor belts sweeping constantly along as the uniformed checkout workers swept items over the laser pricers by their registers.

"Even on a Thursday night," Jake commented as he pushed past a pair of elderly women standing next to a pyramid of Coke cases, "this place is a zoo. There must be five hundred people in here."

Most of the aisles on the other side of the checkout counters seemed crowded, and there were shopping carts parked almost everywhere. Despite the chaos, there was something calming about the sight of the supermarket; the familiar setting made everything that had happened in the past two days seem surreal and foreign. The turbulent normalcy of the market seemed to render Calvin's brutal death impossible. Here, people were going about their lives, sharing a common experience with Americans in every city across the country. Brett wished that she were one of them; innocent, unknowing, buying food for dinner or groceries for the week, worried only about freshness and value.

But she knew too much; there was a good chance the seemingly haphazard scene was actually something much more sinister. The boxes and cartons and plastic wrappers themselves were reaching out with invisible tendrils. Affecting wants, needs, choices.

"Let's start with the shelves with items that have been around since Ted Conners's death," Jake said. "That way, we'll be more likely to find packages doused with the compound."

They turned into an aisle stocked on both sides with canned soups. Brett recognized most of the brands—Campbells, Chunky, Dinty Moore. She saw a fair number of Tucker products—covering nearly half of the shelves to her right, three quarters of the ones on her left. She moved the tiny camera strapped to her palm back and forth, filming as much of the aisle as possible. Up ahead, two teenagers were looking through a shelf of tomato soups, perhaps searching for a particular brand. Beyond them, a woman in a sundress was bent over a shopping cart, placing cans of diced carrots next to a sea of bagged vegetables. And just a few feet to Jake's left, a tall brunette in a spandex athletic outfit was filling a blue basket with boxes of rice.

"Okay," Brett said, her voice low. "Start spraying. Try to be as inconspicuous as possible."

Jake strolled a few feet forward, the spray bottle crooked to the side, pointing out from beneath his right arm. He sprayed a thin mist at the shelves as he went, covering the cans of soup, even managing to hit the spandex woman's basket and her collection of boxed rice. He returned, spraying the other side, then brought out the fluorescing lamp from under his other arm. Brett made sure the camera was properly aimed as he flicked the switch.

The sheer brightness of the glow caught Brett by surprise. It looked as though every third can had been coated with the compound—without regard for brand or content. Brett was even more shocked when she glanced at the spandex woman's basket. Every box of rice glowed, sending up a sphere of color almost the same shade as the basket itself. The woman's eyes went wide, and she held the glowing basket as far away from her body as possible.

Jake coughed, turning off the ultraviolet lamp. The cans went back to their natural colors, and the woman looked up, confused. Jake mumbled something about "market research," and continued down the aisle, gesturing for Brett to follow. When they reached a more empty section—a shelf cluttered with boxes of rice and pasta—he again reached for the spray can. A second later, every third box of rice and pasta glowed bright blue.

"It must be some sort of a test run. The treated products are made by different companies, without any regard for content or price. And if that woman's basket means anything—the test run is a success."

Jake turned toward a half-full shopping cart that had been abandoned in front of the rice shelf. There were more than thirty different items in the cart: cereal, canned fruit, bags of bread, cooking items, household cleaners. Jake leaned over the cart, spraying the serum over every package surface. Then he held up the fluorescent lamp.

The cart turned a magnificent shade of turquoise. Perhaps twenty-five of the thirty objects were coated with Compound G. Brett held her hand out to the side, using the camera to catch the cart and the glowing blue rice boxes on the shelves. She filmed until the glow dimmed away to nothingness.

"I'm betting we'll find the same level of contamination all over this supermarket," Brett said, using her thumb to turn off the video camera. "And maybe in other supermarkets in town as well."

"If we don't stop Tucker and Alaxon from getting together—we'll find Compound G on every shelf in every supermarket in the country." Jake lowered his voice as a lanky young man separated from the crowd of shoppers in the soup section of the aisle and ambled in their direction. "I think we've got enough to open a major investigation. We should get outside and call Sandler—"

Jake paused, looking down the aisle. Brett followed his gaze, and saw that the long-armed man was still moving toward them.

He stopped just a few feet from Brett. She made the sudden mistake of making eye contact—then stifled a cough. The man's eyes were like the bottom of a frozen, dead lake.

"Excuse me," he said, in a low voice. "I think that's our shopping cart."

Brett glanced behind Jake—and saw another man standing on the other side of the metal cart. This man was big, maybe six-three, with wide shoulders, wearing a denim jacket and green army pants. He had a Chicago Cubs baseball cap pulled down low over his forehead; even so, Brett could see the spider web of raised pink scars that covered both of his cheeks.

Brett turned back to the gawky man in the bad suit. She could feel Jake squaring his shoulders; obviously, he felt the same sudden discomfort that was flowing through her body. There was something off about the two men—the way they were looking at one another, as if reading cues.

"Whoops," Jake said, his hand drifting up toward the panic button hanging against his chest. "Our mistake."

"Not your fault," the gawky man responded, taking another step forward. "They all look the same. The trick is to ignore the cart, focus on the products. The brand names. Everyone's got his own favorite brands. That's the beauty of free choice. Isn't that right, Mr. Pierce?"

The scarred man grunted from beneath his baseball cap. Brett stepped back, her hand touching her husband's hip. She saw Jake's finger touch the panic button again and again. Any moment, the two ex-cops would come running down the aisle. Maybe it was a false alarm—but it was better not to take a chance.

"Thanks for the philosophy lesson," Brett said, shifting to step past the gawky man. "We'll be more careful next time—"

The gawky man suddenly slid to his left, blocking the aisle. Brett started back, nearly slamming into Jake.

"The thing about free choice," the gawky man said, opening his jacket and withdrawing a long hypodermic needle. "Is that you've always got to consider the consequences. That's just good business sense. Every strategy has its own set of repercussions. Mr. Pierce and I are experts at repercussions."

Jake yanked Brett behind him, pushing her back against the rice shelf. Her gaze remained pinned to the hypodermic in the gawky man's hand. She couldn't identify the clear liquid inside from that distance, but she guessed it was something lethal—perhaps potassium chloride. *Christ.* Her head started to spin.

"This is insane," she hissed, panicking. "There are witnesses everywhere. You won't get away with this."

"Your optimism is quite charming," the gawky man said, glancing over his shoulder. "But the other shoppers are much too busy exercising their free choice to get in the way. Certainly, this is no greater a degree of difficulty than a trauma room in a crowded ER."

Brett's jaw clenched. She looked into those dead blue eyes and saw pure violence staring back at her. She felt Jake's hand touching her behind his back—he was telling her to get ready. She was shocked at the aura of calm he was giving off. But then she understood. It wasn't calm—it was desperate anger. Jake had been pushed too far.

"Careful," the gawky man said toward his scarred partner. "They're getting that trapped look in their eyes—"

Suddenly, Jake's right foot shot out and hit the shopping cart dead center. The cart skidded forward, slamming into the scarred man's knees. The man went down, cursing, and

Jake whirled in the other direction, hurling the fluorescing lamp at the man with the syringe. The lamp slammed into his shoulder, shattering, sending him staggering a foot back. Jake grabbed Brett's arm and yanked her forward. They skirted past the shopping cart and around the fallen man, and Brett saw a flash of movement as he caught her by the ankle. She screamed, trying desperately to kick free of his firm grip. His other hand raced forward and Brett saw a long serrated blade arcing toward her leg.

Her mind froze and her body took over. Her arms swept out, her hands clawing at the shelf to her right—knocking a dozen heavy bags of rice down on top of her prone attacker. The bags landed with a heavy thud and the man's hand opened. She leapt free, catching up to Jake as he turned the corner toward the produce aisle. She could hear footsteps behind her and fought the urge to look back. But as she passed Jake on her left she couldn't help but glance over her shoulder.

The slight man was barreling toward them, his face contorted in an almost ecstatic rage. He had the syringe in one hand, and his other hand was reaching into his jacket, touching the dark handle of a gun.

"Jake!" Brett shouted, terrified, as they rushed between a covered salad bar and a metal rack filled with cantaloupes, "He's got a gun!"

Jake didn't look back. There was a large gathering of shoppers ten feet ahead of them in front of a stand full of on-sale watermelons. A few more seconds and they would be lost in the crowd.

"Keep moving!" Jake shouted back at her. "Don't stop until you're outside!"

Suddenly he threw himself to the left, leaping halfway up the rack of cantaloupes. After a loud metallic crash, the rack gave way. An avalanche of the round melons cascaded into the aisle, bouncing across the floor, smashing headlong into the salad bar. There were shouts from up ahead, people turning, and Brett slowed despite Jake's counsel. She watched as her pursuer stopped at the head of the salad bar, his hand frozen in his suit jacket, the syringe hidden behind his back. He seemed uncertain whether to continue after them with so many people watching. Maybe he had expected this to be much easier—definitely, he hadn't counted on Jake's quick actions. From his eyes and his demeanor it was obvious he was a professional—and normally two doctors would have had no chance against him. But this was not a battlefield. This was a supermarket. As level a playing field as Brett could imagine.

Before the man could decide what to do next, Jake was on his feet in the sea of melons, his legs apart, his thighs tensed. Brett recognized the stance. *A soccer player lining up for a penalty kick.*

Brett's mouth went wide as she realized what Jake was about to do. *Jake, you fucking maniac—*

Suddenly his right foot whipped forward, sending a cantaloupe the size of a volleyball whizzing through the air. The melon smacked full force into the blue-eyed man's chest, exploding on impact. The man reeled back—and suddenly a second cantaloupe hit him dead in the face. There was a loud, sickening pop and his head jerked back, his hands rising to his shattered nose. A third melon slammed into his stomach and he doubled over, dropping to his knees. Then Brett saw the scarred man skid around the cor-ner—and she grabbed Jake's wrist, pulling him toward the crowd of shocked onlookers.

"You're insane, you know that?!"

Jake was breathing heavily as they pushed through to the glass exit, his face red with adrenaline. "Coach used to make us run header drills with honeydews. If you catch 'em just right, they don't explode. Good thing that guy never played college soccer."

"He could have shot you!" Brett responded, angry. "Christ, Jake, they could have killed both of us."

Her shoulders shook from the realization that they had just narrowly avoided death. She barely felt the ground beneath her feet as they burst out into the warm night air. There were police officers rushing past them into the super-market, but nobody seemed to pay them any attention. "And what happened with the panic button? Where was the fucking cavalry?"

Jake pointed across the street, toward the green Chevy that was still double-parked on the other side. They raced past their own car, weaving through the slow traffic moving down Boylston. Jake reached the side window of the Chevy first. Inside, the thick necked ex-cop looked up, shocked. A cell phone was pressed against his ear. His partner was adjusting the rearview mirror, scanning the street behind them, completely unaware that Jake and Brett just escaped death.

"Where the hell were you guys?" Jake shouted, as Brett looked back toward the supermarket, searching for any signs of their two assailants. "We were nearly killed in there!"

"Why didn't you hit the button?" Kendrick shouted back.

Jake ripped the plastic circle off of his chest, breaking the string, and tossed it onto the man's lap. "If I'd hit the fucking thing any harder, I would have broken my finger."

The other ex-cop was already out of the driver's side, rushing toward Brett, a semiautomatic pistol held low in his hands. "How many of them?"

"Two," Brett answered, still scanning the front of the supermarket. There was no sign of either assailant. "But they're probably long gone."

Kendrick was hitting the button with his thumb, still holding the cell phone against his ear. The receiver sitting on the dashboard in front of him buzzed loudly, the sound reverberating off the Chevy's windshield. "Well, it works now. There must have been some sort of interference in the supermarket."

"Forget it." Jake grabbed the phone from him. He yanked Sandler's card out of his pocket and began dialing. Brett watched him, slumping against the car, her chest heaving. The fear was beginning to hit her as she thought about the syringe and the serrated knife blade. Then she remembered what the gawky man had said about the trauma room and the crowded ER.

That man had killed Calvin Johnson. Tortured him, then strangled him with an IV wire. Although Jake had managed to beat him in an absurd way—this was anything but comical. These people were cold-blooded killers. Brett had seen it in those horrible, dead blue eyes.

"Mr. Sandler," Jake said into the phone, his voice a little too loud. "We've got our proof."

He looked back at Brett, and she held up her right hand, showing him the tiny camera still strapped to her palm. Then she cursed her stupidity, as she realized she could have filmed their assailants—making it easy for homicide cops to identify them. But her mind had been frozen by the sudden attack. She had never been so close to death.

"Brett," Jake said, touching her shoulder. He had finished with the phone, and was leaning against the Chevy next to her. "Are you okay?"

"I think so." Brett pushed thoughts of her father out of her head. "Jake, those men were going to kill us."

Jake brushed her hair with his hand. He was trying to appear calm—but she could tell he was as scared as she was. "It's all going to be over soon. Sandler has everything ready on his end. Tomorrow morning his people are going to swarm Alaxon's offices in the Prudential and shut them down. He's also going to stop the stockholders' meeting in the Hynes. With our evidence, he thinks he's going to get indictments by tomorrow afternoon. And then he's going to start the conspiracy investigation into the four murders—and tonight's attempted murder."

Brett listened, but the words seemed faraway. "So tomorrow morning we go back to our normal lives?"

She almost laughed at her own statement. Their lives would never be *normal* again. Jake still had the compound in his body—and there was no way to know, yet, whether its effect on his sperm was permanent or temporary. And both of them had dead friends to mourn—friends who could never be replaced.

Still, they were alive. She leaned her head against Jake's

shoulder, listening to his pounding heart echoing through her ears.

"Sandler asked if we wanted to be there when he makes the arrests," Jake said. "He said if we wanted, he'd have our escort bring us up to Alaxon's headquarters tomorrow morning, a few minutes after the federal marshals arrive."

Brett looked at him. "What did you tell him?"

"I said I'd ask my wife and call him back."

Brett paused. She felt sudden tears burning behind her eyes. "I want to face them, Jake. I want to face the people behind Calvin's death."

Jake nodded. It was the answer he had hoped for. He finished for her, echoing her thoughts with his own.

"I want to look the bastards in the eyes."

24

Jake watched the sun rise from the window in his study, his fragile emotional state stirred by the tendrils of color that tracked across the deserted street below. His fingers drifted down the cool glass pane, tracing the shower of morning light; there was something cleansing about dawn, and Jake felt the pain and turmoil of the past few days begin to burn away. The situation was far from over—but the path to resolution seemed clear.

Jake pushed his desk chair back from the window. Behind him, every inch of floor and furniture was covered by a sea of computer printouts and open textbooks; unable to sleep, he had spent most of the night delving into the strange world of chemical pheromones, hoping to understand the compound that had taken refuge inside his body. The sad truth was, there wasn't a whole lot known about the class of chemicals, or their role in human life. Even in the insect world, pheromones were more an accepted phenomenon than an understood chemical process. Certain proteins released by one creature bound themselves to receptor sites in the endocrine system of another, causing a chain of glandular and synaptic reactions. Beyond that model, very little was understood. According to Jake's texts, there had been no successful trials of mammalian pheromones; the chimp video represented something brand-new, a step beyond the current state of research. Although Jake would have to run a series of similar tests on the chemical himself before he could declare Heidlinger's compound a true success, from what he had witnessed in the supermarket, he had already suspended his disbelief. Compound G was a odorless, tasteless, nearly invisible protein—an agent of attraction; if it were not for two unfortunate side effects, its presence might never have been discovered at all.

Jake rubbed his hands against his eyes, turning away from the window. In light of the true nature of Compound G, the two side effects seemed almost trivial. The existence of a mammalian pheromone could very well change the structure of society. Misused—such as Alaxon's spraying of products in a supermarket—a pheromone could challenge the very notion of individual free will. Decisions made because of a chemical were not real decisions at all. They were physiological responses.

The potential of a chemical like Compound G was terrifying. There was no telling what would happen if the pheromone were disseminated on a national scale. Or what other uses a company like Tucker National could come up with, profit being the only motivation. Jake had to make sure the truth behind Compound G was exposed—before the buyout went through.

Only then would he be able to concentrate on the less significant—but personally critical—side effect. At the thought, his gaze shifted to the closest open text, where a brightly colored cross-section of the male reproductive system lay spread across two glossy pages. His shoulders sagged—and he chided himself for his pessimism. It was too early to make any conclusions.

He had gone through the subject in his head a hundred times—and he was still left with two distinct possibilities. If the compound was affecting merely his sperm—then it was only a matter of waiting until the protein naturally left his system, and he would return to a fertile state. On the other hand, if the compound had affected his spermatogonia—the glandular machines that created his sperm in his testicles—then the situation would be permanent. He would never be able to give Brett children.

At the moment, his only real option was to wait until the compound drained—through natural, metabolic processes—from his system. He and Brett had already spent two hours emptying their house of every store-bought item they could find. Then they had used antiseptic and antibiotic cleansers to scrub their refrigerator and cabinets, testing afterward for any remaining traces of the chemical. Throughout the cleaning process, they had carried on normal, married-life conversation, consciously avoiding the one thing on both of their minds: *Is it already too late?*

Jake slammed the textbook shut. The sound had barely finished echoing off the study walls when a quiet cough sounded from the doorway. Jake turned and watched Brett enter. She was dressed in a dark, velvety shirt that matched her short hair and tight charcoal slacks. Her eyes looked wired, as if she hadn't slept much, either. She held two steaming mugs of coffee in her hands.

"It's almost nine," she said, handing him one of the coffees. "Did you sleep at all?"

Jake shook his head. "You?"

"I'll sleep when this is over. Every time I close my eyes, I see that man, that scarecrow with the horrible eyes."

Jake sipped his coffee, glancing back out the window. He could see the green Chevy parked a few feet from their driveway, but for some reason it didn't make him feel very secure.

"And you think he works for Alaxon?" Brett asked. "A hired gun?"

Jake shivered, remembering the look on the man's face as he had approached with the syringe. "Maybe, but for a guy like that I don't think it has anything to do with money or career. He looked like he was enjoying himself. We were very lucky, Brett. Let's hope our luck holds through the rest of the morning."

He saw the Chevy door swing open, Kendrick heading toward the house. It was time to go. Jake rose from his seat, gulping down the coffee. He was still wearing the same clothes from yesterday—but he didn't care. He was going to face the monsters who had killed his best friend and almost ruined his marriage.

"Do you have the camera?" he asked.

Brett tapped her pocket. Jake finished his coffee.

"Let's go bring them down."

Four sets of footsteps reverberated through the cement walled parking garage as Jake, Brett, and the two security guards approached the bank of elevators carved into the stark white cinder-block wall. They had chosen to enter the building by way of the parking garage to avoid the short walk through the crowded mall upstairs. Jake could feel the weight of the enormous glass-and-steel skyscraper above them. It loomed atop three underground floors of parking and two floors of high-end retail shops. The mammoth building had been visible throughout the short drive from their South End apartment, and Jake had kept his eyes trained on the sheer glass picture windows of the top few floors. Of course from that distance the windows were nothing but tiny strips of reflected sunlight, but he tried to imagine the scene inside. Arthur Sandler and his team of federal agents bursting into Alaxon's headquarters, reading search warrants, sequestering files, slapping handcuffs onto businessmen's wrists. He wondered if the same team of agents would stream down into the Hynes Convention Center to close down the stockholders' meeting. Or would there be a second raid simultaneous to the first? As he and Brett had driven past the Hynes en route to the base of the Prudential, he hadn't noticed any police cars or flashing lights anywhere near either building; he had assumed that Sandler would want to keep a low profile until the situation was under control. There would be plenty of time for press conferences and public explanations later.

Jake glanced at the rows of parked cars behind them; the vehicles filled nearly every space in the underground garage. He wondered how many of the cars belonged to undercover federal agents. He was bolstered by the thought, and he put his arm around Brett's shoulders, his excitement rising as they reached the bank of elevators.

Each of the six elevators led to a different set of floors. The two bodyguards guided them directly to a pair of doors set a few feet apart from the elevators, with a single listed destination. "Mr. Sandler left the elevator unlocked for us. It's the private penthouse lift, a straight shot to the CEO's office on the fifty-fourth floor."

Kendrick hit a button by the elevator, and the doors whiffed open. He ushered Jake and Brett inside and then took position next to his partner near the elevator controls. The doors slid shut, and the elevator jerked upward. Jake leaned back against the wall, watching the digital floor display count upward in bright red strokes. Trying to relax, he rubbed his sweaty palms down the sides of his slacks. He felt a hard lump in his front pocket—and raised his eyebrows. Then he remembered. He was still wearing the same pants from yesterday. He still had the Viagra paperweight Stan Humphrey had given him in his pocket. He thought about showing it to Brett when the elevator suddenly slowed, the red display numbers blending together as they neared the penthouse floor.

"Get ready for the fireworks," Jake said, stretching his calves. He held his breath as the double doors slid open.

There was a short hallway in front of them, leading to a closed wooden door. Kendrick stepped out of the elevator, checking the hallway with quick flicks of his eyes. The other guard held the door open as Jake and Brett moved behind Kendrick. As they approached the wooden door, they heard a quiet metallic click, as if it had been unlocked from the inside.

The wooden door swung inward, and Jake stared past Kendrick into the front entrance of a magnificent, circular office. The office was at least thirty feet across, banked on two sides by a massive, curved window with a view of the downtown. Most of the office floor was covered by a thick white shag carpet, and the walls were lined with creamy marble.

Jake followed Kendrick through the doorway, Brett and the other bodyguard a step behind him. In the very center of the office, standing on a raised marble dais, towered a huge television screen. The screen was nearly six feet tall, the glass curved slightly outward to contain a monumental vacuum tube. The television was on, the screen giving off a blue glare.

In front of the TV was a glass coffee table and a leather couch. Behind the couch, there was a spiral stone staircase, and beyond that, the showcase of the office—the strangest terrarium Jake had ever seen. The tank ran the entire length of the back wall of the office, and was well over ten feet high. It was filled with shiny black sand; within the sand, Jake could see little flecks of movement. He shivered, remembering what Stan Humphrey had told him about

Simon Scole's obsession. Then he forgot about the tank as his eyes focused on something just a few feet ahead of Kendrick, leaning against the wall.

A hockey stick—with a scrawled signature running down the wood. Alex's prized possession. Jake's teeth came together and he stormed past the heavyset bodyguard. Brett rushed after him, her voice concerned. "Jake, where are Sandler and his federal agents?"

"I'm right here, Dr. Foster," came Sandler's voice from an alcove behind the television set. Sandler stepped into view, his patented smile above his cleft chin. Jake paused, still a foot from the hockey stick. He watched as a second man stepped out of the alcove. The man was tall, well-toned and handsome—but there was something off about his appearance. His hair was too bright, almost yellow, and his skin was too smooth—as if he had caked on layer after layer of tan makeup. Still, he was dressed impeccably, and his stance was confident and controlled. Jake tried to guess his age—but he could have been anywhere from fifty to seventy.

"Jake, this is Simon Scole, CEO of Alaxon Industries. I believe you've already met his son Malthus, VP of Research and Development."

Suddenly, the door to the office clicked shut behind Brett. Jake felt Kendrick's hand land on his shoulder—not comforting, but controlling, pinning him in place. His pulse rocketed as he looked past Kendrick and saw the gawky man from the supermarket leaning against the door, his arms crossed against his chest, a cruel-looking automatic held expertly in his right hand. Large black bruises covered the skin beneath both of his eyes, and a taped strip of white gauze covered his bashed-up nose. He looked at Jake, an angry grunt escaping through his teeth.

Then there was another sound from across the room—footsteps against stone. Jake turned and watched the man with the scarred face and the baseball cap moving down the spiral staircase. His hands were deep in the pockets of his denim jacket.

Jake's heart froze. He stared at Sandler, trying to form words.

"I'm sorry," Sandler said, "but there are bigger issues here than you realize. It's unfortunate that it has to end like this—but I don't see any other way."

"You lying bastard." Jake started forward, but Kendrick's hand held him tightly in place. His stomach clenched, his mind trying to comprehend the scene before him. It made no sense—Sandler came from one of the richest families in Boston. He was the attorney general, running for governor. One day he hoped to be President. *One day he hopes to be President. . . .*

A thought formed inside Jake's mind. Compound G had potential that went far beyond packages on a supermarket shelf.

"Compound G," he whispered. "You want to use its power for yourself. In your campaign for governor. Maybe one day to run for president."

The pheromone was designed to attract without any indication that there was something chemical going on. Content didn't matter—as long as the packaging was coated with Compound G. It was a politician's dream.

"Jake," Sandler said. "It's not the enormous leap of ethics you might imagine. I spend hundreds of thousands of dollars designing the perfect television spot to attract voters. I spend thousands more running slogan tests, choosing photo angles, picking the right music to play behind my campaign speeches. I even have an entire staff of Harvard MBAs researching the right color combinations for my posters and ads. All this in an attempt to subliminally draw in voters. Alaxon's product is simply the next logical step."

Jake trembled, aghast at the idea. Voters drawn to a candidate because of a chemical reaction enacted by his posters and ads. It didn't matter that most of the voters never met him face to face—the pleasurable memories associated with his picture and his campaign paraphernalia would be enough to give him the necessary edge. He'd win the presidency for sure.

"You've been working with them all along," Jake whispered. "You're a part of this."

"Not exactly," Sandler said. "I only learned of the Compound a few months ago, when I received a fax from one of Alaxon's employees. But I recognized the potential immediately."

"But the side effects," Brett said, her hands jerking nervously as she eyed Malthus Scole. There was something strange about her movements—but Jake guessed it was just a reflex reaction, a symbol of her inner fear. Malthus was still leaning against the door, watching the exchange with a bored expression on his face. "The infertility and the DIC."

"Compound G 'enjoys' an acceptable level of product liability," Simon Scole suddenly interrupted. His voice was rushed, his hands checking the knot of his tie. "The cigarette companies were willing to put up with much worse. A few hundred deaths and a few million more infertile men is far better than widespread lung cancer and emphysema, don't you think?"

"But the murders," Jake started—but Simon Scole cut him off with a flick of his hand.

"That's enough, Dr. Foster. Arthur and I have a stockholders' meeting to attend. I'm sure my son and his associate will be happy to respond to all of your concerns."

Simon moved gracefully across the office, Sandler a step behind him. Malthus held the door open for him, his head slightly bowed. Jake watched, stunned, as the two men moved past. Then Kendrick and the other bodyguard followed, silent as well-trained dogs. They had been a part of this as well, pretending to protect Jake and Brett while keeping an eye on them. Jake wanted to leap out and grab Sandler by the throat—but Malthus was standing too close to Brett, the automatic still gripped in his hand. And the scarred man had reached the bottom step of the spiral stairwell, his hands still deep in his pockets. Any sudden movement would be suicide.

"Malthus," Simon said, as Sandler and the two bodyguards exited the office. "Take good care of our guests."

Then he paused in the doorway, looking at Jake and Brett. His eyes were as dead and merciless as his son's. "Try not to make too much of a mess."

He stepped out of the office, shutting the door behind him. The second he was gone, Malthus's posture changed. His spine straightened and his head jerked up, his bruised face going strangely calm. It was as if some string holding him down had suddenly snapped. His eyes burned into Jake, and a half-smile touched his lips. He waved the automatic toward the center of the room. "I don't think you'll catch me by surprise this time around, Dr. Foster. On your knees in front of the television."

Jake stared at the barrel of the gun, his body paralyzed. In the supermarket, there had been no time for fear—he had simply reacted. Here, reaction seemed impossible. Panic had already set in.

"Mr. Pierce, perhaps they need a little incentive." Malthus nodded toward the scarred man, who drew his right hand out of his pocket. He was holding a long, serrated knife. Jake's stomach turned over. He could hear Brett struggling to breathe next to him. His mind spun, jagged thoughts screaming through his head. He had to do something. He had to protect Brett—

Suddenly, Malthus slid forward and grabbed Brett by the arm. He threw her toward his scarred partner. Fiery anger ripped up Jake's body as Brett landed on her knees in the center of the office, just a few yards from the base of the spiral stairs. Without thought, Jake leapt at Malthus.

There was a flash of movement as Malthus easily sidestepped his attack. A long, muscled arm wrapped around his throat, lifting him back off his feet. He felt the barrel of the automatic pressed hard against the side of his head. Malthus leaned close, whispering in his ear. "Gallant, Dr. Foster. But gallantry has no place here. This is purely business. And one of the cardinal rules of business is to set realistic goals."

Jake gasped, struggling for air. The man's strength was unnerving; his muscled arm felt like an iron rope against Jake's throat. Jake felt himself being dragged forward, then shoved down onto his knees. He was facing the enormous television screen, just a few feet from Brett. There were tears streaming down her cheeks as she watched him suffocate. The scarred man was standing over her, spinning the serrated blade between his hands. "No," Jake said, choking. *God please no.*

"Mr. Pierce," Malthus's voice echoed in his ears. "I'd like to have a private moment with my new friend."

Jake's panic climbed as he watched Pierce grab Brett by the hair, half-lifting her to her feet. She shouted Jake's name, but her voice sounded miles away. Pierce started back up the staircase, dragging Brett with him. Brett struggled—until the scarred man held the blade up to her face, shaking his head. Then Pierce yanked her forward.

Jake's vision swam as Brett disappeared up the stairs. His eyelids rolled shut, green spots spinning in front of him—and he knew he only had a few seconds left before he lost consciousness. He had to act. Now.

Focusing all of his energy into his thighs, he jerked upward, driving his head backward into Malthus's face. He felt his skull connect with soft flesh and Malthus cursed, letting him go.

Jake coughed, gasping for air as he shook his head, finding focus. Malthus staggered behind him, blood streaming from his already-injured nose. He stopped in front of the massive television screen, his body lit up by the glowing blue pixels. The automatic was still in his right hand, and he was blinking rapidly, trying to clear his vision. Jake knew he had only a few more seconds.

Without conscious thought he reached into his pocket and yanked the heavy glass paperweight free. He cocked his arm, ready to let fly—when a sudden idea hit him. He adjusted his aim and flung the paperweight as hard as he could. It whizzed past Malthus's ear and hit the television screen dead center.

The heavy object collided with glass pressurized at fourteen pounds of pressure per square inch. There was a flash of bright light, followed by a massive roar. Jake dropped to the floor as a burst of heat swept over him. The glass came a moment after the heat—a thunderous gale of shards speeding through the air as fast as bullets. Malthus's body caught the brunt of the explosion. He jerked upward, screaming, as the glass and heat hit him, lifting him over Jake's prone body, sending him crashing into the coffee table. The table collapsed under his weight and he hit the ground rolling, slamming into the base of the leather couch.

The heat quickly dissipated. Jake scrambled to his knees, shaking glass out of his clothes. He was bleeding from a dozen places and he could feel tiny cuts and abrasions all over his body, but nothing serious, no deep punctures or dangerous burns. He glanced at the blackened vacuum tube lit by flickers of orange flame and shook his head, amazed.

Then he heard motion from the direction of the couch, and he swung his head away from the television. Amazingly, Malthus was crawling to his knees. His suit jacket was shredded, and blood streamed from gashes all across his back. Part of his blond hair had singed away, and one of his oversized ears hung in tatters from his head. The automatic was gone, probably buried under the shattered coffee table. But somehow, Malthus was still conscious.

Jake leapt to his feet, his eyes wild. He didn't have time for a protracted fight. *Brett needs me.* He caught sight of Alex's hockey stick still leaning against the wall. He grabbed the stick in both hands and whirled toward Malthus.

Malthus had made it to one knee, using the couch for leverage. He saw Jake holding the hockey stick and a strange smile crossed his bloody lips. His voice slipped out between pained gasps.

"That's not your sport, Dr. Foster."

You fucking monster! Jake swept forward, no longer in control. He swung the hockey stick with full force, catching Malthus dead in the jaw. With a loud crack, Malthus's body flipped over the back of the couch. Fabric tore as his suit jacket caught on the leather—and a half dozen tiny white objects spiraled into the air. One of the objects hit Jake in the chest and landed on the couch. He looked down—and his soul caught fire.

It was a finger bone—a man's ring-finger severed just below the second knuckle. Jake's muscles spasmed as the anger swept through him. He raised his eyes, watching Malthus struggle to his feet in front of the massive curved terrarium running along the back wall of the office. Blood poured now from an open gash in Malthus's jaw, and his eyes were half-closed, his body kept aloft by willpower alone.

But Jake felt no mercy. This man had mutilated his best friend. This man had tried to kill him—and his wife.

Brett.

Jake's ears rang as he rushed forward. Malthus sensed him coming and raised his arms—but Jake was powered by an internal force greater than anything Malthus had remaining in him. He swung the hockey stick with all his strength, hitting Malthus in the dead center of his chest. Malthus crashed back into the terrarium, disappearing in a spray of broken glass and shiny black sand. Jake felt something land on his right arm—followed by a sharp stinging. He looked down and saw a tiny red ant hanging from his flesh by a pair of oversized mandibles. He cursed, shaking the ant away.

Then he looked down at the destroyed terrarium. He could see Malthus's leather shoes sticking out from beneath a sea of black sand and shattered glass. The sand was undulating, thousands of tiny red ants scurrying frantically across the surface. Jake trembled as he poked one of Malthus's shoes with the hockey stick. *Nothing.*

Jake sprinted toward the spiral stairway. He took the steps two at a time, the hockey stick gripped in his right hand. Above him he saw a glass door, beyond that a glowing, glass-walled hallway. He hit the door with his shoulder, bursting onto the skywalk. To his left, all of Boston splayed out below him, a postcard lashed by orange tongues of midmorning sun. He could see the harbor in the distance, streaks of aquamarine glistening beneath puffy white cottonball clouds.

Ahead, the skywalk opened out into a vast cement glade, bordered on four sides by a three-foot-high metal railing. The open cement was at least fifty feet across, ending in a raised helipad painted with a bright yellow circle. A sleek-looking helicopter sat on the pad, its rotors still, the black glass windows staring like the eyes of an ugly steel insect.

A few yards to the left of the helicopter, right up against the railing—Jake saw two figures locked in a violent struggle. He sprinted across the skywalk and tore onto the cement glade, his eyes focusing on the two figures. He could see Brett on her knees, both hands locked around the scarred man's wrist. The serrated blade was inches from her face.

A sudden, fiery, primal rage possessed Jake. The hockey stick forgotten, he lowered his shoulders and hurled himself across the cement glade. As he came within five yards of Brett she saw him, her eyes wide—and she instantly read his mind. She dropped prone, twisting her body out of the way. The scarred man looked up—a second too late.

Jake's shoulder slammed into the side of Pierce's ribcage. As the impact reverberated through him, Jake lifted with his thighs, gaining leverage—and Pierce's body jackknifed over the top of the railing. At the last second he slashed out with the blade—barely catching Jake across his right bicep. Blood sprayed lightly and Jake collapsed, grabbing at the wound as he fell backward. His eyes widened as he watched the scarred man teeter for a frozen second—then the assassin disappeared over the side of the building. Jake reflexively reached out for him with his good arm—missing the denim jacket by inches.

He leaned over the railing, watching the man spinning like a starfish as he plunged downward. Fifty yards below the helipad was a wide concrete ledge covered in satellite dishes, phallic black antennas, and wide, circular spotlights that guide helicopters in at night. Jake had less than two seconds to wonder what the man was going to hit.

With a distant, sickening crack, Pierce landed spread-eagle in the center of one of the spotlights. Instantly, a bloody spiderweb exploded across the glass. Jake turned away—and met Brett's eyes. She was still sitting on the concrete ground, her back against the railing. She looked like she was near shock. Worried, Jake dropped next to her, holding his bleeding arm. The sight of his injury cut through her glaze. She began to check him for damage. Her fingers stopped shaking as she expertly probed the nasty slash.

"You'll need stitches," she said, her voice barely audible. "But it doesn't look serious."

Jake nodded, tearing away a section of his left sleeve. Brett tied the thin material around the wound, doing her best to stanch the bleeding. Jake watched her as she worked, emotion moving through him. He realized he was shaking as hard as she was. He had almost lost her.

"Jesus, Brett—"

"It's okay, Jake. We're both okay." She leaned into him, embracing him with both arms. He felt tears burning at his eyes.

"Sandler betrayed us. The stockholders' meeting is going on right now. There's no way we can expose them in time. The compound will roll out on a national level before we convince anyone that the attorney general is in on the conspiracy."

Brett had gone strangely calm. She reached into her pocket—and pulled out the palm-sized video camera. "Maybe not."

Jake raised his eyebrows. He suddenly remembered seeing her moving her hands when she had asked Sandler about the side effects. He hadn't guessed that she was going for the camera. He had underestimated her. She hadn't been paralyzed by fear. "How much did you get?"

"Enough. I got them both together, comparing themselves to the cigarette companies."

"An admission of guilt," Jake whispered. "We need to get this down to the convention center as quickly as we can."

Brett nodded past the helicopter. "There's a second exit just behind the copter. I made a break for it before Scarface tossed me against the railing."

Jake shivered and then pushed the thought away. There would be time for that later. "We just need to find a way to get the video evidence out to the stockholders—and to the public."

He stopped, realization hitting him. He grabbed Brett's free hand. "Sandler said the entire meeting was being shot on closed-circuit TV—and simultaneously broadcast on CNN and MSNBC. If we get down there in time, I can hook up the camera to the system."

Brett's dark eyes shone. "We can expose them at their own convention. Jake, it's perfect."

A second later they were both up and moving toward the second exit.

25

The stinging was relentless; a thousand needles dug through every inch of his skin, injecting drops of pure acid directly into his nerves. An angry, sweltering pain, as if his skin itself had gone bad, curdled off his bones in violent twists. The stinging moved in waves up his legs, across his stomach and chest, up his neck, across his cheeks. Tiny knives dug into the soft skin of his groin, into his ears, up his nostrils. His lips and eyes swelled as the daggers bored into the soft tissue, and suddenly the blackness receded, replaced by something blazing red: *rage*.

Malthus opened his swollen eyes. The bright light of the

office burned into his retinas, and he blinked hard—but he couldn't get his vision to clear. The liquid redness tinged everything. He slowly lifted his head—and felt the ground quiver with movement beneath him. He looked down his body—and saw that he was lying half-buried in a sea of dark silicon beads and broken glass. Then his eyes focused on his bare arms and the skin showing through the torn material of his suit. *Ants.* Thousands of them, crawling frantically over his skin, hanging by their mandibles, stingers jabbing again and again and again . . .

Malthus groaned and struggled to his feet, sluggishly slapping at the tiny creatures, trying desperately to shake them free. His blood dripped from dozens of cuts, and he could feel larger shards of glass burrowing into his back and shoulders. He had lost a lot of blood—his jaw was slick with it from the blow of the hockey stick, and a hot river ran from his mangled right ear—but that was only part of the sluggishness. The ant venom was overpowering his system. He could taste the bitter foam in his mouth, could hear the vile ringing in his ears. *Just as Father had described.*

He knew he didn't have much time. The ant bites and the blood loss would combine to incapacitate him. His father would find him lying in the demolished remains of his prize terrarium—overcome by a doctor with no combat training. His father would call him a failure, would tell him what he already knew—that he was worthless, that he was nothing, that he did not belong in the corporate world. It would be like the Air Force all over again; and this time, not even a whore with an endless heart could help him start over.

He staggered across the office, refusing to let the fatigue pull him to the ground. He passed the destroyed television set, stumbled around the spiral staircase, then lurched forward into the alcove that contained his father's desk. Behind the desk, concealed in the stark white wall, was a door. The door came open as his hands touched a plate halfway up its face.

He stumbled into the small executive bathroom. The room was dazzlingly clean, with two sinks, a stall, and a small, glass-walled shower. His father had told him that one day—once he proved himself—he might have an executive bathroom of his own. Tears burned his swollen eyes as he realized that day would never come.

He pushed the shower door open and pulled himself inside. His hands found the faucet control and a jet of ice-cold water crashed down on his head. He watched swirls of dark red blood twist across the tiles. He felt the cool streams wash the ants off his body, dulling the horrible stinging, pushing a burst of new life into his fatigued muscles. He clenched his teeth, letting the water soak through his tattered suit, letting the water cleanse away his failure, letting the water focus his mind.

It's not over yet, damn it. He was still alive, still conscious. If the two doctors had also overcome Pierce—then they were still somewhere in the building, or nearby. Malthus doubted they would give up; he had seen the determination in Jake Foster's eyes. They would try to disrupt the stockholders' meeting—and that meant Malthus still had a chancc to stop them. He still had a chance to show his father that he wasn't a failure.

He reached forward with a swollen hand and shut off the faucet. He raised his eyes, ignoring the red glare that still tracked across his vision. His pain no longer mattered.

I still have a job to do.

26

Brett burst out of the elevator into the marble-lined lobby of the Prudential a step behind Jake, the video camera held tightly in the palm of her right hand. Her pulse was rocketing so fast that she felt lightheaded, and she could taste her own sweat on her lips. Her arms still ached from her struggle with the scarred man; when she blinked, she saw the serrated blade swinging down toward her face, saw her hands go up at the last second to catch his wrist, saw the smile burst out between his scarred cheeks, his huge muscles barely flexing as the blade moved down, down, down. . . .

Brett slammed her feet against the black marble floor, shaking the image away. She had to keep her focus; catharsis could come later, after they had exposed Alaxon and Compound G. She owed it to Calvin and everyone else who had suffered because of Simon Scole's company—she had to keep her head until this was over.

She focused on Jake as they barreled across the lobby and out through the revolving glass door that led into the brightly lit Prudential Mall. The makeshift bandage on his bicep was soaked through with blood—but it didn't seem to be slowing him down.

They moved through the short section of mall that connected the base of the Prudential Building with the Hynes Convention Center. The mall was crowded, mostly with office workers and retail clerks arriving from the many levels of parking beneath the massive conglomerate of shops and restaurants. They skirted past a booth cluttered with cellular phones, swept past a pair of ATM machines—and arrived at the brass doors that led to the convention center. The doors were propped open, and a sign just inside read: TUCKER NATIONAL STOCKHOLDERS, MAIN HALL.

A second later they were through the brass doors and rushing across the polished stone lobby of the convention center. They passed a security desk on their left, but the two security guards didn't even look up as they rushed by. Brett guessed the stockholders' meeting was open to the public—not that anyone outside the business world and the financial media would have any interest. The average American didn't know what went on within the hallways of these skyscrapers—and they didn't really care. As long as the products arrived on the supermarket shelves, as long as their favorite brands ended up within reach. They didn't have to worry about conspiracies and cover-ups; that was what governments were for. Men like Arthur Sandler, watchdogs to make sure big business played fair.

Brett's lips came together as they approached a pair of massive wooden doors at the back of the stone lobby. She heard the echo of an amplified voice coming from inside— and a smattering of applause from a gathered, rapt crowd. She wondered how many similar meetings were taking place across the country at that very moment. How many other convention halls were filled with men and women in business suits—*playing fair*.

Her stomach crawled as she and Jake pushed their way inside the double doors. The cavernous room measured about one hundred feet across, with twenty-foot ceilings and high, windowless walls. Above, a massive chandelier glowed bright orange, tiny teardrops of crystal flickering in gusts of air-conditioned air. Beginning just a few feet in front of Brett was a sea of metal folding chairs—maybe three hundred, set up in rows of twenty, stretching from wall to wall. Every chair was occupied, most of the occupants men in gray or blue suits. At the end of each row stood a color television set next to cone speakers on top of rolling AV carts. Most of the businessmen and women had turned in their chairs to watch the screens—though a few were still facing forward, choosing authenticity over technology—despite the obvious advantages of the latter. Brett followed their lead, squinting to see over the heads of the audience in front of her.

A high stage took up the front of the vast room, and in

the very center of the stage stood a wooden pulpit. The man
behind the pulpit was barely visible from Brett's distance; a
small, bald, shriveled, froglike old man, seated in a cushioned wheelchair, partially hunched over, speaking softly
into a microphone. In front of him, a huge television camera was operated by a man wearing a CNN baseball cap. A
few feet behind the camera were two more metal folding
chairs, occupied by two men Brett easily recognized. Her
mouth tasted bitter as she moved her eyes from Sandler's
square jaw to Simon Scole's yellow hair.

"Look at the bastards," Jake whispered. "So damn smug.
This is their moment."

Brett unhooked the video camera from her palm. She
pressed a button on the side of the tiny device, rewinding it
to a digital marker she had punched in when she had started
filming Sandler and Simon Scole. "Let's ruin it for them."

Jake took the camera from her and moved quietly along
the back of the great hall. It took Brett a second to realize
where he was going; then she saw the AV control board in
the back corner of the room. The board consisted of a four-
foot-long, desk-shaped counter, covered in diode-lit levers
and flashing buttons. Hundreds of wires ran out the back of
the board and down across the stone floor, twisting like
sleeping black snakes toward the television sets standing in
the aisles. Brett saw two oversized wires protruding from a
panel in the direct center of the board, weaving down the
side of the hall toward the stage. Jake seemed focused on
the panel and the two large rubber wires—and it was obvious the two wires were the main audio and video lines,
through which the froglike man was broadcasting.

Jake slowed his pace as they approached the control board. Anxiety swept across his eyes—and Brett saw the young man seated behind the board, his hands folded against his chest, a bored look on his face. He was dressed in a gray sweatshirt and dark jeans, and seemed much more interested in something on the far side of the room than in the board in front of his face. Brett followed his gaze and saw a team of CNN reporters standing behind a pair of television cameras.

Brett had a sudden idea and touched Jake's arm, stopping him. "Give me a second. I think I can get you a few minutes alone with the control board."

She wiped sweat from her brow and strolled forward. She stopped just a few inches behind the young man and leaned over his shoulder.

"Excuse me," she said in a soft voice. He looked up, startled, and she smiled amiably, pointing toward the CNN reporters by the far wall. "Sorry to bother you. I'm an associate producer with CNN. We're having a bit of trouble with one of our cameras, and our cameraman needs a second pair of hands. Since his assistant recently quit, leaving us shorthanded, he suggested that you might be able to help us out. It will only take a few minutes."

The young man's eyes lit up. Then he threw a distressed glance at the AV board in front of him. "I'd love to help. But I'm not supposed to leave the board unsupervised."

Brett patted his shoulder. "I can watch the board for you. I can't help fix a camera—but I know how to work sound and video controls."

The young man paused for less than a second. Then he

smiled. "Okay. Just keep an eye on the sound levels. If the old guy starts coughing again, make sure you bring it down a bit so he doesn't burst a few eardrums."

The kid rose and started across the hall toward the CNN cameramen. Brett gestured toward Jake, and he rushed forward. It would take the kid only a few minutes to push through the crowded hall—but Brett hoped a few minutes would be enough. Jake had minored in electrical engineering in college—and he'd been raised by an engineer father.

Brett stepped back, giving Jake room. He dove right for the center panel, testing the plastic with his fingers. He pulled gently at the two main wires and them looked at his wife.

"We need to pry this open," he whispered. "Help me look for something sharp."

Brett ran her gaze around the AV board—then she noticed a small vinyl bag on the floor near her feet. She grabbed the bag, tore it open—and saw a handful of various screwdrivers, wrenches, and wire cutters.

"Will this do?" she asked, showing Jake a long screwdriver.

Jake grinned, taking the screwdriver from her. He carefully jammed the blade into a crease in the plastic AV panel and slammed his palm against the handle.

There was a sudden crack, and heads turned in the nearby back row. Brett tried to look calm, pretending to check the sound levels as Jake pried the broken plastic aside. She watched him peer down into a spaghetti sea of different-colored wires. She wondered if the open AV board presented a danger of electrocution. She knew Jake was skilled—but she had seen plenty of engineers come into the ER half-dead from electrocution.

She held her breath as Jake shoved his hands into the sea of wires and gently began to disconnect some of the copper leads from the board. Every few seconds he glanced at the nearest television screens, making sure he hadn't yet disconnected the main input. Then he took his hands out of the board and opened the back of the video camera, revealing a pair of silver connecting screws. He looked at Brett—and she nodded.

Jake reached back into the board and yanked a pair of wires free. A sudden murmur broke across the hall as all of the television screens simultaneously went black. The froglike man on the stage pushed his wheelchair back with a squeak, and Sandler and Scole both stood, scanning back toward the AV board. Brett heard a shout from the direction of the CNN reporters—but she kept her focus on Jake and the camera.

Jake had the two wires extended as far as they could go. He attached the copper ends to the connecting screws on the camera. Then he turned the camera over and hit the play button.

Suddenly, Arthur Sandler's face appeared on every television screen in the room. The murmuring stopped, as all attention shifted to his charismatic smile and cleft jaw. His voice echoed through the great hall.

"I spend hundreds of thousands of dollars designing the perfect television spots to attract voters," he began. "I spend thousands more running slogan tests, choosing photo angles, picking the right music to play behind my campaign speeches. I even have an entire staff of Harvard MBAs researching the right color combinations for my posters and ads. All this, in an attempt to subliminally draw in voters. Alaxon's product is simply the next logical step."

There was a loud gasp from somewhere in the audience, then a few heckled shouts in Sandler's direction. Sandler was holding his palms out in front of him, trying to say something, but nobody seemed to be listening. All attention remained pinned to the television sets.

The televised exchange continued a few more seconds—and then Brett heard her own voice echo through the hall. "But the side effects. The infertility and the DIC."

The camera angle shifted, and Simon Scole moved into view. His face was cold and businesslike as he waved her concerns away. Brett was so overcome by the victorious rush, she caught only the last two sentences of his ghastly rationalization—more than enough to seal both Alaxon and Arthur Sandler's fates. "The cigarette companies were willing to put up with much worse. A few hundred deaths and a few million more infertile men is far better than widespread lung cancer and emphysema, don't you think?"

The video image jittered—then the television screens went blank. Shouts exploded from the gathered stockholders, and Brett stepped next to Jake, her eyes focused toward the stage. The froglike man in the wheelchair was staring in shock at the two men to his right. Simon Scole's face had turned pale—even beneath his thick makeup. And Sandler's jaw quivered as he scanned the back of the hall. Then his eyes landed on Jake and Brett—and his mouth went wide.

A barrage of pointed questions erupted from the corner

filled with CNN reporters. Certainly, there would be much explanation necessary before people realized what they had just witnessed—but now Tucker could not possibly get away with rolling out Compound G on a national level. The buyout would never take place. Brett smiled, realizing that it was really over, she and Jake had really won—

She saw the shape out of the corner of her eye a bare second before it hit Jake from behind, sending him careening into the closest row of occupied chairs. There was a loud metallic crash, followed by screams as people dove out of the way. Jake landed prone, the shape straddling his back. Malthus Scole's suit was completely shredded and soaked through with blood. Part of his right ear was missing. Every inch of his skin was marred by raised, bright red bumps. Most of his hair had been singed away, and his jaw looked crooked, definitely broken. Besides the obvious trauma to his body and clothes, for some reason he was soaking wet. Water dripped down as he raised his right arm.

Then Brett saw the long black knife clenched in his hand and her mind snapped back to life. She lunged forward, screaming for help—but pandemonium had broken out; people in business suits crashed into one another as they tried to get away from the crazed man. Brett and Jake were on their own.

Brett threw herself at Malthus, her hands grabbing for his raised wrist. Before she reached him, his other hand flicked back—an indifferent, effortless motion. His open fist collided with her cheek and she spun off her feet, falling onto her chest. Something hard jammed against her ribs, knocking the air out of her. She gasped, black spots appearing in front of her vision. She crawled to her knees, coughing, then looked down—and saw the screwdriver lying on the cement floor.

Her eyes narrowed. She grabbed the screwdriver and whirled around. Malthus was still on top of Jake, his arm raised, the blade hovering pendulously above Jake's squirming body.

Without pause, Brett leapt forward. She closed her eyes and thought of Calvin as she swung the screwdriver with all her strength—jamming the long blade into the direct center of Malthus's back.

Malthus's head jerked up, his body convulsing. His hands came open and the serrated knife clattered harmlessly to the floor. He staggered to his feet above Jake, his hands reaching desperately behind his back, his fingers clawing at what they could not reach.

He turned, facing Brett, his mouth wide open, blood trickling from the corners of his lips. Brett's eyes shifted down—and she saw the sharp tip of the screwdriver jutting out just below Malthus's sternum.

With one final gasp of strength, Malthus hurled himself forward, his swollen blue eyes boring into Brett's skull. She stepped aside, and he crashed into the AV board. The force sent him halfway over the board, his wet arms slamming into the open bed of wires.

There was a painfully bright flash, followed by a loud electric crack. Flames leapt up from the AV board as Malthus's body jerked spasmodically, an animalistic scream bursting from his lungs. A clanging fire alarm erupted from somewhere above them, drowning out his screams, and he staggered back, still convulsing from the electric shock. Then, suddenly, his knees gave out. He collapsed, smoke rising from his blackened arms. His head lolled to one side, hitting the cement floor.

Brett felt Jake grab her from behind, pulling her tight against him. He was breathing hard, staring down at Malthus's back. Frantic footsteps approached from somewhere behind them, and distant sirens blended with the fire alarm. Soon police and firefighters would arrive—and Brett and Jake would have a lot to explain. But with their video evidence streaming out over CNN, Brett doubted they would have much trouble proving their story. Soon the entire world would know about Compound G.

She watched in silence as the serpents of smoke rose from Malthus's dead body. Then she leaned heavily against Jake's chest, shutting her eyes.

27

Brett ran her hands up her naked body as she rose above Jake, feeling the warmth of her skin, the coursing thrill of her impending orgasm. The scent of sex was strong in her nostrils, and the echo of the bed's overused springs reverberated through her ears. Her shoulders rolled back as she felt Jake slide deeper into her, and her lips opened, a short breath escaping. It felt so damn good she wanted to cry out—but instead she leaned forward, locking eyes with her husband. There was no sense of distance in his gaze, no hint of distraction. Brett smiled—*because this is how it's supposed to be.*

The wall next to the bed was bare, the basal body temperature chart crumpled up in the wastebasket on the far side of the room. The support pillow Brett's mother had contributed was banished to a closet downstairs, next to a dozen Tupperware containers filled with every hormone-measuring device Jake had brought home over the past year. It was late afternoon—and they had already had sex three times within the past forty-eight hours. Neither of them had mentioned ovulation, cervical mucus, or female hormones.

Nor had they spoken of the political fallout of the past two days. Neither one of them had brought up the headline blazing across the cover of the *Boston Globe* that sat on Jake's desk in their office. The headline told them only what they already knew—that Arthur Sandler had resigned from office, pending a federal investigation into his role in the Alaxon scandal. And that Simon Scole was out on bail—although conventional wisdom said there was no way he would beat the case being developed against him by the new attorney general.

At the moment, the continuing fallout seemed insignificant. Compound G and ASD were distant nightmares, and even their own celebrity in the wake of the Alaxon scandal could not touch them. Their phone was unplugged, their beepers deactivated. Nothing existed beyond the confines of their bedroom.

Tomorrow, they would both return to work. Jake would start the process of finding a new lab to continue his study of ASD. Meanwhile, Brett would begin to rebuild her ER, which was still reeling from Calvin's loss.

Together, she and Jake would learn to live with the repercussions of the past week and the losses they'd endured: Calvin, Daniel Golden, and Stan Humphreys, whose body had been found in a dumping ground owned by Alaxon Industries. Most of all, they would learn to live with the effects of Compound G. If Jake's ASD was permanent, they would search for a cure. If it was temporary, they would restart their quest for fertility; this time, they would go about it as loving partners, not obsessed scientists.

Brett still wanted a child with every fiber of her being. But now she also understood that there were equally important things in her life.

She reached down with her hands and touched Jake's chest. She could feel his heart beating beneath his skin. She closed her eyes, gasping, as the moment approached.